ROGUE GOLIATH

ROGUE GOLIATH

John R. Monteith

STEALTH BOOKS

Rogue Goliath

Copyright © 2015 by John R. Monteith

Stealth Books

THE NEXT GENERATION IN PUBLISHING
COMING IN BELOW THE RADAR...

www.stealthbooks.com

The tactics described in this book do not represent actual U.S. Navy or NATO tactics past or present. Also, many of the code words and some of the equipment have been altered to prevent unauthorized disclosure of classified material.

ISBN-13: 978-1-939398-45-1

Printed in the United States of America

To Aida

My Chaldean Queen

CHAPTER 1

Lieutenant Sung-woo Yoon wiped sweat from his brow and glared at the chart. Deep inside North Korean waters, the *Kim Jwa-Jin* violated international law and defied a hostile seven-hundred-ship navy to find it.

Yoon's mental clock ripped off seconds counting the surfaced South Korean submarine's exposure to spying eyes and radar systems. Body heat from scared shipmates made the unbathed armpit stench heavy, and he welcomed his captain's order to sniff fresh air.

"Lieutenant Yoon, lay to the forward hatch. Equalize pressure, open the hatch, and retrieve the infiltration party."

Yoon marched by men hunched over consoles and then stepped through a doorway. After passing empty racks in the berthing area, he stopped below a machined ring. He palmed a handle, twisted it, and heard hissing heat race into the cool night.

Impatient, he cracked open the hatch, and residual positive pressure propelled the steel plate backward over its hinge. His fingertips burned, and he licked his abraded skin.

"Damn it," he said.

A dome of starlight appeared, and a talking silhouetted head interrupted his view.

"Infiltration team of four with one detainee, requesting permission to come aboard."

"Permission granted," Yoon said. "Hurry, and have the last man close the hatch."

A black figure in a wetsuit dropped before him and hit the deck plates with cat-like grace. The rifle over his shoulder jiggled as the compartment's newest occupant stepped aside and stooped to remove his swimming fins.

The captain's voice rang through the door.

"Did you get him?"

The commando tore back his hood, exposing cropped black hair and a young but stern face.

"Yes, sir," he said. "Justice is served."

The next commando landed with grace but retained his fins while joining the first in reaching back up into the gaping hole.

Boots glistening with seawater jutted into the compartment, and the swimmers grabbed rope-bound ankles. Fists above the hole grasped a drenched camouflage jacket while lowering the prisoner. Hands bound behind his back, the captive appeared sullen as the commandos yanked him aside. The final two warriors then landed in sequence, the last man swinging down the hatch.

Shifting his weight against the slight rocking, Yoon reached and pulled the hatch into its seating. He torqued the handle, driving the locking bars into place. He then yelled towards the doorway.

"Hatch is secure!"

"Submerge the ship," the captain said. "Make your depth thirty meters. Make turns for ten knots."

The deck dipped downward, and Yoon leaned forward, dropped his head, and exhaled. Time's forward march resumed its normalcy as he sensed the Sea of Japan swallowing the *Kim*.

The absurdity of surfacing in enemy waters frazzled his nerves, but employing frogmen required the vulnerability since the *Kim*, a *Type 214* German-designed submarine, lacked a lockout chamber.

Yoon feared that if the submarine evaded prying Chinese satellites, North Korean radar systems, and spying merchants, the kidnapping of a high-profile person would attract attention and invite a North Korean armada to vengeance.

Trying to convince himself that the reward merited the risk, he looked at the prisoner. From the mission brief, he expected the junior admiral of the Korean People's Navy who had eight years earlier orchestrated the two-submarine ambush that had split the South Korean corvette *Cheonan* in half.

Yoon also remembered that a strong power base craved revenge. Since an ensign killed aboard the severed corvette had married into the Samsung family, political pressure had driven the National Intelligence Service to identify a target of vengeance.

Patient, diligent spying had unveiled the North Korean admiral's identity and his residence on his country's east coast. Then came the plan for his kidnapping and arrival aboard the *Kim*.

With the submarine slithering into the waters, Yoon indulged himself in hopes of bringing the admiral to trial. Then his optimism faded, and his time slowed to a glacial tick.

The frogman he recognized as the leader, an army captain from the 707th Special Mission Battalion, withdrew a knife from its sheathe and sliced up through the captive's bonds. The captain then pressed the weapon's hilt into the admiral's hands, arming him.

The admiral drove the blade into the stomach of the nearest commando while the army captain withdrew a pistol, leveled it at his teammate's head, and pulled the trigger. Crimson droplets sprayed the piping behind the victim.

The final commando turned and reached for a firearm, but his leader sent two rounds into his chest. The captain then hoisted his rifle over his shoulder, lowered it, and leveled it.

As he stepped through the door, he sent surgical rounds into Yoon's crewmates. Screams of terror and protest rang from the control room, rousting Yoon into action. He darted towards a dead commando to retrieve a rifle, but the admiral's voice stopped him.

"Don't bother."

The admiral aimed a dead commando's pistol at him. The muzzle flashed, and lighting pulsed through Yoon's belly. He collapsed to the deck and remained conscious as the strange tragedy continued to unfold.

The admiral followed the rogue army captain into the control room, which an eerie silence had overcome. Alone, Yoon turned his awareness inward to discern if he needed to prepare to meet his maker, but he sensed his life force remaining within him.

Each breath bringing agony, he concluded that the bullet had bored holes through his intestines but had missed nerves and bones. He pressed his hand against the entry wound and rolled to his knees. He tried to stand, but pain stopped him. Content to drag himself, he slithered towards the control room.

He needed to warn others.

Grunting with each inch he gained, he feared his crew would die before he could raise the alarm. Then a presence startled him.

A young acne-faced seaman, a cook's assistant named Hong, spoke in a quivering voice.

"What's wrong, sir? I was sleeping when I heard gunfire."

"We're under attack. Grab the microphone at the control station."

Hong stared at Yoon.

"Go! I'll tell you what to say."

The youngster stepped through the doorway and yelled.

"I have the microphone, sir."

"Security violation. Captain Tong is a traitor and is killing us. Announce it!"

The assistant's shaky voice squeaked over the loudspeaker.

"Good, Hong. Now say that Tong is heading aft. All hands grab small arms and weapons of opportunity."

Hong's second announcement carried less fear.

"Good," Yoon said. "Now say that the prisoner is armed too. There are two assailants. The other army commandos are dead."

The cook's voice rang out again, parroting Yoon.

"Any man who can reach berthing, do so," Yoon said. "I have three rifles and two pistols salvaged from the dead commandos. We will make a stand here."

When Hong finished the final announcement, Yoon called him to his side.

"You did well, Hong. How are you with a rifle?"

"Not so good, sir. I barely qualified in training. I'm better with a shotgun."

"We don't have that luxury. They may double back at any moment. Get me a rifle so I can defend our position."

Hong struggled to lift a corpse's head and slip the rifle free.

"Hurry!" Yoon said.

He broke the weapon free and handed it to Yoon.

"Now grab a weapon. Pick a pistol or a rifle, your choice."

Yoon studied his weapon. It felt lighter than the standard issue K2 assault rifle, but its shape and function appeared similar to that with which he had trained. He unfolded the stock, and its mass felt negligible, made from a lightweight plastic reserved for special users who valued every spared ounce.

Hong returned to his side with a rifle.

"Right choice," Yoon said. "Even if you're a mediocre shot, you'll do better with a rifle covering the length of the control room. Come, prop me up behind the doorway."

"Which side, sir?"

"To the right. I will shoot left-handed so that you can shoot normally."

Hong stooped and yanked his jumpsuit collar. Yoon clenched his teeth and growled as pain shot through him.

"Lift me. Lay me against the doorway."

The cook obliged and balanced Yoon's torso between a bulkhead and an air reducer. The reducer's corners dug into his ribs, adding frustration to the flame burning his entrails.

As a test, Yoon leaned his torso against his supports, lifted his rifle, and aimed it down the control room. The sickening sight of bodies littered his vision, and his belly pain consumed him. He lowered the rifle, relaxing his stomach muscles and welcoming the reduced agony. He would fire if needed, but it would hurt.

As Hong hid behind the doorway's opposite side, Yoon heard stirring behind him. He winced in pain as he turned to see three men who wielded wrenches as clubs creeping towards him.

The eldest, a senior chief petty officer, studied the carnage and revealed wide eyes to Yoon.

"What the hell's going on, sir?"

"Captain Tong is killing everyone," Yoon said. "He must be trying to take over the ship. The prisoner is armed and helping him."

Senior Chief Nang surveyed the dead commandos behind him, and then he stared at the motionless bodies of his former shipmates on the other side of the door. Yoon watched acceptance register on his face as his features relaxed.

"Then I guess we're in a gunfight, sir," he said. "Are you strong enough to give orders?"

"I am, at least for now. I'm losing blood."

Nang barked an order, and two crewmen departed.

"They'll fetch the first aid kit from the torpedo room, and we'll patch you up the best we can, sir."

"Senior Chief Nang?"

"Yes, sir," Nang said.

"Grab a weapon."

The veteran stepped away, stooped over a corpse, and came back to Yoon with a pistol.

"What's your plan, sir?" Nang asked

"I hadn't thought too far into the future."

"You know you're in charge now, right, sir?"

Yoon looked at the bodies of his former commanding officer and executive officer. Death had promoted him to the senior sailor.

"I know."

"You need to do something."

The two younger men returned with a first aid kit. The senior chief popped it open, ripped bandages from their wrapping, and pressed gauze against Yoon's belly.

"Let's roll you over, sir."

Nang added cloth to the exit wound and mummified Yoon's gut with tight bandages underneath his ribs.

"Good, sir?"

He felt weak, and a mild chill enshrouded him, but intuition told him he had survived the worst.

"Good for now. We need to establish communications with each compartment. Let's see who's able to fight."

"We would be better positioned if we advance into the control room. We'd also assure ourselves control of the ship's systems. Can you move, sir?"

"I need help, but yes. We'll take position around the periscope, and we'll have two riflemen watching the aft door to the compartment. I won't be able to fight, but I can give orders if you recline me against the control station. "

"You heard him, men. Take rifles and take cover behind the last seats of the tactical system."

The men obeyed.

"Are you ready, sir?"

"Unless I say stop, ignore my screams."

Yoon clenched his jaw and stifled a yelp as Nang helped him to his feet. They staggered to the control station where the veteran lowered and reclined the lieutenant.

"Should we announce our new position, sir?"

"Yes. We need to risk open communications to fight as a team. Hand me the microphone."

The veteran obeyed, and Yoon clicked the handset.

"This is Lieutenant Yoon, the new commanding officer. Captain Tong has teamed up with the captive, and they have killed much of the crew. But there are survivors, and we are fighting back. We are armed, and we have secured the control room. Everyone contact the control room if you can, but do not expose yourself to danger."

"Well said, sir," Nang said.

"I can do more."

He lifted the microphone again.

"We know our ship better than our adversary. Use your knowledge to hide. Use your knowledge to arm yourself. We will unite and take back our ship."

He winced, lowered the handset, and waited.

"What if they're all dead, sir?" Nang asked.

Three more survivors emerged from the berthing area in varied states of fatigue and fear. They had reached the gun locker and appeared with shotguns and rifles.

"Excellent!" Yoon said. "We now outnumber them fourfold, and we're better armed."

"But Tong," Nang said. "He's a trained killer. And what if the supposed admiral is also an enemy commando in disguise?"

"I don't think so."

"Why not, sir?"

"Because he shot me, and I'm still alive."

The senior chief nodded.

"I'm going to advance our position farther aft, sir. We need a clean line of site to guard the door."

The macabre aura of corpses surrounding him had dulled Yoon's senses. As he focused on them, he wanted to respect his former shipmates, but necessity trumped decency.

"You need to set up a bulwark before doing so."

"A bulwark?"

"A mound behind which you will stand and aim your weapons. It must be made of a material dense enough to stop bullets."

"What do you have in mind?"

Yoon nodded at the dead.

"Them."

The control room became less stifling as the survivors dragged the deceased from Yoon's sight. After half the corpses had disappeared behind electronic cabinets, Nang returned alone.

"I've got three rifles and three shotguns aimed at the door. I don't care what sort of training Tong has, the only way he's coming into this room is full of holes."

"Keep piling bodies, Senior Chief. You need to be ready for anything. I don't remember if he had grenades."

"I don't remember either, but I'll keep dragging bodies back there. Here, take this."

Yoon accepted a pistol and rested it beside his hip. As he watched the senior chief carry away bodies, he thought he sensed the ship slowing. He craned his neck towards a display and verified that speed tapered towards zero. Tong had cut propulsion.

Nang returned to his side.

"All stop, sir. What's he up to?"

"It means Tong wants us to be found. This is deep treason, and there must be enemies with knowledge of our mission and location. We need to retake this submarine quickly and leave."

"You mean to storm the engineering space?"

Yoon pictured Tong waiting in ambush and considered it insane to challenge the commando's defensive position.

"He controls propulsion, and we're dead in the water until we change that. We either wait for barbarians to hunt us down in foreign waters, or we face danger on our own terms."

"So be it."

"Since I can't move, I insist that you prop me outside the door so that I'm the first target he sees when we open it."

"I can't ask you to, sir."

"It's an order. If I die, you'll be in charge. After you regain control of the ship, you must make five knots southwest for ten hours. Then due south for twenty hours. Then southeast for ten hours. At that point you will be safe to attempt communications."

"Sir, are you sure we need to take such drastic measures?"

A surge of belly pain reminded Yoon of his desperation. He envisioned Captain Tong having sent a beacon to the North Korean Navy announcing his position, and he wondered why a depth charge hadn't ended his life.

Then inspiration struck.

"We have no choice," he said. "But we can turn the odds."

"How?"

"Choke him out. We don mobile breathing units, start a fire, and open the door."

"Starting a fire is suicide."

"Not if we contain it. Grab a pot from the galley and make a small bonfire. We only need smoke."

The senior chief frowned in thought, and then his face lit up.

"I've got just the thing, sir. I'll be back."

The veteran fetched his ingredients and then returned cradling a pot in front of his midsection. He lowered it beside Yoon. It contained printer paper, the splintered wooden shards that Nang had broken from the former executive officer's stateroom chair, and a bottle of goryangju liquor.

"Goryangju?" Yoon asked.

"Eighty proof. I keep a bottle for the men in the torpedo room. It helps the hours pass faster during our watch."

"This should work."

"Darn right it will, sir."

"Before you do, bleed air from the forward banks to make sure most of the smoke gets pushed into the engineering space."

"Right, sir."

The veteran stepped away and traced piping to a valve. He twisted it open and followed the tubular metal downstream to a handle. He yanked it, creating a hiss and popping Yoon's ears.

One by one, the survivors marched by Yoon to the berthing area to grab mobile breathing units. One of them grabbed the pot and the combustibles. Nang grabbed the last two units and helped slip the mask over the officer's face.

Mask electronics amplified the senior chief's voice.

"We're ready, sir."

"Help me up."

Yoon's adrenal glands pounded his body with epinephrine and exorcised his belly pain. His heart raced, and he prayed that he wasn't condemning his men to death.

Nang lifted Yoon by his armpits, and fire filled his belly. The lieutenant gnashed his teeth as the senior chief helped him walk outboard a row of electronics cabinets.

At the compartment's bulkhead, he turned and saw rifles and shotguns poking over a bulwark of bodies. They reached the door.

"Lay me here," he said.

He heard his buzzing amplified voice from his breathing unit's mouthpiece echo off the bulkheads as Nang lowered him against a cabinet facing the door.

"Give me back my pistol."

Nang handed him a weapon and then sprinkled alcohol into the pot beside him. The other survivors had piled stuffing from chair backs beside the vessel to provide more fuel, flame, and fumes.

"Whenever you're ready, sir. We've all got our masks on. I'll stay here with you. You scan to the left after I open the door, I'll scan to the right."

"Very well," Yoon said. "Wait until I give the order to open the door. Light it up."

Nang lifted a lighter from his coverall pockets and ignited a wad of folded paper. Tossing it into the pot, he stepped back. Flames danced, pulsing heat over Yoon's face and floating smoke into the overhead piping.

"More smoke," Yoon said. "Keep adding fuel."

Darkening gray wisps filled the air.

"When I say, open it ten centimeters."

"Yes, sir."

"Now!" Yoon said.

The senior chief cracked open the door, giving Yoon an angle of view into the engineering space. Hands trembling, he peered through his facemask at his wavering pistol sights.

A minute passed as eternity, and smoke billowed through the door. His heart skipped a beat as he heard coughing on the other side, and he knew that Tong had been waiting in ambush.

A second man began coughing, and the hacking became intense. Yoon heard the clanking of lockers opening as his adversaries sought breathing masks. Then he heard the hiss and snap of air hoses mating with air lines.

Lacking mobile breathing units, his adversaries were tethered to air manifolds. They could move short distances between manifolds, or they could discharge their weapons. But they would be challenged to do both while finding cover.

He thought he had the advantage. Then he heard a loud, repeating clink.

"That sounds like he's trying to manually blow the after ballast tanks, sir," Nang said. "He's knocking the valve open."

Yoon's heartbeat accelerated.

"Head to the control station, pump all water to after trim tanks. Then flood water from the sea into our auxiliary tanks."

"Sir?"

"He's trying to surface the stern! He wants us to be found now. You have to make us heavy and counter his efforts, or we'll breach the surface."

"I will see to it, sir."

A minute later, Nang returned.

"It's done, sir."

"How can it be done? You weren't gone long enough."

"I set the system up for continuous flooding and pumping. He won't surface us."

Yoon felt the deck tipping as Nang looked into the engineering space.

"They've retreated to the reduction gears, sir."

Yoon nodded and then looked at the mound of bodies.

"Climb over, men. It's time to move."

The survivors crawled over their buttress of corpses and huddled by Yoon's side.

"The senior chief will open the door. I will fire three rounds of suppression fire. Then the first two of you go in and hide behind the diesel generator. Once inside, use the generator for cover as you move deeper in. Then the next two men will enter and hide behind the near end of the generator."

In the smoke, Yoon saw heads nod.

"Ready, Senior Chief?"

"Ready, sir!"

"Open!"

The door crashed back on its hinges. Yoon leaned, stifled a grunt as fire blazed in his abdomen, and aimed his pistol. Three pops rang from his weapon, and he lowered it.

"Go!"

Two figures blocked his vision while passing through the door. He aimed at two humanoid figures and fired more rounds.

"Go!"

Two more men passed.

"Senior Chief, stay here with me and take aim. We have six guns against their two. We can do this."

Nang rotated his rifle barrel through the doorway, leveled it, and fired. Yoon's ears rang, and a cacophony of shrill noises rang from the room as weapons spoke.

He then discerned the gentle grinding of polished gears, and he realized that Tong had restarted the shaft.

Then, a cracking explosion echoed.

After a moment of disorientation, Seaman Hong's voice passed through the doorway.

"He's blown up the shaft! The shaft is sliding out the back of the ship! It's sliding out the back!"

Recognizing that a severed shaft would create a morbid hole in the ship, Yoon realized that Tong was committing mass suicide. He wondered if such madness represented the backup plan, the makeshift reaction to the crew's smoking and storming of the room, or if it had been the traitor's original intent.

"Senior Chief!" he said. "Secure the stern bearing, now!"

Nang darted into the engineering space, and Yoon crawled behind him. When he reached the propulsion control station and shut off the main motor's electronic power, he noticed that the shooting had stopped. Craning his neck, he saw the two adversaries lying on the deck.

One of his men lay dead, but his senior chief had reached the end of the compartment, his foot flailing in the air as he reached behind the motor to cause the bearing's emergency seal to clamp down on the shaft.

Nang then wiggled backward, crouched, and yelled.

"Shaft bearing is secure!" he said. "The shaft is stopped."

"We're safe then," Yoon said. "At least for now."

CHAPTER 2

Yoon watched Nang stagger to him while balancing against the steepening decline. He estimated that the *Kim* had assumed a twenty-degree down angle.

"Head forward and level the deck," he said.

Nang departed, and a new person took place beside the lieutenant. The young face of Seaman Hong appeared smashed and swollen behind a mask.

"What should we do now, sir?" he asked.

"Get the men tending to any wounded," Yoon said. "I'm fine. Check the others."

While the youngster surveyed his shipmates, Yoon saw that his surviving men appeared uninjured.

Then Nang returned, his eyes wide behind his mask.

"Sir, don't panic. I'm fixing the problem."

"What is it?"

"Our depth."

Yoon bore the pain of twisting to view the gauge behind his shoulder. He read the value, and coldness consumed him. He whispered the number.

"Five hundred and fifty meters."

"But we're rising, sir. I'm pumping water off. I know I made a mistake by taking us too deep, but I'm fixing it now."

Yoon waved his palm and shook his head.

"You almost killed us. By our design depth limits, we should already be dead. But you can't blame yourself. You kept us from surfacing, and we are still alive."

"I'm sorry, sir. I'm taking us up slowly. Look, we're at five hundred and twenty meters now."

"I will trust you. Looking over my shoulder is excruciating. Come. Help me to the control room. We'll keep rising, and then I'll take us shallow to ventilate."

"We have no propulsion, sir. The shaft is severed and useless. We're stranded!"

Dead in the water, betrayed, and outnumbered by a factor of hundreds of potential hunters in the enemy's fleet, Yoon felt overwhelmed. But he had survivors to lead, and he would give them every chance to return home.

"But we have our ship back," he said. "We may be stranded and with structural damage due to the depth excursion, but we have communications and an arsenal. No matter who may pursue us, I refuse to die without a fight."

An hour later, he pressed his pectoral muscles into the crutches Nang had retrieved from the medical locker. With a new oxygen-generating canister in his mobile breather, he inhaled his facemask's fresh air and leaned over a sonar display.

"Nothing," he said.

"Nothing?" Nang asked. "I can't see us being that lucky."

"I see a half dozen fishing vessels, but there's nothing with the clean propeller blades of a warship. And no sounds of aircraft."

"Can you really hear aircraft on sonar, sir?"

"Depends how close they are. Same with warships. But let's call it a blessing that our sensors hear nothing of the sort."

"We're going shallow, then?"

"We have thirty minutes before sunrise. It's now or never. Man the ship's control station."

Nang sat before a panel.

"I'm ready, sir."

"Make your depth twelve meters."

"Make my depth twelve meters, aye, sir."

The senior chief jostled a joystick, pumping water from centerline tanks into the sea.

"Slowly, Senior Chief. We can't correct any overshoot by driving ourselves back down."

"Slowly, aye, sir."

He released the stick.

"Twenty meters, sir. Eighteen. Sixteen."

"Too fast! Flood the tank!"

"Flooding. One thousand pounds of water... two thousand."

"Stop!"

"Holding at fourteen meters, sir."

"Pump five hundred overboard."

Nang jostled the stick.

"Thirteen meters. Twelve and a half. We'll hit twelve soon."

"Raise the induction mast."

A hydraulic servomotor clicked over Yoon's head.

"Induction mast is raised."

"Commence snorkeling."

The ship shuddered with the gentle, sound-isolation mounted vibration of a diesel engine.

"Do you want to raise the periscope, sir?"

"No. I don't want to increase our radar cross section."

Clean air displaced the floating gray clouds. The lieutenant looked to Seaman Hong, who stood by his side.

"Give it a test."

The youngster pulled the mask from his face, inhaled, and started coughing. He pressed the plastic back into his cheeks and gasped for breath.

Yoon wanted to lower his induction mast to eliminate the risk of eyeballs, radar systems, and infrared sensors seeing it, but he remained patient, optimizing his opportunity to clean the air.

Ten minutes later, the atmosphere appeared pristine.

"Try it again, Hong."

The seaman nodded, lifted his mask, and expanded his lungs. "It's fine, sir."

"Secure snorkeling. Lower the induction mast."

Servomotors clicked again.

"Help me with my mask, Hong."

Yoon winced as the seaman pinched a tuft of his hair while lifting the straps from his head. He wiped sweat from his cheek onto his coverall sleeve and scratched his nose.

"Thank you."

"You're welcome, sir. It's good to breathe real air again."

"Right," Nang said. "That's much better."

"Now you can inspect the hull," Yoon said. "Pick a patch of hull between ribs and peel back the lagging, Senior Chief."

"What am I looking for?"

"I'm afraid you're looking for warping."

"Are you serious, sir?"

"We hit nearly six hundred meters before you pulled us out of our descent. I'm serious. The metal of our hull can't withstand that much stress and retake its normal shape. Take a look."

Yoon watched Nang crawl behind a tactical system console and prop his back against one of the ship's circular ribs. He pulled a flashlight from his jumpsuit, turned it on, and popped it into his mouth. Flipping a corner of insulating lagging, the senior chief craned his neck and stared.

He wiggled free and returned to Yoon.

"You're absolutely right, sir. If the rest of the ship is like what I just saw, we must look like a big metal concave caterpillar."

"That's why our next step is calling for help," Yoon said. "We're stranded and damaged structurally."

He had loaded a message into the *Kim's* radio queue, and he decided to send it to a satellite from his radio mast. The electromagnetic burst would be detectable to eavesdropping systems, but he needed to take the risk.

"Raise the radio mast."

A servomotor clicked.

"The radio mast is raised, sir."

"Transmit one outgoing message."

"The message is transmitted, sir. Satellite confirmation is verified."

"Lower the mast."

The finality of taking his last calculated risk calmed him. If calling for help had doomed him to being discovered, he would die knowing he had given himself a chance to be rescued.

Accepting his decision, he sought productive activity to make the *Kim* seem more like a combat vessel and less like a coffin.

"Senior Chief," he said, "gather the men and start placing the deceased into the freezer," he said.

"I'll see to it," Nang said.

As his traumatized team dragged their former friends into cold storage, Yoon pressed buttons on a console, invoking a chart. He studied sea currents to predict his drift over the upcoming days.

The water would drag him north, and then it would buttonhook him back south, keeping him in hostile waters. With Tong's treason, he expected an armada to know his exact location, and escape would require assistance. He felt more assured of his decision to transmit his plea.

But the lack of an attack confounded him. The *Kim* drifted over the horizon of the enemy coast, within easy reach of its hunters. Where were the helicopters? Where were the patrol craft? Or was his enemy stalking him with the dozens of silent assassins of its submarine fleet?

He toggled the screen to a view of the sounds the *Kim's* hydrophones heard. Seeing no assailing forces, he yielded to paranoia.

"Something isn't making sense," he said. "We should be under attack already."

Thinking he spoke to himself, Yoon hadn't expected a response. Nang's reaction startled him.

"I may have an answer for you, sir."

He twisted his pained abdomen to see the senior chief and Hong carrying a body into the compartment. Instead of continuing to the freezer, they stopped and lay the body below Yoon.

He looked down and saw the admiral staring back at him with tormented but living eyes.

"We found him alive, sir."

"I see that."

The captive groaned, and Yoon scanned his body for wounds.

"He's barely hit. Just his leg and his arm."

"That's right, sir. Looks like he just played dead."

Yoon glared at the man.

"Coward."

"I think not, young man. It's not cowardice to preserve one's life when no noble death is before him."

With Tong dead, he viewed the prisoner as the target of his revenge. He considered kicking him, but he remembered his wound.

"Bandage him," he said. "Then tape him to a chair."

With the captive's torso mummified to a seat in front of a tactical console, Yoon hobbled on his crutches towards him.

"Tell me what happened to you tonight, starting with your abduction."

"I had been asleep for approximately two hours when your men broke in through my bedroom window. I live in private quarters on the base with my wife. She was visiting her mother, leaving me alone in the house. I assume that her absence played into the timing of my abduction."

Yoon realized he suffered from restricted knowledge. The *Kim*'s crew knew where to drop off the commandos and where to gather them. Their activities on land had been a planned secret, and he had to trust the admiral's account of the tale for lack of dissenting evidence.

"How did they get you off the base?"

"They drove. Rather, they made me drive. They changed into naval officer uniforms in my house and rode with me in my car. Then they made me drive to their assault craft on an isolated stretch of beach. It seemed to be a very simple and well-planned operation."

Yoon judged the man as cooperative.

"Simple, until something went awry," Yoon said. "I saw the captain free your bonds and hand you a knife, which you immediately jabbed into the stomach of a commando. That was premeditated. When did the captain confide his plan in you?"

The admiral pursed his lips in thought, measuring his words.

"When we reached the beach, he sent his men ahead to secure the area. He shocked me with his direct candor at that point."

"What did he say?"

"He said I was condemned to stand trial for the sinking of the *Cheonan* and that I would certainly be found guilty and executed."

"Did you sink the *Cheonan*?"

"Me? Personally? No."

"But were you responsible?"

"Yes. I designed and authorized the mission."

From the corner of his eye, Yoon saw Nang raise his palm and then backhand the side of the admiral's face.

"Senior Chief!"

"Sorry, sir, but he deserves no less."

"Get back and sit down, Senior Chief."

As Nang retreated across the room, Yoon winked at him to infer that he approved his violence.

"He won't do that again," Yoon said. "Now, what did the captain say to compel you to join him in his treason?"

"Given my situation, I was agreeable to any option to improve my lot. He said he wanted to take me captive himself and hold me hostage for ransom. I needed to only assist him in turning on all of you, and the attack was to begin as soon as he set foot aboard the ship."

Yoon wanted to believe him, but it seemed like self-indulgence to hope that Tong hadn't intended to call upon the enemy fleet to pursue the *Kim*.

"You want me to believe that this was motivated by greed?"

"I have no evidence to the contrary."

"What was his plan with the submarine?"

"He shared with me in the engineering space that he planned to kill most of the crew. He would leave just enough of you alive to drive the ship to a safe coastline."

"Why would we comply with him?"

"He was ready to offer you your lives in exchange for your assistance. He was also going to appeal to your sense of mission accomplishment by pointing out that he would eventually deliver me to justice, for a price, of course."

"What went wrong?"

"You started the fire."

Yoon stifled a surge of pride and humbled himself by recalling that the fire was obvious in retrospect. It was one good idea in a string of many he would need to survive.

"That caught him off guard?"

"He was waiting for you to barge into the engineering space. I believe he expected you to be desperate and angry enough to challenge him directly. He would have gunned you down, probably only injuring the last men to keep enough manpower to operate the submarine."

"Then the fire thwarted his plans?"

"Yes. When you cracked open the door and the smoke rushed in, I noted a shift in his demeanor."

"How so?"

"He seemed defeated for a moment, but not desperate. More angry, as if you had ruined his mission, but you hadn't condemned him to death. He still behaved as if he were in charge of his destiny."

"Commandos are trained to be confident."

"I understand this. I am merely telling you what I saw."

"I see. Why are you being so cooperative? Why should I trust you?"

The captive looked up at Yoon.

"Because I want you to succeed in your mission of bringing me to justice. Despite the threats of your traitor, I believe that your judicial system provides me my only chance of survival."

Yoon found the logic sound and prodded further.

"What about the shaft?"

"I suspect that his backup plan was to cripple this ship, surface it, and hail my countrymen. By doing so, he probably expected to seek asylum with my people. I see no other rationale for him having plastic explosives with him for use on your shaft."

"That would explain why we haven't yet been hunted down. Your countrymen don't know where we are. Tong wasn't planning to tip them off. They only know that you have been abducted."

"I can only assume you are right. But they will come, and when they do, I will suffer the same fate as you. Like you, I have no wish to die by torpedo or depth charge."

Yoon straightened his back.

"Senior Chief, set up a two-man watch rotation on the prisoner. Give him water but no food until I say so. When he claims he needs to use the head, contact me."

"Aye aye, sir."

Nang selected the first two armed sailors to stand guard over their prisoner.

"Help me to the captain's stateroom."

With pictures of the former captain's family on a small desk, Yoon found his new quarters alien. But he wanted to assert his responsibility for the survivors' safety, and that included taking residence in the commanding officer's quarters.

"Help me into the chair."

The senior chief lowered him, and he tested varied reclining angles until he found one that minimized his pain.

"Sit, Senior Chief."

In the tight space, Nang angled his knees to avoid bumping Yoon's as he sat.

"What do you think, sir?"

"I want to believe what he said because it maximizes our chances of survival if Tong never sent our location to our adversaries."

"But you're skeptical."

"Maybe just paranoid."

"After what just happened to us, I don't think anything we could think about is paranoid."

"Good point. So we believe his story for lack of a better one."

"I don't see another option, sir, unless there's something we've missed."

"I don't think we've missed anything, but we need to sleep on it. We need to set up a new watch rotation to monitor sonar, watch over the prisoner, and monitor the battery."

"Right, sir. You're not planning on running the electrolysis system, are you?"

"I'm thankful that we can generate electricity while submerged, but we won't need the extra power for days."

In search of pain relief, Yoon shifted his weight.

"We have enough men and the right mix of skills. I'll set up a new watch rotation."

Yoon entertained thoughts of returning home to his fiancée. He hoped that the fleet would let her know that he was okay and, more importantly, take action to rescue him and the other survivors.

He would wait until nightfall to float a radio antenna to the water's surface to listen for messages from the fleet. Until then, he would seek ways to turn his disadvantages into opportunities.

He had a prisoner, and he had a mission of getting his submarine home.

CHAPTER 3

Jake Slate stared at his beer.

"I can't drink this," he said.

"It's okay, honey," his wife said. "I'm driving tonight. Live it up."

"I mean I don't think I want it."

"Get something else. That beer looks kind of light anyway. Get something stronger."

"No, I mean I don't want any beer."

"You want some scotch? I think this place has that single malt you get when we go out. The good stuff, but not the great stuff."

"Glenfiddich, aged twelve years. I'm sure they have it. That's not the point. I don't feel like drinking."

She frowned.

"Are you sick?"

He glared at her.

"Linda!"

"What?" she asked. "It's a fair question."

"I'm not sick."

"Then what's wrong?"

"Those pills Pierre told me to take. The naltrexone. The Sinclair Method he made me try. I think it's working."

"What's that again?"

"You know. If I'm going to drink, I take the pill at least an hour before starting. Then it blocks receptors in my brain that create a desire for additional alcohol."

A waitress arrived and announced the content of the meals as she lowered a salad before Linda and a steak under Jake's nose. After she departed, he slid the beer aside.

"I told you about the pills, right?" he asked.

"Yeah, but I thought they were only supposed to slow you down. I didn't know they would stop you altogether."

"I knew it might stop me," Jake said. "But I didn't believe it until I felt it. It sort of snuck up on me."

"That's good, right?"

"I don't know. I feel like Pierre just force-fed me a solution to a problem I didn't have."

"What's that supposed to mean?"

"He pressured me into taking the pills a few months ago. I didn't want to offend him. So I did it."

"For him, huh? You could have stopped without him knowing it. He lives halfway across the world for God's sake."

"The next time we talk, he's going to ask about it, and I can't lie to him."

"You aren't doing this of your own free will at all?"

Jake lowered his gaze. She was right.

"Maybe I was a little curious."

"Curious to see if it would work, or curious to see if you needed it?"

"God damn it, woman!"

Her expression turned dark.

"Watch your language."

"I told you not to accuse me of having a drinking problem."

"I didn't accuse you of anything."

"The hell you didn't! You just asked if I needed a treatment for alcohol use."

He carved a piece of red meat and lifted it to his tongue. The filet melted in his mouth. He remembered she was a teammate and not an adversary, like he viewed most people in the world.

"Sorry, honey," he said.

"I only asked because you've said that you wanted to cut back."

"Yeah, cut back, maybe, but I wanted to still be able to enjoy it when I want. This has made the entire craving go away. I'm not sure I know what to do if I can't get blitzed once in a while."

"Maybe that means you have to deal with all the problems in your life you haven't dealt with yet."

He watched her chew on a fork full of romaine lettuce.

"One reason I married you is because you're direct."

"This is going to be good for you. Not drinking, I mean."

"Let's see about that. This may not even be a permanent feeling. Maybe it's just a temporary reaction."

As the phone beside his untouched beer vibrated, he glanced at the contact's name and felt exhilarated and scared. From the corner of his eye, he saw fear cast shadows over Linda's face.

"Who is it?"

The name issued from his tightening throat as a whisper.

"Pierre."

"Oh, no. Not again," she said. "What's he want?"

"I don't know. It's just a text saying to call him as soon as I can speak freely."

"I don't like this, Jake. You've paid your dues over and over again. Can't we just live in peace?"

"Honey, this is my job. It's my purpose to respond when he calls me. I can't just live a life of leisure all the time."

"If you need a purpose, you could spend all your money and time volunteering for the Church. You don't have to run off and risk your life whenever Pierre feels like making a buck."

"I send tons of money to oppressed Iraqi Christians through the Chaldean Church because the rest of the world has forgotten them."

"I know, and Bishop Kalabat appreciates it as much as I do, maybe even more so. You do it for me and my family members who've been forced into exile because you know it's the right thing to do, but you don't get any satisfaction from it."

"I don't share your passion for the Church."

"Not yet, you don't. But I have faith that you will someday."

"Maybe. I'm still doing my research. Give me time."

"I know. You need to deal with your anger, first, anyway. Cutting back on the drinking will help."

Jake doubted anything would help. A deep anger burned within him, and he identified himself with the emotion. He wondered how other people could appear so calm with the tragedy of human existence when the concept infuriated him.

"I admit that not drinking could help," he said. "But forgive me if I'm not optimistic."

"Well, that's at least something that could help you. But what about me? Pierre's going to give you some job now where you risk your life for a bunch of strangers, and I won't even know where you were. I have to see stories of naval battles on the news and guess if it was you or not."

"If you knew where I've been or where I'm going, you'd be a kidnapping target."

"I'm probably a target anyway. The FBI can only protect us so far. I may as well know what you're doing."

"Not unless you want to live on the run."

"I'm not abandoning my kids."

"Then you have to keep living in ignorance."

"I don't have to like it."

"I didn't say you had to. Let's just try to enjoy dinner. I'll contact Pierre when we get home."

At home, Jake flopped into the leather chair and tapped a security code into his computer. A glance through his office door's window showed Linda reclining on a couch, watching television while trying to ignore him.

The French accent of his friend and mentor, Pierre Renard, filled the soundproofed room.

"How are you, my friend?" Renard asked.

"Not so bad," Jake said. "Those pills you gave me kicked in with a vengeance tonight. I couldn't drink. I lost my appetite, so to speak."

"Wonderful! That's how it's supposed to work."

"I guess. But I feel like you robbed me of an old friend. Alcohol has gotten me through a lot of rough patches. When the world shits on me, I need a place to go to recover."

"The world shat on you frequently through your young adulthood. But now you are in your mid-thirties and in charge of your destiny. You are no longer the victim of a broken home or the malice of the United States Navy. The sooner you realize that you are ready to exorcise your demons, the better – for all of us."

"You make it sound easy."

"I did not say it was. And if you desire to drink again, you can always redevelop the bad habit. At least now you know you can turn it off when needed. You have options."

"Well said, my friend. Options. I suppose you contacted me to grant me yet another option to save the world."

"Indeed. Mind if I smoke?"

"I'm looking at your handsome mug on a liquid crystal display. It won't bother me."

"Force of habit."

The Frenchman's steel blue eyes glistened as he lifted a gold-plated Zippo lighter under the tip of a Marlboro.

"Have you given up trying to quit?"

"It depends on my stress levels. I do rather well during my normal routine, but I can't risk the distraction of the unsatisfied craving while planning a mission."

"Good segue. What are you up to?"

"Our first rescue mission."

"Someone is paying you to be a mercenary coast guard instead of a mercenary navy?"

"That's a moderately accurate analogy. But I have yet to see a coast guard that operates submarines."

"But it is a rescue mission, meaning you're not planning for me to kill anyone, right?"

"Correct. You'll be commanding the *Specter* with the usual veterans on your team to establish a protective perimeter. Terry will command the *Goliath* for the rescue. Of course, our clients want one of their own submarines involved, as a matter of national dignity."

"Who's the client?"

Renard exhaled smoke in a drama-building gesture that Jake considered too perfect to be accidental.

"The Republic of Korea Navy needs our services in extracting a stranded *Type 214* submarine from hostile waters."

Memorized images and specifications of vessels on both sides of the Korean Peninsula flickered through Jake's mind.

The North Koreans had ships, aircraft, and submarines of substandard capability, but they made up for technical shortcomings with quantity and diligence. With more than seven hundred vessels, they could protect their coasts, and with planning and training, they could sink their prey, as they proved against the *Cheonan* eight years ago.

On the southern side of the conflict, Jake considered South Korea's German export *Type 214* design to be comparable in capability to his *Specter,* one of Renard's two *Scorpène* class submarines. Having commanded the *Specter,* one of its twins, and similar vessels for a decade, he had resolute confidence in the submarine and in his ability to lead it.

"If the South Koreans need help saving a *Type 214*, something bizarre happened. They're a good navy, maybe lacking in creativity and risk-taking, but they're as disciplined as any. A South Korean *Type 214* should be able to hold its own against anything the North Koreans can dish out. It can hold its own against the Chinese, too. What the heck happened?"

"Treason," Renard said. "They won't yet share the nature of their operation other than it was an insertion and extraction of frogmen on the east coast of North Korea, but I expect they will once they see my ships committed to their cause. One of the frogmen turned on his comrades and the crew, and he managed to crack the shaft with explosives."

"Damn. That's harsh."

"Indeed. I'm told that a fifth of the crew survived. They remain submerged and undetected to this point, but apparently, whatever their mission, it's created quite a flurry of activity from the North Korean fleet. Almost two hundred ships are already deployed in a hunt, and more are deploying."

"When did this all happen?"

"Coming up on thirty-six hours ago."

Jake performed quick time and distance calculations, using common submarine transit speeds.

"That *Type 214* should be home by now, but the North Koreans must know that it isn't. They must have spies at every South Korean naval base."

"That's exactly why they've increased their operations tempo instead of decreasing it. They suspect something went wrong for their adversary. They suspect a South Korean submarine was involved in an assault against them, and there's a submarine still missing from its home port. They smell blood in the water."

"The *Goliath* is capable of underwater transport of submarines, right?"

"It is indeed. I have amassed too many enemies to always transport my submarines above water where they are exposed. I needed the *Goliath* to be completely functional when submerged as well. Of course, it's slower when submerged, but I think you'll be quite impressed when you study its capabilities."

"I can't wait to see it."

"Terry sings praises about it. Sometimes I suspect that he would rather command it more than the *Specter* or the *Wraith*."

Jake recalled having befriended Terrance Cahill when he commanded an Australian submarine. Cahill had lost command of his ship by violating his admiralty's orders and firing on a Chinese submarine to protect Jake during an operation in the Spratly Islands. When Renard had offered Cahill a job commanding one of his submarines, Jake had welcomed Terry as his peer.

"If Terry likes it, I'm sure it's a good ship."

"It's one of a kind. But it's a necessity for me to have the flexibility of high-speed, long-distance transport of my submarines with the ability to submerge and hide. The *Specter* and the *Wraith* may have air-independent propulsion, but without nuclear reactors, they can't cover the distance between theaters of operations fast enough for our clients."

"Sounds like the *Goliath* should have been nuclear, at least ideally, if you could have afforded it."

"The finances of purchasing and maintaining a reactor were unfavorable. However, you can consider it a hybrid of a surface combatant, a submarine, and a cargo vessel."

"So it has a cannon? Missiles?"

The Frenchman smirked.

"Two railguns – my personal favorite armament. Heavy reliance on electricity, low reliance on ammunition storage space."

"Cool. What about anti-air missiles?"

"Splintering rounds from railguns and a point defense laser backed by a phased array tracking system."

"Air-independent propulsion?"

"Six MESMA systems of the *Scorpène* design."

"Six? No shit?"

"The *Goliath* needs to sustain transport speeds underwater while carrying a *Scorpène* vessel as its cargo. You understand the power needs of such a requirement."

"Heck, yeah, I do. This ship sounds awesome. No wonder Terry likes it."

"He's already in surfaced transit to our clients with the *Specter* aboard the *Goliath*. It's costing me an arm and a leg in fuel, but he's making thirty-two knots. He's covered half the distance from Taiwan and will arrive at Donghae in eighteen hours."

Jake opened up a new browser and started shopping for a first class ticket from Detroit to Seoul.

"Who's his crew on the *Goliath*?" he asked.

"He recruited a young but skilled officer from an *Anzac* class frigate to be his executive officer. Apparently, talented sailors can be lured from the Australian Navy by money as easily as French sailors."

"Are you sure the guy can handle being inside the *Goliath* underwater for long stretches?"

"He was instrumental in shaking down the ship during trials. He kept his composure during submerged operations, at least outwardly. The rest of the crew is made of many submarine veterans, and I'm sure he felt adequate peer pressure to remain calm."

"How big is the crew?"

"The ship is quite automated. Only twenty-six men, which Terry found quickly. His network with his former shipmates is impressive."

"Will you send me the technical specs for the *Goliath*?"

"Of course. You won't be aboard it, but you'll need to know its capabilities."

Renard drew from his Marlboro and exhaled smoke.

"I imagine you want to know how I found this opportunity."

"I figured it was Her Majesty, the Queen of the CIA."

"More or less," Renard said. "She's pulling the strings and assuredly using this crisis to increase her political clout, but she deemed herself far too important to call me personally. She had an underling connect me with the South Korean admiral in charge of the recovery."

"Don't take it too hard. You know better than anyone how people use people - underlings as you call them - to build images of self-importance and power."

"True, but she's still a bitch."

"A useful bitch. She connects us to the people who need us."

"Indeed. And those people need you in a briefing room in Donghae in twenty hours. I'll forward you the details of your travel requirements, a summary of the mission, and technical specifications."

"I'm looking online now, but I don't see a flight that can get me there that fast."

"I'm sending a private jet that will take off in two hours and take you to Los Angeles. You can catch a flight from there. I've saved you the trouble and already purchased your ticket."

"How long is the mission?"

"A week, plus travel time. If you can't succeed in that time frame, then the South Koreans will take matters into their own hands and risk open hostilities to recover their countrymen."

Being called to save lives without killing excited Jake.

"Okay. Sounds like a good mission. I'm on my way."

"Bon voyage, my friend."

Jake stood, left his office, and walked into the living room. Linda looked at him with concern.

"You're leaving, aren't you?"

"Just for a week and a half or so."

"When do you leave?"

"I have about an hour."

"An hour? Can't Pierre ever give you more warning?"

"No. He has to react to opportunities."

"Are you scared?"

"No."

"You're never scared. You always think you're invincible. But I'm terrified that one day your luck's going to run out."

"Don't talk like that, honey. I'd never take a risk that I thought would separate me from you."

He sat on the couch and hugged her. She squirmed, and he let her go.

"Pierre's plans are foolproof, honey."

She rose from the couch and walked away.

"Where are you going?"

"I don't share your optimism," she said. "I'm going upstairs to pray."

CHAPTER 4

Lieutenant Commander Dong-suk Kye suppressed the mocking voice in his head that reminded him about his ship's quarter-century technology disadvantage. His nation had commissioned his *Taechong* class patrol boat before his birth.

But it was fast, and Kye believed he could inspire his crew to overcome its technical shortcomings.

Sea spray pelted his cheeks as *Taechong Nineteen* sliced the waves. He turned and ducked through a door into his ship's bridge.

"All stop," he said.

The helmsman repeated and carried out his order, and the undulations of the deck plates subsided.

"Prepare to deploy the sonar suite," he said.

His officer of the deck, an ensign, barked back.

"The sonar suite is ready, sir. Speed is above the maximum of eight knots for sonar deployment."

"Very well," Kye said. "Report when speed decays to eight knots."

"Do you want a backing bell, sir?"

"No. Continue coasting."

Kye knew that South Korea's frontline submarines could remain silent while hearing his loud ship from great distances, and he refused to facilitate their efforts by reversing his propellers and churning water. Though a young man, he valued patience, and he waited for his ship to slow before extending its sonar system into the flowing water.

"Speed is eight knots, sir."

"Lower the sonar suite."

The clunk of a hydraulic servomotor signaled the extension of *Taechong Nineteen's* hydrophones into the sea. Kye wondered if a

South Korean submarine circled underneath his keel, waiting to crack it.

"Prepare to transmit active, half power, three hundred and sixty-degree search, twenty-degree wide beams. Transmit."

Shrill high-frequency chirps echoed from the water, through the gunship's hull, and into his bones. He had announced his presence to all nearby naval vessels, yielding a temporary advantage to any submerged foe.

If his risk of filling the ocean with sound merited a silent torpedo under his keel, his first warning would be the deck plates shattering his shins. But he waited with confidence, checking his fear and trusting fate to give him time to listen for acoustic waves bouncing off his enemy's hull.

And he expected an enemy.

The revered admiral who had sunk the South Korean warship *Cheonan* in 2010 had been abducted, and evidence suggested an amphibious operation. Spies kept tally of which South Korean warships deployed and returned, and a *Type 214* submarine, the *Kim*, remained at large.

Why the assailing vessel stayed at sea remained a mystery. Some in Kye's admiralty suspected a trap for the armada sent to hunt it. Others considered it a justified prize gifted by a quirk of fate. Kye understood it as his opportunity to enforce justice.

His orders made no stipulation about bringing the admiral home alive. Kye's gunboat, and the hundreds of other ships and aircraft that sought the assailant, were to thwart the adversary's effort to use the admiral for mockery – at all costs, including the loss of members of the hunting party or the admiral's demise.

"No return, sir," the ensign said.

"Stow the sonar suite," Kye said.

He waited a slow thirty seconds for the sphere to return to its nest within *Taechong Nineteen's* bilge. The delay equated to half a nautical mile of a theoretical hostile torpedo's inbound travel, with his ship in a deaf state, having stowed the mechanism to hear it.

Speed offered his only salvation from unknown dangers.

"Sonar is stowed," the ensign said.

"All ahead full," Kye said. "Steer course two-two-zero."

He resisted the urge to review the nautical chart – a paper version, unlike the electronic versions his adversaries enjoyed. The overhead image of his waters, his location within them, and the boundary of his ship's search zone lived in his mind.

The old gunboat rumbled, and sea spray pelted the bridge windows as he placed distance between his hide and any would-be pursuing torpedo. Nearing the edge of his search boundary, he ordered *Taechong Nineteen* slowed and its sonar suite lowered.

"Prepare to transmit active, half power, three hundred and sixty-degree search, twenty-degree wide beams. Transmit."

As underwater sonic energy announced his vulnerable, motionless position, he awaited an acoustic return.

A wailing chirp. Then nothing. Another wailing chirp. Then again, no return. Four more repetitions, and no sign of an adversary.

Then, on the next transmission, his sonar operator shouted across the bridge.

"Active return! Range, five and one half nautical miles. Bearing three-one-two."

"Cease transmissions!" Kye said.

He marched across the bridge, brushing the backs of startled crewmen. When he reached the sonar monitor, the operator stepped aside, giving him a view of fuzzy green lines.

His eyes counted outward five concentric circles and settled on a faint constellation of green dots that traced the linear blob of an acoustic echo. He stepped back and let his executive officer, a lieutenant, satiate his curiosity.

"That's near the limit of our system's range, sir," the executive officer said.

"The acoustic environment supports it," Kye said. "The background noise is low. The surface layer runs deep. We can hear reliably to that distance, and that's a submarine."

"Shall I prepare rockets, sir?"

"Yes," Kye said.

The executive officer stepped to a console and tapped buttons.

"Warming up the weapons, sir. Fifteen seconds remaining before warmup is complete."

"Very well. Hold your fire until you hear an unequivocal order from me to launch."

His pulse raced, and he grabbed the sonar operator's arm.

"Can you hear anything?" he asked. "Incoming weapon seekers, high-speed screws, cavitation, launch transients?"

The man pulled his earpiece upward to talk.

"No, sir. The target's too far away."

"Prepare to transmit," Kye said, "bearing three-one-two, half power, twenty-degree beam. Transmit."

The chirp reverberated through his bones.

"Active return! Range, five and one half nautical miles. Bearing three-zero-eight."

"The bearing has changed," Kye said. "The target's evading."

"Shall we take the shot, sir?" the executive officer asked.

"I will press the button myself," Kye said.

He stepped to the weapons console, flipped up a guard, and pressed a red button. The rippled hiss of rocket exhausts made him cringe, and as the sounds subsided into the distance, he raised binoculars from his chest to his face.

Plumes traced a horseshoe of radiance against a blue sky, but he noticed fingers missing in the claw of contrails. He concluded that two rockets had failed to fire.

"Hang fire, tubes three and fourteen," the executive officer said.

"Very well. Eject tubes three and fourteen."

While his crew cleared the dud canisters from the launcher, he lowered his optics and watched his flying weapons converge in the distance.

White water droplets danced and dipped as the rockets dropped charges. He waited as the bombs sank to their detonation depth of one hundred meters.

Explosions rumbled, and spherical arcs of aqua bent the sea's surface.

"Transmit again, bearing three-zero-eight, half power, twenty-degree beam."

"Transmitting, sir."

He felt and heard his gunboat's chirping wail.

"No return, sir."

"Prepare to transmit, bearing two-seven-zero to bearing three-five-zero, half power, twenty-degree beams. Transmit."

"Active return, sir! Range, four point nine nautical miles. Bearing two-eight-six."

Kye recognized the brilliance and bravery of his adversary as he announced his next moves.

"The target turned towards us," he said. "Since my attack assumed that the target would turn away, I have miscalculated, and my depth charges missed. I will engage the target with two torpedoes. Prepare torpedo one for launch on bearing three-zero-six. Prepare torpedo two for launch on bearing two-six-six."

"Weapons are warming up, sir," the executive officer said.

"Very well."

"Torpedoes one and two are ready."

"Launch torpedo one," Kye said.

He heard compressed gas spit a cylinder from a launcher located amidships on the gunboat's starboard side.

"Torpedo one is away, normal launch," the executive officer said.

"Very well. Launch torpedo two."

The second weapon hit the water, and Kye stepped to his sonar operator.

"Do you hear our torpedoes?"

"Yes, sir. Running normally."

"Listen for enemy torpedoes."

The operator nodded.

"Anything yet?" Kye asked.

"Nothing, sir."

"We probably won't hear them coming, and I'm not waiting. Stow the sonar suite."

"Wait! High-speed screws, sir!" the sonar operator said.

The enemy submarine had launched at least one torpedo at him, and immediate speed meant life.

"Continue stowing the sonar suite," Kye said. "Helm, all ahead flank."

The helmsman acknowledged the order and rotated the engine order telegraph. The gunboat's stern dug into the water, and the ship lurched.

"Left standard rudder, steer course one-three-five."

As the old vessel rolled and shook, Kye wished for wings. With scant knowledge of the trajectory of the submarine's retaliatory salvo, he fled with blind hope.

Despite its age, the boat flew, and like a sprinter, it reached its top speed in seconds. Kye preferred his odds over those of his adversary.

Minutes elapsed, and he feared that his rattling ship would break apart. But *Taechong Nineteen* held together, and he sensed he would survive. To convince himself, he left his executive officer in charge of conning the vessel and left the bridge. After passing through a doorway, he descended stairs, turned, and then opened a door to the weather deck.

The ship's self-generated artificial wind whipped his cheeks. He trotted aft, bending around the starboard torpedo nest and then ducking under the emptied rocket launcher.

Reaching the fantail, he popped open a rusted locker and withdrew a sound-powered phone headset. He slipped it over his ears and screwed the set into a circuit.

"Bridge, fantail," he said. "This is the captain. Communications check."

"Fantail, bridge," the executive officer said. "Communications check is satisfactory. Any sign of incoming weapons, sir?"

"Negative. But maintain flank speed."

"Maintain flank speed, aye sir."

Near the horizon, the ocean erupted, and Kye realized that one of his torpedoes had detonated. For a moment, he thought he had scored an absolute victory – one dead adversary and his ship unscathed. But then, as the rumble of the explosion reached his ears, he saw a contrail rise from the water.

Then the contrail disappeared.

Phantom torpedoes drifted to the back of his mind as he digested the latest menace of a submarine-launched anti-ship missile. A canister had breached the surface. The weapon had then ignited, flying into the sky and revealing its exhaust. Then it had reached a waypoint and turned towards *Taechong Nineteen*, becoming an invisible spec.

His ship lacked the technology to track the missile, much less shoot it down. His heart climbed into his throat, and he forced himself to spit out an order.

"Incoming missile! Deploy chaff!"

The fake wind carried the popping thud of canisters belching metal into the sky. He doubted the airborne shards would fool the incoming missile's seeker, but he lacked better options.

He surprised himself with his next thought – calculating missile flight time. Assuming ten nautical miles distance at launch and a speed of six hundred knots, he decided his men had less than a minute to react.

But it was plenty of warning to abandon ship.

He opened his mouth to give the order, but then he reconsidered, wondering if his admiralty would view such compassion as cowardice.

"Prepare damage control teams," he said. "Don firefighting gear and man hoses."

He waited as time accelerated with his anguish.

"Damage control teams are manned, sir," the executive officer said.

"Have you sent our tactical data to the squadron?" Kye asked.

"Yes, sir. We will be credited with the sinking."

A sick feeling overtook him. Replaying the vision in his mind, he tried to convince himself that his torpedo's explosion had followed the enemy's missile launch. Perhaps his eyes had missed the contrail's early evidence.

No, he concluded. The detonation had preceded the incoming missile, and submarines with cracked keels don't launch missiles.

His torpedo had hit something else.

Staring at the water churning behind his propellers, Kye recalled the nautical chart, and in a moment of stunning clarity, he understood.

The enemy had fled into the search area of a friendly *Sango* class submarine, drawing his torpedo towards his countrymen and killing them. A pit burned in his stomach until the howl of the approaching missile rattled him.

He looked up, and a deafening sound carved an arc over his head. His startle reflex scrunched his lean frame, and he felt a shockwave catapulting him as he lost consciousness.

Salt water burned his abraded leg, waking him as he bobbed. The pain heightened the anger surging within him when he noticed the billowing flames and black smoke enveloping his ship. He hoped that men would survive and that the ship would stay afloat, but he knew the blast had rendered his vessel useless.

Kye raised his hand, screamed, and smacked the water.

He had used the proper search technique to find his adversary, and he had been decisive in his attack. But somehow, with an inexplicable mix of skill and luck, his enemy had achieved a resounding victory.

A solitary thought pushed all others aside.

Revenge.

CHAPTER 5

Terry Cahill commanded the world's most versatile vessel.

He stood at the corner of the bridge that jutted from the ship's starboard bow. Through the polycarbonate windows that interlaced steel bars backed and reinforced for submerging, he watched the long prow slice through the waves at the *Goliath's* maximum encumbered speed of thirty-two knots.

A glance over his left shoulder showed the laser cannon's raised hatch on the left half of the ship. With the entire twenty-six man crew tending to propulsion and preparing to submerge the vessel, he expected the laser's covering, which seemed part of another vessel, to sheathe the weapon from corrosive saltwater.

A farther twist of his torso revealed the *Goliath's* cargo, the *Scopène* class submarine, *Specter*. Rising at forty-five degrees, arms reached upward from the *Goliath's* starboard hull to ribs that embraced rolled and arced steel plates, which supported a mesh-like grated rubberized surface to cradle the *Specter's* underbelly.

Spray shot from the sea, offering periodic kisses to the cradle's underside, which extended convex shapes downward. The pontoon-like ballast tanks below the bed offset part of the cargo's weight when submerged.

From his elevated height on the bridge, he saw the hydraulic presses that worked with gravity to hold the *Specter* in place.

To Cahill, a former submarine commander, the world on the water's surface felt alien and exposed. Though it would restrict his speed, he welcomed submerging the *Goliath*. His mercenary boss, Pierre Renard, had just sent a message that Chinese warships sprinted on a course to intercept him.

"Making turns for eight knots," he said.

He tapped a capacitive touchscreen, and the *Goliath's* hardened, redundant array of hard drives and data cables sent a command signal to slow both of the ship's electronic drive motors.

Liam Walker, his executive officer and a former mariner from an *Anzac* class frigate, kept his binoculars pointed at the window.

"Doesn't it feel weird to give a command to yourself?"

"No," Cahill said. "I've always believed that it's more efficient to do something meself when I can do it faster than telling someone else to do it."

"Suit, yourself, Terry. You blokes were always more informal on submarines."

Hearing an underling address him by his first name gave him mixed emotions. It reminded him of the abrupt end to his naval career when the Australian admiralty had stripped him of command for shooting a limpet torpedo at a Chinese submarine. His less-than-lethal attack's success and tactical genius had failed to spare him from punishment.

Released from his nation's service, he had accepted Pierre Renard's offer to join his mercenary fleet as its second commanding officer, in the mold of Jake Slate.

"Shall I secure the turbines, or would you prefer the honor?" he asked.

"Given how advanced this ship is," Walker said. "I'm surprised you just can't think it and shut them down."

"Very well," Cahill said. "Duly noted that me executive officer is too lazy to secure the turbines. I will handle it meself. Securing turbines."

He pressed an icon on the touchscreen and then tapped a pop-up confirmation image. A message told him that the ship's twin gas turbines were spinning towards silence.

"Head valves are shut," Walker said.

Cahill smiled.

"I see that. I see the indication, and I see it in the high-resolution display from one of our topside cameras. This ship feels like a two hundred million-dollar video game."

"If you ever spent time in engineering, you might think otherwise. Grease is still grease, and oil is still oil."

"Very funny," Cahill said. "Why don't you tell me how our propulsion system is doing?"

Walker lowered his optics to his chest, nodded at a monitor, and reached out a finger to a touchscreen.

"Both gas turbines are secured," he said. "All six MESMA systems are running normally, bearing the electric strain. Propulsion is running on air-independent power. Maintaining eight knots."

With the liquid oxygen and ethanol-fueled, French-designed MESMA air-independent propulsion modules, Cahill appreciated his abundance of underwater power.

"Are we ready to dive?" he asked.

"The ship is, but I may not be," Walker said. "It still gives me the willies. I sometimes wonder why I signed up for this."

"You signed up for a quadrupling of your pay."

Cahill tapped an icon to open his microphone and send his voice throughout the ship.

"Prepare to dive," he said. "All stations report status."

He looked to Walker to digest the reports that all intakes except seawater cooling systems had been sealed.

"Starboard MESMA units report ready to dive," Walker said. "Starboard engine room reports ready, as does starboard weapons bay."

For his present deployment, Cahill's modular weapons bays each held a BAE Systems railgun, both of which could employ guidance from the four-paneled phased array radar system mounted high on his catamaran's elevated stern sections.

"Port MESMA units, port engine room, and port weapons bay are all ready to dive," Walker said. "The *Specter* reports ready for dive, as well. Its ballast tank vents are verified open so that it can submerge with us."

Cahill maintained communications with the skeletal crew aboard the *Specter*. The submarine needed its staff in case the *Goliath-Specter* tandem faced unforeseen crises, including conflicts that required the submarine's weapon systems.

He used a touchpad and mouse buttons to restrict his voice to the ship he transported.

"*Specter, Goliath,* are you there, Henri?"

The French accent sounded familiar.

"*Goliath, Specter,* I'm here."

Through the shared data feed, Cahill saw the status of the submarine's systems.

"Your tactical system is down," he said.

"I will bring it up when submerged," Henri said.

"The Chinese have dispatched a *Type Fifty-two* destroyer and a *Type Fifty-four* frigate to investigate us."

"I see that on the data feed," Henri said. "You don't intend to engage them, do you?"

"No, Pierre forbade it. The goal is to evade them. But I will engage them as a last resort. Deploy your towed array sonar and have Antoine ready at his sonar station."

"I will. Are you also going to deploy the *Goliath's* towed array?"

"Yes, to train and observe me new sonar crew's ability, but I want Antoine listening from the *Specter.* I will consider him the standard by which I judge the others."

Cahill paused for a last look at the sun, tapped icons, and then stepped to the aft of the bridge. Behind and below his window, bubbles rose from the *Goliath's* submerged ballast tank vents under the starboard hull.

"Ten meters," Walker said. "Eleven. Twelve."

As the *Goliath* sank, bubbles burst from its cargo tanks under the *Specter.* Waves swallowed the rounded midsection of the transport ship's starboard hull as the seas reached the *Specter's* beam. As water displaced air from the main ballast tanks, gentle spray shot up from vents atop the submarine.

He looked to his monitor at the information that pressure sensors draped under the submarine fed to the buoyancy management system at his fingertips. Seeing a registered downward force, he knew that water filled the *Specter's* ballast tanks, making it heavier than the water into which it submerged.

Aqua crests lapped the bridge windows, refracting sunlight into Cahill's eyes. He turned away, and a quick glance over his shoulder revealed waves reaching the *Specter's* conning tower. His continued assessment of the submerging evolution revealed that the port and starboard weapons bays at the sterns of his ship remained visible above the sinking transport vessel, as did the now-sealed laser cannon pod on the port hull's bow.

"Fifteen meters," Walker said.

Water crept up the bridge windows, and sunlight yielded to the overhead artificial illumination.

"Twenty meters," Walker said. "The ship is submerged. The cargo is also submerged."

"Very well," Cahill said. "Make your depth forty meters."

From the corner of his eye, he watched his executive officer tap a touchscreen. The deck took a slight downward angle, the sea over the windows became dark, and then the ship leveled.

"Steady at forty meters," Walker said.

Cahill touched his screen.

"Coming right to course zero-four-zero," he said. "I'm making sure we don't drive underneath this Chinese patrol."

"I'd be surprised if they don't just give up and go home after they figure out that we can play submarine whenever we want."

An ominous feeling – a possible shadow of a memory from his prior clashes with the Chinese Navy – overcame Cahill. He stiffened his back.

"I'm afraid I don't share your optimism," he said. "You have the bridge. I'm heading below."

He passed through a door, latched it behind him, and descended a steep stairway to a tight, odd-shaped compartment under which welds held the rakish bow module to the cylindrical, submarine-based section.

As he reached for a watertight door, a peek in the bilge revealed the inverted triangular keel section, which provided stability and added buoyancy, continuing underneath the ship. Swinging the door open, he stepped through its machined frame and into the familiar, circular-ribbed world of a submarine.

Lacking a torpedo room, the *Goliath* presented Cahill its tactical control room as its first cylindrical compartment. Four men staffed the space, with three seated in front of consoles and a supervisor hovering over them.

"Good afternoon, sir," the supervisor said.

The young leader had been an officer aboard Cahill's submarine prior to quitting the Australian Navy for lucrative mercenary adventures. He retained his habit of addressing Cahill as 'sir'.

"What's on sonar?" Cahill asked.

"Nothing, sir."

"Keep listening. I'll buy a coldie for the entire sonar team if you guys can hear any war vessel before Antoine does from the *Specter*."

Knowing that the left half of his ship lacked a tactical team, he saw no reason to repeat the beer-inspired challenge to anyone within the port hull. The far side of the *Goliath* held a smaller crew that tended to propulsion and weapons. To reach the starboard hull to eat, the port-side team needed to crawl through the catwalk welded behind the aftermost support beam.

He continued his sternward walk, passing electronic cabinets that appeared where he would have expected a conning platform and periscope on the *Specter*.

With the elevated bridge pod atop the starboard bow and with cameras mounted atop the weapons bays in the sterns providing external views, the *Goliath's* design omitted half the standard submarine control room. Renard had instead allowed for a larger crew's accommodation area, which he extended into the control room, to add both crew comfort and extra buoyancy for carrying the *Goliath's* heavy cargo.

As Cahill passed into the elongated berthing area, a sailor's snoring matched the modest rhythm that rocked the ship. Placing his weight onto the balls of his tennis shoes, he crept into the ghost-silent scullery and then continued to the mess hall.

A few men played cards at a table. Cahill nodded and continued to the first MESMA section, testing his memory to recall the term MESMA as an acronym for the French-designed Module-Energy, Sub-Marine, Autonomous ethanol-liquid-oxygen propulsion plant.

Unlike the *Specter*, which used one MESMA plant, the *Goliath* contained six, three per each catamaran-inspired hull, providing his ship the bulk of its cylindrical length. With half the battery capacity and twice the mass of the *Specter*, Cahill relied upon its MESMA plants for undersea power.

The transport ship's builders had removed the aft battery cells from each hull to provide buoyancy while connecting the forward cells in series to maintain proper voltage. With two men operating each plant under a pair of roving supervisors, the MESMA team comprised the largest unit of Cahill's crew.

The hiss of steam filled the section, and he felt heat waft over him. With his jumpsuit unzipped and flopped over his waist, a technician Cahill had recruited from a civilian power plant exposed a sweat-marked tee-shirt. He was examining gauges on a control station as his partner, an Australian Navy recruit, climbed up from the lower deck and joined him.

"Running like a champion," he said. "It's a temperamental system, but I can keep it running, even all out when you need it."

"I know you can, mate. That's what I pay you for."

Twenty-five meters and two MESMA plants later, Cahill pulled an industrial-strength paper towel from a roll on a bench and ran it across his face. The fabric became moist, and he dropped it into a waste bin bolted against a rail. He bid farewell to his third MESMA team and ducked through another watertight door.

Above, wide air ducts fed a large gas turbine engine – a fixture he found bizarre on a submerged vessel. Loud and inefficient at the low powers of a submarine battery's charge rate, the engine better served surface ships to enable their great speeds. For the hybrid *Goliath*, a gas turbine in each hull allowed direct feeding of the ship's motors for rapidity while surfaced, and the MESMA units combined with the undersized battery cells provided the undersea propulsion.

"How are we doing?" Cahill asked.

A man in coveralls seated before a control panel turned, looked up, and then nodded towards the electric motor at the tapering cylindrical stern.

"Fine, Terry. It's running quiet and reliable. This *Scorpène*-type engine room is a quality design."

Cahill glanced aft and saw the top of the electric motor, which the Taiwanese builders had sunk into a custom recess for the *Goliath*. The motor drove the starboard shaft, which stretched below his view through the tapered keel and through the stern bearing at the ship's tail. He then opened a hatch above him that Renard had retrofitted onto the engine room's angled slope, reached upward to handles, and pulled himself through.

Closing the hatch, he noticed the quietness of the weapons bay. He climbed a ladder and entered his ship's aft space.

The railgun was unimposing, deceptive in its lethality. With its barrel aiming forward, the weapon system impressed Cahill with its compact size. The greatest mass rose behind the breach to absorb recoil, and as he walked deeper into the bay, he stood on his tiptoes to reach the top of the cannon.

The small space below the gun and above the engine room held its rounds, but with electricity providing their muzzle speed and their kinetic energy making them lethal without warheads, numerous rounds fit within their tight packing.

Although he disliked reliance on moving parts, the electric motor-powered hatch above him and the hydraulic lift which raised the railgun through it had proven reliable in trials. But he demanded that a man be stationed in each bay to manually jack up the weapons or clear jammed rounds if needed.

"What are you doing, Terry?"

He looked to the smallish man who reclined in a cot reading a book under a recessed curve in the hull.

"Just admiring me ship, specifically the railgun. I needed to see it, just in case we need it against these Chinese mongrels."

"There's nothing else like it," the man said. "I never thought I'd be submerging on a surface ship, or tending to railguns on a submarine. I'm still not sure what we are."

"We're an armed transport ship," Cahill said.

"It's still weird, though I don't mind it for the pay."

"I consider meself lucky that Renard thought of building her. Look at what we're doing now."

A light source flashed by one of the polycarbonate windows that offered a thin panoramic view around the top of the bay. He recognized it as some form of biological life, ignored it, and continued his speech.

"If Renard hadn't designed a high-speed transport, the *Specter* wouldn't be able to reach Korea from Taiwan in time to be of any use. And if we couldn't submerge, we'd be fighting off Chinese ships that outgun us. No, mate. This ship isn't weird. It's bloody brilliant."

A sound-powered phone chirped by the man's head. He reached, tore it from its cradle, and lifted it to his cheek.

"Starboard weapons bay," he said.

He extended the phone.

"It's for you."

Cahill stepped forward and took the handset.

"Captain," he said.

"Terry, it's the bridge," Walker said. "We've got important news from Renard. It's not much data, given how low the bandwidth is on our submerged communications wire."

"I understand the bandwidth constraints. No need to defend yourself if the news seems cryptic. What did he say?"

"He said the Chinese warships have stopped."

"Well, that's good. Did he say anything else?"

"Yes."

"Spit it out."

"Helicopters," Walker said.

"Helicopters? Nothing else?"

"No. I'm afraid not. Not with the limited bandwidth. It was a four-word message. Chinese warships stopped. Then a hyphen. Then the word helicopters."

A sinking feeling filled Cahill's stomach.

"Helicopters," he said. "That one word says enough."

"The Chinese have sent helicopters after us?"

"That's right," Cahill said. "Man battle stations."

CHAPTER 6

Cahill stood on the *Goliath's* domed bridge.

"We'll maintain course and speed," he said.

"You don't want to reconsider surfacing?" Walker asked.

"No."

His executive officer squinted and frowned, his quizzical look casting shadows over his eyes.

"There's no other way to shoot down helicopters."

"I understand," Cahill said. "But we're not going to shoot them down. We're going to avoid them."

"If we surface, turn east, and sprint, we can test their flight range. If they pursue us, we'd have plenty of time to shoot them out of the sky before they could reach torpedo launch range."

Cahill appreciated his executive officer's spunk, and he allowed the debate.

"True," he said, "but that would delay our arrival. Every minute of delay is an extra minute the North Koreans may stumble upon our clients' survivors."

"You'd risk driving underneath the helicopters to save time?"

"Yes."

"Is this normal courage for submarine officers, or are you just one of the gutsiest?"

"Hard to say, mate. You'll have to trust me."

"Well then, what's your strategy? Just drive straight and hope we don't get discovered?"

Cahill pondered the answer and realized he was ignoring an important parameter.

"More or less," he said. "But you've given me an idea."

He tapped his screen to contact the *Specter*, and Henri's French accent rose from the loudspeaker.

"Yes, Terry?"

"Can you launch a bathythermograph?"

"Ah, yes. I see. It would be an interesting activity. You hope to discover an acoustic layer."

"I do, but that didn't answer the question."

"Of course. The unit would clear the hydraulic supports from the countermeasure launcher, but what portions of the *Goliath* it might hit on the way down is a matter of speculation."

"May as well shoot it now, before the helicopters are close enough to hear any banging."

"I understand," Henri said. "I will see to it. I need fifteen minutes to backhaul a countermeasure and insert a bathythermograph."

"Very well, Henri. Launch it when ready."

He terminated the communications with the *Specter* and shot a glance at his executive officer.

"Okay," Walker said. "I give in. What's a bathythermo-whatever? Some sort of temperature sensor?"

"Correct. You shoot it from a submarine, and it stays tethered to the launcher until its line breaks. It tells you what the temperature is all the way down."

"What's the point? We can't dive anywhere near as deep as the bottom."

"Sound will bounce off the bottom, or it might curve away from it. Sound will also bounce off the surface but usually curve back up to bounce off it again. Sound's behavior is predictable based upon pressure, salinity, and temperature, but temperature is the overriding factor."

"What's it all mean?"

"It means, that if the sound velocity profile is favorable, you can find a good depth for listening for other submarines. Or you can find a good depth where you can hide with your sound being trapped in a layer of water."

"Hide, as in hiding from helicopters?"

"Perhaps. Depth may provide us protection, and I want to know where that protection might begin."

Cahill looked at the overhead view of icons on his screen. With the Chinese warships and helicopters outside acoustic detection range, their stale location data had decayed to a guess. A glance at his executive officer's slumped shoulders showed him lamenting the same staleness.

"How close do the helicopters need to be to hear them?" Walker asked.

"That's an answer of mixed parameters and mixed emotions. For a conventional submarine, hearing a helicopter only means that it's close enough to be dangerous. However, on this beauty, hearing a helicopter may provide enough warning to surface and fight."

"I see," Walker said. "Now I understand how you've mitigated the risk. Unless one lowers its dipping sonar right on top of us, we'll have a chance to fight back before we would find ourselves underneath a torpedo."

"Right. Helicopter torpedoes have less range than heavyweight torpedoes, which means a helicopter needs to get closer. That gives us reaction time before one can launch."

"But if a hostile helicopter achieves a position atop of us, we're dead, right?" Walker asked.

"Yes. Quite dead, barring a miracle of this ship's size or speed granting us a second chance."

A green icon glimmered on Cahill's screen, and he tapped it to accept a voice connection with the *Specter*.

"Cahill," he said.

"This is Henri, sir. I'm ready to launch a bathythermograph."

"That was fast."

"Antoine had already thought of it and had a unit staged by the launcher."

"Are you waiting for an order? I said you could launch when ready."

"Not waiting. Just informing you. I didn't want to surprise you in case this creates a metallic transient noise."

"Very well. Launch it."

Moments later, Cahill heard a subtle thud. As he questioned if the sound of the sensor's launch were real or imagined, a loud clank confirmed that the unit had banged against a support arm on its journey to the depths.

"Thank God there's nobody close enough to hear that," Walker said.

"Agreed. But let's trust and verify."

"Verify? You mean to risk a radio transmission?"

"Perhaps," Cahill said. "But first let's see if Pierre's already doing us the favor of transmitting useful information. As long as I've made noise, I may as well risk exposing our radio antenna for a download."

A frown cast a shadow over Walker's face.

"What's wrong?" Cahill asked.

"I'm not sure that Pierre isn't already doing us the favor. Look at his low-bandwidth transmissions."

As Cahill called up a history of recent transmissions from Pierre Renard, he recalled the communications protocol.

Renard had borrowed the bandwidth of high-endurance P3 Orion aircraft that the South Korean Navy flew to communicate with its submarines. With the *Goliath* submerged, the water above its antennas absorbed the electromagnetic energy of all but the aircraft's lowest transmission frequencies. Low frequencies meant low baud rates and lethargy of information flow.

Every minute, Renard sent a fifty-character message of gibberish so that the *Goliath* could verify its low-frequency reception. When the Frenchman needed to send a message of content, the characters changed, and an algorithm in the transport vessel's radio system raised an alarm if it recognized English words.

As Cahill studied the history of symbols, he noticed numbers that appeared meaningless. But equipped with Walker's queuing, he noticed the pattern, and then he noticed an error in the system.

"Good gracious, mate," he said. "Nice catch, Liam."

Walker nodded and smirked.

"I'll make note to have the system updated to recognize the word 'helo'. Apparently, such shorthand escaped the grasp of those who wrote the English detection algorithm."

"Right," Cahill said. "He's sending us coordinates of helicopters. Helo one and then helo two, each with latitude and longitude to the sixth decimal."

"Right."

"Are you checking this on the chart?"

"Already ahead of you. Done."

On Cahill's screen, the icons of two helicopters jumped through hyperspace and appeared ahead of the *Goliath's* track. Twenty miles separated the ship from the nearer aircraft.

"Damn," Cahill said. "Those pilots have made good guesses on where to look for us."

"When do you start to worry?"

"Worry? I don't intend to worry. But I will shoot them down before they approach within five miles."

"Should we maneuver?"

"No change to course or speed. That's just a guessing game the way helicopters maneuver so quickly. But depth is still in play. Time to check on the sound velocity profile."

He opened the channel to his cargo submarine, and he heard a new French accent.

"*Specter*, Antoine here."

"Antoine? Where's Henri?"

"He's right here beside me in the control room, but he knew that you wanted to ask about the sound-velocity profile. So he had me answer. I just finished computing it. Do you want me to send you the graphical data?"

"No. Just let me know if there's a layer I can dive below."

"It's close to your diving limits. There's a layer at one hundred and eight meters. You're only designed for one hundred meters. So it's a coin toss if one hundred meters will mask any of your noise. The *Specter* will be exposed above the layer, unless you go to one hundred and fifteen meters."

Cahill's mind stalled as he faced the hardest decision in his short tenure as the *Goliath's* commanding officer. Seeking the acoustic layer would risk overpressure damage but improve his chances of unfettered travel. Staying shallow would hasten surfacing if he needed to fend off his hunters.

"Terry?" Remy asked.

"Yes, yes, Antoine. We'll stay shallow. Thank you for the information."

"Okay. I will listen for helicopters, then."

As Cahill secured the voice channel, he noticed an icon appear eight miles from his ship.

"You see the update from Renard?" Walker asked.

"Yes. Remind our tactical team to listen attentively for active transmissions from helicopter sonars."

A red light pulsating on his screen caught Cahill's attention, and an unsolicited report from the *Specter* rang through the bridge.

"Active transmission, bearing three-one-nine," Remy said. "Variable-frequency dipping sonar. Probable Harbin anti-submarine warfare helicopter."

Cahill confirmed the bearing against that of the closest helicopter.

"Very well, *Specter*," he said. "Probability of detection?"

"Less than fifty percent. The sound power level is small. I heard it on my bow array sonar. I don't have it on any conformal hull sensors or towed array."

Cahill forgave the *Goliath*'s sonar team for failing to hear the sonic threat since his ship lacked a bow array sonar.

"What do you want to do, Terry?" Walker asked.

He thought about doing nothing, counting on the helicopter to pick up its dipping sonar and reposition itself farther away. But he concluded that his patience for cat and mouse games with the Chinese had worn thin.

He grabbed a microphone and raised it.

"Prepare for rapid surfacing," he said. "Ready all weapon systems. Translator, lay to the starboard bridge."

"Now you're thinking like a surface warfare officer," Walker said. "You may want to remind Doctor Tan that he's our translator and not our guest. He may not understand that laying to the bridge means getting his ass up here."

Cahill spoke into the microphone.

"Anyone who sees Doctor Tan, help him find his way to the bridge immediately."

"This is what happens when you hire an academic," Walker said.

"Do you know anyone else with sea legs who's fluent in English, Mandarin, and Korean and supposedly conversant in Russian? We're lucky Renard found him."

"Good point," Walker said. "Pierre seems to be really good at finding people."

"Line up our communications system for high-frequency voice, maximum power."

Walker tapped his screen.

"High-frequency voice is lined up for maximum power."

"Very well. Make your depth twenty meters."

The deck angled upward, and as the darkness surrounding the windows became turquoise, he heard a knock at the door.

"Come," he said. "Enter the bridge."

A small man with disheveled black strands atop a wide head stepped through the doorway. Large eyes stared back at him through thick glasses.

"Welcome, Doctor Tan."

"I came as fast as I could."

"Are you ready to speak with an authoritative voice?"

"I am always ready. This is our agreement."

"Good. Take the microphone. You will be hailing the pilot of a nearby helicopter and warning him to fly away from us. Can you handle it?"

"Of course. I have no more desire to die than you."

"Ready for rapid surfacing," Walker said.

With the *Goliath's* generous electric power and low-diving depths, Cahill had high-displacement, centrifugal trim and drain pumps at his command. The rapid surfacing procedure included driving upward and spitting water from the trim tanks.

"Rapid-surface the ship."

The world titled upward, and within seconds, sunlight bathed the room as the deck rocked and bobbed with surface swells. As he looked on the expected bearing of the helicopter, he instructed Tan.

"They're out there somewhere," he said. "Hail the pilot."

As Tan rattled off words in Mandarin, Cahill glanced at his cargo. Through downward facing grates, water gushing from the bottom of the *Specter's* ballast tanks spilled through the rubberized mesh of its cradle.

His executive officer, binoculars pressed against his face, called out and reminded him to look for the airborne threat.

"Phased array system is already tracking the target," Walker said. "And I see it now, too. It's definitely a Harbin."

"Aim both cannons to land rounds half a mile in front of the target," Cahill said.

"Cannons are ready."

"Any response, Doctor Tan?"

"None. I've hailed three times."

"The helicopter is moving towards us," Walker said.

"Prepare to launch one round from each cannon."

"Ready," Walker said.

"Fire."

The boom from the starboard railgun preceded the supersonic crack from the port hull's weapon. Flying at seven times the speed of sound, the rounds splashed in seconds.

The low-altitude trajectories traced hazy tubes of vapor, and the supersonic impacts reminded Cahill of cruiser-sized shells shattering the sea's silence. Mounds of water rose from the waves, erupted, and burst forth inverted fountains of fury in front of the aircraft.

But the helicopter climbed above the shooting droplets, recovered its path, and kept coming.

"Tell them that I will blow them out of the sky if they come within five nautical miles," Cahill said.

Tan nodded and barked out commands in Mandarin with a renewed zeal, but the helicopter continued.

"Prepare one round from each cannon to land five hundred yards in front of the helicopter."

"Weapons are ready," Walker said.

"Fire."

The rounds splashed, but the second helicopter joined the first in a direct sprint towards the *Goliath*.

"Six miles to the nearest helicopter," Walker said. "Twenty-one to the second helicopter."

"Set the system to automatically shoot the nearer helicopter if its range reaches five miles exactly. No more warning shots."

"Automatically?"

"I don't want us nitpicking about tenths of miles and last chances."

"The system doesn't allow that," Walker said. "At least not that I know of."

As Cahill placed his finger over the weapons control screen, he made a mental note to ask Renard for a software upgrade to improve the automation of the railguns.

"Then release the cannon controls to me," he said, "and countdown the range to the nearest helicopter in tenths of miles."

"Five point five miles," Walker said. "Five point four."

"I sure hope these mongrels don't test me."

"Five point three. Five point two."

"Damn them," Cahill said.

His finger twitched.

"Nearest helicopter is changing course!" Walker said. "It's circling us now, keeping a range of five point two miles."

"At least their crew has shown they can listen," Cahill said. "Train the port cannon on the closest helicopter. Train the starboard cannon on the other. Shift propulsion to the gas turbines as soon as they can bear the load."

"Weapons are trained," Walker said. "Head valves are opening. Gas turbines are spinning up."

Cahill stepped back and sat in the captain's chair.

"That's it?" Walker asked.

"That's it. They would have tried to attack us by now if that's what they meant to do. Whether that was their original intent or not, I don't care. Seeing our railguns and phased array radar system has deterred them. From here, they'll just follow us and take video until they satisfy their curiosity or until they reach their fuel limit."

"You're sure you don't want to shoot them down, just to be safe? I don't trust the Chinese."

"Nor should you, but they don't have suicide wishes. As I said, I'm not shooting down helicopters today. I'm avoiding them."

Walker pointed at the nearer aircraft.

"You call that avoiding? I feel compelled to wave at the pilot."

"Then wave, mate. I'll give meself full credit for avoidance if we can keep this an aggressive but nondestructive encounter."

"You're the captain."

"Indeed I am," Cahill said. "Set course for Donghae, maximum speed until we arrive."

CHAPTER 7

Sinking into his crutches, Lieutenant Yoon digested the tactical
scenario. Information from friendly airborne radar systems fed icons
on his monitor, pinpointing the enemy's search assets. The *Kim*
remained outside the detection range of his hunters, but he wondered
how long his luck could last.

Senior Chief Nang interrupted his thoughts.

"The welding is complete, sir. I took pictures on my phone."

He extended his arm, and Yoon looked at the screen. Chains
designed to hoist torpedoes connected the severed sections of the
submarine's shaft.

"It's been a few years since I welded, but I think I did a
pretty good job," Nang said. "It should hold the shaft in place if the
stern bearing fails."

"Good," Yoon said. "But I question if it could take the stress
of torque, even at a crawling speed."

"I wouldn't risk it, and I hope we don't have to find out. But
if the rescue effort fails, we may have no other choice."

"We'll test your workmanship only if necessary. At the
moment, we're safe. We're ten miles from the nearest threat."

"Ten miles isn't very far, sir."

"I am grateful that our adversary had no information on our
location when they began to hunt us. That uncertainty is why the
nearest gunboat is ten miles away. That uncertainty is why we are
still alive. I'll take ten miles distance as opposed to five miles or one
mile."

"You could plant a torpedo underneath that gunboat, and
then the nearest threat would be fifty miles away, and the object ten
miles away would be a sinking hull instead of a potential problem."

Yoon leaned into his crutches, extended his arm, and ran his
finger from the central icon to the second-nearest threat symbol, a

red square representing a decrepit frigate. At fifty nautical miles, the target steamed outside the reach of his torpedoes, but he knew that his submarine could handle the old surface combatant if it shortened the distance between them.

"I know how to deal with surface ships," he said. "I can kill them with torpedoes or missiles. They don't concern me."

As the words left his lips, he regretted the artificial bravado.

"But the intelligence report stated that a surface ship nearly sank the *Gwansun*, sir. If a gunboat can come that close to sinking our sister ship, then anything in our enemy's arsenal poses a threat to us."

"But it did not sink our colleagues. Instead, the *Gwansun* retaliated and destroyed its attacker, and it also took a *Sango* class submarine to the grave with friendly fire. I would call that a resounding victory."

"Victory? Narrowly escaping a relic gunboat? Stumbling upon a *Sango* by blind luck and using it as a decoy for a hostile torpedo? The *Gwansun* was supposed to remain submerged and undetected on its way to help us. I consider it survival by the grace of God."

"It survived," Yoon said. "It's still a victory, and it's still coming to help us."

"How can you be sure, sir? Our adversary could have followed the *Gwansun* here. This could be a trap. "

"What sort of trap?"

"A *Sango* submarine could have trailed the *Gwansun* here, waiting for it to make noise when it tries to help us."

"What of it? Then we and the *Gwansun* would dispose of that *Sango* submarine with torpedoes."

Again, he sensed that his boldness sounded forced.

"Even if that were so, the explosions would attract the North's entire navy," Nang said. "You must face it, sir. Our only act of defense is firing a weapon, and if we detonate a weapon near our ship, we announce our position and commit suicide. Even with the *Gwansun's* help, we need some good fortune to get out of this predicament."

As he shifted his weight between crutches and lowered his head to the tactical monitor, his stomach sent a burst of pain up his torso. He pressed his palm against his bandages.

"You're right, Senior Chief. We don't know who's listening for us. There may be a *Sango* within strike range, there may be a helicopter that's approached since our last intelligence download, and there may even be a gunboat atop of us that escaped radar detection. We need to act as if all sound is deadly."

"I'd like to think that our rescue planners thought of that."

Yoon nodded, keeping his gaze on the screen.

"The *Gwansun* is supposed to be half a mile behind us now," he said. "I find it eerie that our sister crew is so close and we can't hear them. I'd like to verify their presence, but we can't risk the exposure of any communication."

"I'm sure they can't hear us either, sir. Not while our propulsion plant is secured."

"I'd bet a month's pay that they've already passed underneath our hull and have visually located us through their periscope," Yoon said. "Finding us is not the issue. The issue is them having a chance to surface and send divers over the side to create the towing connection."

Nang scratched his chin and sat beside him. Facial oil glistened under whiskers, and the body odor reminded Yoon that his surviving crew hadn't showered in days.

"You think that's the only issue, sir? Getting divers over the side to wrap tow ropes around our stern planes?"

Yoon reflected upon the plan. The *Gwansun* would settle stern-to-stern behind the *Kim* and attempt to tow it backward by wrapping lines around the welded, static portion of its stern planes.

"Yes. The *Gwansun's* crew can't deploy swimmers any easier than we can. It's a surfacing exercise, which requires waiting until nightfall, and they face the added challenge of an alerted enemy that's scouring the waters for us."

"Nightfall was forty-five minutes ago, sir. Per plan, they have already succeeded in deploying divers."

Yoon dropped his head as he realized he'd lost track of time.

"Don't worry about it, sir," Nang said. "I see deploying the *Gwansun's* swimmers as only the second greatest challenge."

Yoon glanced to the senior chief, twisting his torso with deliberate care. He noticed sly wisdom in the man's eyes.

"Then what's the greatest challenge?"

"Our hull damage."

"If you mean our lack of structural integrity, that's why the *Gwansun* will use a nylon line and move slowly. The line will flex, in addition to being quieter than chain."

The veteran's eyes glimmered.

"That's the point, sir," he said. "The noise. I don't know if anyone has thought this through, but any attempt to tow us risks making a loud creaking noise from every piece of our hull. We took too much damage when we went deep."

"Surely, our rescue mission planners thought of this."

"I'm sure they thought of it. But how good do you think the data is on a damaged submarine's hull noise signature? I'm betting such data has never been gathered for any submarine, much less this class of submarine."

Before Yoon could answer, he heard a dull thud. He looked up and noticed it had traveled from the after compartments.

"They're here," he said.

"The *Gwansun*? That could be the sound of rope sliding over our stern planes."

"Get back there," Yoon said. "Investigate."

After the senior chief departed, Yoon heard the rubbing noise rise and then fall to silence. Then he felt a slight lurch backward.

Ecstasy consumed him as the *Kim* started moving. But then Nang's omen came true - a wretched, agonized shriek erupted from warped, protesting metal.

"Stop!" he said.

His command echoed in the control room, reaching nobody else's ears. But the *Gwansun's* sonar operators proved their attentiveness to his symbolic plea by noticing the condemning cacophony. The sound ceased as the rescue submarine stopped dragging his ship.

His ecstasy became fear as he accepted that the *Gwansun's* efforts failed. The noise precluded being towed, and he was stranded beyond his nation's ability to help. Worse, the attempt had just revealed his position to his hunters, and adrenaline coursed through him.

Nang returned, his eyes wide.

"They were surely attempting to tow us, but the noise was worse than I had feared. At least they were smart enough to stop towing us immediately."

"We need to prepare to fight," Yoon said. "I'm sure we just revealed our bearing to the nearest gunboat. I can only pray that no other hunters heard us to allow triangulation of our position."

He looked to a tactical monitor and toggled its view to raw sonar data. Curiosity replaced his fear.

"What's this?" he asked.

"You tell me, sir. I don't deal with those fuzzy lines."

"That's our colleagues on the *Gwansun*. See how fast their bearing is changing? They're moving away and ahead of us on our starboard side."

"What's going on, sir?"

"They're heading after the gunboat."

Yoon shifted his gaze to the bearing of the North Korean hunting ship. The lines representing its noises intensified, and he stifled a cry of pain as he reached down for a headset dangling beside the console and lifted it to his ear.

He heard the rhythmic chop of high-speed screws.

"And the gunboat is accelerating towards us," he said.

For a long minute, silence ruled the control room. Yoon glued his eyes to the sonar system, and when he looked up, he noticed a handful of his surviving crew gathering.

He addressed his new audience.

"Who's guarding the prisoner?"

His new onlookers mustered two names, satisfying him.

"What's going on, sir?" Nang asked. "You're seeing a lot but not saying much."

"I need to see this in the tactical system."

He called up a new screen and entered his estimate of the *Gwansun's* velocity, based upon the maximum acceleration and speed of his own ship. The system matched the history of bearings to his comrades and estimated their course and location.

He then updated the enemy gunboat's velocity to its maximum speed, starting at the time of the *Kim's* accidental groaning steel noise. The outcome inspired him.

"Our colleagues on the *Gwansun* are leading the hunters away from us."

"What's that there, sir?" Nang asked.

Yoon refocused on the sonar display and noticed bursts of sounds from the bearings of his countrymen. He then stiffened his back, grimaced, and pressed the headset to his ear.

"Torpedo launch," he said. "It's a Seahake Mod 4, from the *Gwansun!*"

"Excellent," Nang said. "No time wasted. Decisive!"

"Decisive indeed. Whether or not the gunboat radioed its discovery of our noise to its fleet, the explosion will confirm our presence. Rather, God willing, it will confirm the presence of the *Gwansun*. I believe that the commander of the *Gwansun* is trying to protect us by pretending to be us."

"Right, sir. The enemy has no definitive evidence of two submarines. They may believe there's only one of us down here."

During a minute of torpedo travel, Yoon hoped that the weapon would eliminate the gunboat before its retaliation. Then the targeted ship stopped, deployed its sonar system, and blared out acoustic energy.

"Active transmissions from the gunboat," he said.

"Could they possibly hear us?"

"No. We're too far away. But I fear that the *Gwansun* isn't so fortunate."

He listened to his comrades driving away from the gunboat, trying to open range and escape, but then his heart sank.

"Hostile torpedoes!" he said.

"How many?" Nang asked.

The sounds in his left ear seemed like a death knell.

"One," he said. "Now two. Two total."

"Dear God," Nang said. "Can their luck endure another attack? I don't expect there's another *Sango* behind which our colleagues can hide."

Yoon glared at the sonar screen. Traces appeared as visual translations of the hostile weapons' high-speed screws. He stowed the headset, ground his teeth as he reached, and toggled his display to the tactical screen. The system had estimated torpedo speeds, presenting an overhead view of the lethal exchange.

The rescue submarine's torpedo carved a perfect intercept course towards the relic gunboat, but the retaliatory salvo's aim also had merit.

"The *Gwansun* is sandwiched between the torpedoes," Yoon said.

He reached again, bore the pain, and slid the sonar headset over his head to listen with both ears. With his finger, he moved a cursor across his screen to filter the direction of his hearing. To distract himself from the danger his countrymen faced, he focused on their weapon.

"The *Gwansun's* weapon has acquired the gunboat," he said.

"Is it going to hit?" Nang asked.

"The gunboat is accelerating - trying to evade. No! It's too late. Terminal homing."

The rumble filled his head.

"Explosion on the bearing of the gunship. I hear the hull cracking. It's a kill."

Quiet cheers filled the room as Yoon's crew enjoyed the victory but respected the danger threatening their countrymen.

"I think they're on a good evasion course," Yoon said. "They've taken the proper vector to escape the acquisition cone of the trailing torpedo's seeker."

"What about the other torpedo, sir?"

"Not good. It appears to be getting active return from their hull. They just launched effervescent countermeasures."

"Sir?"

"Bubble-makers. A wall of air to acoustically isolate themselves from the torpedo."

He heard the torpedo pass through the bubbles, circle, and regain its target.

"Damn! The countermeasures bought them time, but the torpedo reacquired."

"Are they going to make it, sir?"

"I don't know."

He removed the headset, leaned, and stowed it. He then called up the tactical screen to watch an overhead view of trajectories. Tapping commands, he invoked a projected view of the future.

His heart sank.

"Impact in four minutes," he said.

"What can they do?"

"Sprint, launch more countermeasures, pray. I don't know what else."

During two minutes of quiet desperation, Yoon called up the sonar display on the screen above the tactical scene. He toggled his gaze up and down between the raw sound and the overhead view, hoping for a miracle.

A line grew on the sonar screen.

"There's something," he said.

"Another countermeasure, sir?"

"No. Too crisp. Slip that headset over my ears. I'm done pretending that it doesn't hurt to reach for it."

Nang obeyed.

"Now tap that left icon until the cursor settles under the new trace."

The sound from the new trace confused him. It sounded like the *Gwansun*.

"Now, on the tactical screen, tap the narrowband-frequency cursor. That's right. That one."

A graph of sound-power levels across frequencies up to three kilohertz appeared, representing discrete sounds that comprised the new trace.

"That frequency corresponds to the electric plant. The next one corresponds to the reduction gears. Then those are higher harmonics."

"What's it mean, sir?"

"It means they launched a decoy. An active decoy that's broadcasting sounds just like our class of submarine."

"Is it going to work?"

Yoon recalled his training.

"An advanced torpedo might be fooled into pursuing it, but once underneath, it would notice the lack of steel. A submarine's hull interrupts a torpedo seeker's magnetic influence field prior to detonation. An advanced torpedo would ignore the decoy after sensing no mass."

"What about fooling this old torpedo?"

"God willing, it will work."

He listened as the torpedo intersected the decoy. It circled back once and attacked it again.

"If nothing else, they've bought time. They may yet evade."

The *Gwansun* opened range, and the hostile torpedo continued its loops around the decoy. Yoon sighed in relief.

"Take off my headset," he said. "Our comrades our safe."

CHAPTER 8

Lieutenant Commander Dong-suk Kye stood in the engine room of gunboat *Taechong Twelve*. An overhead-mounted hook and chain network held a diesel engine inches above mounting bolts.

His first act after being plucked from the water and watching *Taechong Nineteen* burn was to salvage equipment and crew from his doomed vessel for transfer to the least decimated ship he could find among the hulks that remained in port.

The missile that doomed *Taechong Nineteen* had hit forward of amidships, costing him his officers and tactical team but sparing much of his engineering team. That played in his favor as he attempted to resuscitate *Taechong Twelve's* engine room.

But he had lost his chief engineer to the damage control effort, and he inherited a new leader for the engineering space.

"What's the problem?" he asked.

The veteran warrant officer, a stranger from *Taechong Twelve's* crew, appeared hesitant.

"Well?" Kye asked.

"Sir, it's just not fitting," the warrant said. "You're trying to patch together this ship from the remnants of *Taechong Nineteen* and at least two other ships. You can't expect parts from one vessel to always fit with another, especially equipment that's been neglected or damaged."

"Have you tried using chains and winches to stretch the base of the diesel so that it reaches the bolts?"

"No, sir."

"Have you tried heating the base of the diesel with hot oil to make it expand?"

"No, sir."

"So you've just stared at it for an hour and have done nothing?"

"Sir?"

"No, no, it's okay. We're all under a lot of stress. We'll have to consider other options, after lunch. Best to rest now and return to this with fresh minds and bodies."

Kye turned and stepped away, scanning the engine room for a certain type of object. A half-meter long torque wrench stowed against a bulkhead caught his attention.

He detached it, lifted it, balanced its weight in both hands, and then he turned. The warrant officer appeared dazed, unsure what to expect. He looked at Kye as the wrench smacked his jaw.

Having stunned his victim, he raised the wrench again and swung it sideways across the warrant's temple. The man fell to a knee. He considered raising the weapon over his head to crash it down, but he decided that risking murder would hinder his desire to hunt the South Korean submarine.

Instead, he kicked the man in the ribs until he lay motionless.

Heaving to catch his breath, he addressed the stunned sailors who surrounded him.

"This man could not find a way to get this ship to sea because he is a coward. He fears danger and will find any excuse to prevent deploying. I will not tolerate cowardice!"

The eyes of the men in the compartment met his to avoid showing fear and fueling his rage.

"Some of you on this ship are survivors from battle under my last command. The rest of you I took from the crews of the ships that were not seaworthy to give you a chance to show your mettle. We are facing the greatest naval effort our nation has seen since the sinking of the *Cheonan*. I don't know you, but you know me by reputation, and I demand that you show competence and courage."

He scanned the room to assure that the men paid attention.

"I found and engaged our enemy's most advanced submarine. I exchanged weapons with it, and were it not for the misfortune of one of our submarines being in the way, I would have sunk it. I will return to sea in a new ship, this ship, and you will perform your duties with courage in support of it."

The faces around him struggled for neutrality, but he knew he struck inner chords.

"Who's my next senior engineering expert?"

A sailor stepped forward.

"I am, sir."

"You have three hours to have that diesel engine installed, five hours total to have it online. Don't fail me."

"I won't, sir!"

"I know you won't," he said. "Even if you need to install it while we are underway."

On the bridge wing of *Taechong Twelve*, Kye raised a radio to his mouth.

"Bring the ship to five knots," he said.

The response from the tugboat captain crackled back, and the vessel moored to the gunboat defied its decrepit appearance by manhandling the naval warship.

Though lacking propulsion during diesel engine installation, *Taechong Twelve* provided a training opportunity for Kye's new crew. He stepped into the bridge.

"Prepare to deploy the sonar suite," he said.

His officer of the deck, an ensign, mouthed a lackluster response.

"I gave you an order, ensign. Speak!"

"Prepare to deploy the sonar suite, aye, sir!"

He watched the young officer fumble for a microphone and speak to a team in the ship's bowels. Blushing, he looked to Kye.

"There's a problem, sir."

"What sort of problem?"

"I don't know, sir. They just said they're not ready."

"Find out why."

The shaken youngster whipped the ringer while lifting a sound-powered phone to his ear. Anxiety and frustration underlay his conversation.

"Hydraulic pressure is low, sir. They're charging the accumulators now."

"Is there not a procedure that requires a verification of hydraulic pressure?"

"Yes, sir."

"Is there not also a manual crank for lowering and raising the sonar suite?

"Yes, sir. But it takes much longer. Minutes."

"Lay to the sonar suite," Kye said. "Deploy the sonar suite using manual override."

The officer acknowledged the order and started off.

"Wait," Kye said. "Inform the senior enlisted man of the team that he has one hour to review the complete procedure with the handling team. Then, he will deploy and retrieve the sonar suite ten times without incident, after this exercise. One mistake, and the count returns to zero. I will see this happen ten sequential times flawlessly."

Five minutes later, the ensign returned, having extended the gunboat's hydrophones into the water.

"The sonar suite is deployed, sir."

"Prepare to transmit active, half power, three hundred and sixty-degree search, twenty-degree wide beams. Transmit."

Shrill high-frequency chirps echoed through Kye's bones as he walked to his sonar operator.

"What do you see?" he asked.

"Nothing unusual, sir. These are our training waters."

"Correct. There's a sunken vessel we use for simulating a bottomed submarine. Show it to me."

The operator pointed at a constellation of green lines.

"Correct," Kye said. "Now, who is your relief?"

"Sir, I'm the only qualified sonar operator. The other was taken by the crew of a deployed vessel."

"I understand," Kye said.

He reached for the ship's announcing circuit and clicked the handset.

"Command Master Chief, report to the bridge."

Two minutes later, a man in his early forties with a leathery face appeared. Unlike the rest of *Taechong Twelve's* crew, the senior enlisted man appeared nonplussed by Kye's dominating style. Though he had not fought with Kye on *Taechong Nineteen*, he was battle-ready, having long ago lost partial use of his arm during a skirmish with a South Korean patrol craft.

"I was watching over the installation of the diesel, sir. What can I do for you?"

"Is there a man on the crew who has expressed interest in learning how to operate our sonar system?"

"None have expressed interest. But one of our cooks has said that he would take any position to escape galley duty."

"Is this cook attentive? Can he learn?"

"He shows good aptitude for a conscript."

"Bring him here and have him start learning. Inform the warrant officer who failed in installing my diesel that I am placing him on galley duty in his stead."

"Consider it done, sir."

The veteran turned to leave the bridge.

"Master Chief?" Kye asked.

"Yes, sir?"

"We will soon practice firing the cannon and torpedoes in the weapons range. Am I going to discover that the team is lacking in knowledge and depth in these critical areas?"

"Lack of knowledge? No. I refused to let my best gunner and torpedo launcher experts be pilfered by the deployed crews. And I personally can back up any of these men should they fall in battle."

"Are you a good shot with the cannon?"

The veteran smirked.

"Sir, if you asked the captain of a *Pohang* class corvette that I hit with nine rounds a decade ago, I assure you he would say that I am."

As the sun set, the departing tugboat drifted towards the horizon, and sea spray pelted Kye's cheeks. Making fifteen knots on one engine, the *Taechong Twelve* drove towards the weapons range.

He heard the door open and the officer of the deck yell.

"Sir, the engine room reports that the second diesel is online and ready to support all loads. He requests all stop to shift propulsion to both diesels."

"Very well. Bring the ship to all stop. Shift propulsion to both diesels."

The officer yelled the order through the open door, and the ship slowed.

"Propulsion is shifted to both diesels, sir."

"All ahead two-thirds."

The gunboat accelerated and then held its speed.

"Bring the ship to all ahead flank."

The officer acknowledged and shut the door. Moments later, the undulations below Kye's feet increased, and he grabbed a rail for support.

Minutes later, the door opened again.

"We've crossed into the weapons range, sir," the officer said. "We have the water space assigned to us, verified empty of other shipping traffic, and we are weapons free against all training targets."

His mind flashed with images of semi-sunken ships that served as targets for gunnery and torpedoes. Seeing no hurry to practice firing, he kept his focus on his gunboat's handling.

"Very well. Continue to the far end of the range. Then conduct a turn with a hard rudder. Maintain ahead flank. Then turn again with a hard rudder the other way. I want to see what this ship can do."

Two hours later, successful ship handling and weapon exercises convinced Kye that his adopted crew was ready. As he leaned over the navigation table, he reflected upon his accomplishment.

Leaderless, with their commanding and executive officers cannibalized to staff seagoing combatants, the men of *Taechong Twelve* had languished in port. Gutted to a skeletal staffing with many enlisted leaders and conscripts stolen away for battle, the crew had awaited a spark. He credited himself with providing that spark and whipping the vessel and makeshift crew into shape in a day.

He summoned his officers to the table and angled a mechanical pencil over a chart showing the Sea of Japan.

"An enemy submarine launched a commando raid off our coast and abducted the hero admiral who led the glorious attack against the *Cheonan*. Now, that submarine has been harassing our ships for three days. There have been attacks here, here, and here. The first was against me when I commanded *Taechong Nineteen*."

He tapped the pencil against the location where a missile had crippled his prior ship.

"Our admiralty believes that the mission against us is intricate. It involves the abduction of the hero admiral, followed by the submarine remaining at sea to entice our fleet to search for it, followed by ambushes from the attacking submarine."

"The enemy has deployed another submarine since the abduction, sir," an ensign said. "Does the admiralty believe it's joining in the attack?"

"Unknown," Kye said. "The admiralty is divided. Some believe it is assisting with ambushes. Others believe it is taking advantage of the distraction created by the first submarine and preparing to launch an amphibious attack against us elsewhere. This is why coastal installations are on high alert. Yet still others believe that the second submarine is nothing but a diversion to dilute our search for the first and to cause us extra panic."

"Do we have orders, sir?"

"No. But we have complete freedom to do as I wish. Nobody thought this ship would be ready, but after a day of hard work and training, I am leading you all into combat."

The faces around him appeared stern, the men hiding their mixes of bloodlust and fear.

"Since I am free of the responsibility of a prescribed search area, I plan to make use of that freedom. I also intend to make use of the weather. Tomorrow will involve mixes of rain and fog, which will reduce the ability of the enemy's radar systems to find us."

"I'm not sure I follow you, sir," his navigator, a lieutenant, said. "In the enemy's eyes, we'll be but one bee in a hive of attackers. Why should attempts to hide work in our favor?"

Kye nodded, impressed that the lieutenant caught the apparent flaw in his logic.

"We're not hunting with the hive," he said. "We're going to maneuver ahead of the enemy and strike at its weakest point."

"Weakest, sir? I consider them weak now. They're in our waters, taunting us, and our fleet is fighting back. You yourself would have destroyed them, were it not for terrible luck."

"That's not their weakest point," Kye said. "The weakest is on their return home, when they think they have achieved victory and believe they are safe. Their guard will be down. That is where we will strike."

He stabbed the pencil into chart, looked up, and saw concern in his men's eyes. Given the location where he jabbed the paper, he excused their fear.

"Here," he said. "Just inside the enemy's waters, where they control the air."

The lieutenant gulped, and Kye heard the tightness in his voice.

"Since we have no anti-air missiles, I recommend that we bring shoulder-launched anti-air weapons with us."

"You're scared," Kye said. "Fear is acceptable. In fact, if you weren't afraid, I would consider you incompetent. But I note your courage in being able to see our weakness against the overpowering threat of the enemy's aircraft. I commend you. And to answer your question, I have already summoned Igla Missile teams to join us. A fishing ship will bring them to us."

"I see, sir," the lieutenant said. "May I ask what your plan of attack is against the enemy submarine?"

"We will be where their commander will least expect us. If he's lucky enough to escape the rest of the fleet, he will let his guard down once in his own airspace. And we will be there, ready to pounce."

CHAPTER 9

Jake Slate stood outside the briefing room in the Donghae naval base. Pierre Renard's steel blue eyes glistened as he inhaled smoke from his Marlboro.

"How were your travels, my friend?" Renard asked.

"Fine," Jake said. "What's my name today?"

"Mister Johnson."

"That's pretty boring."

"They won't challenge its veracity."

The Frenchman tossed the expended butt into a standing ashtray and kissed the air beside Jake's cheeks. The scent of musky cologne and nicotine lingered.

"I regret that we have little time for pleasantries, but there's a special sense of urgency about rescue missions."

Jake stuffed away the sadness of fleeting time with his friend and mentor.

"How long do we have together?" he asked.

"A couple hours at most," Renard said. "I'll be with you on the helicopter ride to the *Specter*."

"The Koreans seem happy to offer you whatever resources you need. Helicopters, submarine communication bandwidth, access to their military leadership."

"They don't quite trust me as well as my Taiwanese clients, but they are committed. And once a Korean team is committed to a plan, there's no derailing them."

"I guess not."

"But for all their efficiency and resilience, they can surprise you."

The comment felt like a foreshadowing.

"What's happened?"

"Our clients tried to handle matters on their own, and nothing good came of it. They tried to tow the *Kim* to safety with another of their submarines."

"I get it that they'd want to save their shipmates."

"But they didn't have complete understanding of the structural damage," Renard said. "The depth excursion apparently weakened the hull enough that the creaking noise created by towing is detectable by even the most rudimentary sonar system."

"So they knew it might create noise, but they couldn't predict how bad it would be. They took a gamble and lost."

"Right. They're lucky that both submarines weren't lost. Escaping the North Koreans required heroics and aggression by the *Gwansun*."

"That's un-Korean to play cowboy like that. They're not natural risk-takers. That's what they hire guys like me for."

The Frenchman lowered his voice.

"It wasn't about risk management," he said. "It was about fear of shame. They consider it shameful to be dependent upon us."

"Shit, Pierre, there's nothing shameful about renting our services. You have a transport ship to cart your diesel submarines across the globe. They don't because they have no reason to build one. It's basic trade economics."

"I agree. But they don't see it that way. So be wary of it."

"Sure, I will. Who's in the briefing room?"

"Staffers. All officers with seagoing experience, but the dozen men in the room are now serving on fleet staff. They're the core of the team that's running the rescue operation."

"Okay. Lead on."

He followed Renard into a stark, three-tiered briefing room of unfamiliar faces. An admiral stood on an elevated stage by the front screen, which showed an overhead view of the Korean Peninsula's east coast. A tall commander beside the admiral translated his boss' greeting.

"Mister Johnson, Mister Renard speaks very highly of you. Admiral Cho welcomes you."

The translator hesitated, and Jake noticed a sense of expectation from the smallish admiral beside him. Having learned politesse over years of military service and mercenary missions, he recognized his obligation.

He marched up the stairs on the stage's edge and sensed Renard behind him, confirming that he had made the right move in approaching the admiral. He extended his hand and offered a slight bow before repeating the gesture with the translator.

"Admiral Cho is pleased to meet you," the translator said. "Please, be seated."

The translator extended his palm to the two empty seats behind the long desk that separated the front row from the stage. Jake followed Renard behind the backs of seated officers and then sat facing the screen. Sinking his buttocks into the seat, he absorbed the information on the wall display.

He assumed that a white X marked the location of the stranded *Kim*, but the lack of English characters befuddled him. He leaned into Renard.

"It's all in Korean," he said.

"The translator will explain."

Jake glanced around the room. Every person other than Renard and himself wore a South Korean Navy uniform, the rankings dropping in proportion to the distance from the screen. He noticed a few young lieutenants in the back row and remembered having been their American equal a decade earlier.

The translator diverted his attention to the room's front.

"Mister Renard, Mister Johnson," he said. "The X you see sixty-five nautical miles east of the adversary's fleet headquarters in Wonsan represents the *Kim*."

Finding it obvious, Jake nodded out of decorum as the translator continued.

"The blue inverted V you see twenty-eight nautical miles west of the *Kim* is the *Gwansun*. The *Gwansun* is risking aggressive maneuvers and outright attacks against adversarial shipping to divert attention from the *Kim*."

Jake considered the *Gwansun's* actions brave. Red icons that represented North Korean warships encircled it, scant miles outside of detection distance.

The translator continued.

"There are almost two hundred and fifty hostile military vessels searching for the *Kim*, and there are countless unknown merchant vessels looking for visual signs of her. The *Goliath* must deliver it to safety as soon as possible."

Stepping aside, the translator lowered his palm towards an inverted blue V stacked on its twin.

"The double blue V represents the *Specter* and the *Goliath*. The *Goliath* will carry the *Specter* to the drop off point, approximately fifty nautical miles north of Kosong."

The passivity of the Korean officers told Jake that they had heard the brief, and since Renard had crafted the plan, he realized that he was getting a special Jake-centric English version. Raising his finger, he interrupted.

"What's special about that location as the drop off point?"

"It's the limit of our air superiority," the translator said.

The admiral stirred beside the interpreter and exchanged words with him in Korean.

"Admiral Cho states that the drop off point may be extended deeper into hostile waters if radar information shows hostile ships and aircraft to be distant at the time of the *Goliath's* arrival on station."

Jake nodded and whispered to Renard.

"Whose decision is it going to be about shifting the drop off point?"

"Guess."

"Shit."

"Don't worry," Renard said. "They're a conservative people. They won't risk putting you or the *Goliath* into harm's way."

"That's what I'm afraid of," Jake said. "Too conservative on the part they control, giving me and Terry more ground to cover underwater."

The translator raised his palm to another X.

"The Liman Current is carrying the *Kim* southward," he said. "If unaided, it would then be carried northeast by the Tsushima Current. Based upon estimated arrival times, the *Goliath* will intercept the *Kim* here, at the loading point. The *Specter* will join the *Goliath* to provide protection."

A sea of red squares representing hostile ships dotted the water between the drop off point and the loading point. Wondering how to navigate through them unnoticed, Jake raised his finger.

"Do you have expectations on how the *Goliath* and *Specter* will reach the *Kim* or how we will get it out of the area?"

"Admiral Cho understands that when your vessels are submerged, they must operate with minimal dependence upon fleet commands. Mister Renard has convinced him of your capabilities and your respect for the situation. You are free to extract the *Kim* as you see fit, and you are free to engage hostile vessels as you see fit. There are no rules of engagement for you – only mission goals."

"What about the *Gwansun*?"

"It will remain at a distance, continuing to provide a distraction. In fact, it has been ordered to attack hostile vessels during the hours we expect the *Goliath* to load the *Kim*."

"That's courageous," Jake said. "A distraction should help us escape. Do we have a prescribed evacuation route?"

"You may evacuate on any route you see fit, and we will broadcast the locations of any threat we can identify. That will obviously be primarily surface ships and aircraft. You will have to evade submarines using your organic sensors."

"Understood," Jake said.

The interpreter stared at Jake until the admiral murmured an instruction to him.

"I think you asked the right questions," Renard said. "You might have taken a bit of the wind out of his sails."

"I didn't mean to."

"Do you have any further questions, Mister Renard or Mister Johnson?" the translator asked.

Jake shook his head, and then the admiral snapped an order. The audience stood, and the translator led a small group in escorting Jake and Renard from the room.

A van took them to a tarmac where they boarded a helicopter. A second aircraft behind his warmed up its engine. Stepping into the cabin and donning a headset, he noticed a muffling of the blades' chopping thump.

He yelled into his microphone.

"Pierre?"

The Frenchman's electrified voice filled his earpieces.

"Yes. I hear you."

"Who's in the other helo?"

"Replenishments for your crew."

"Any key players? I don't suppose I'm training a new executive officer?"

"Negative. Henri will be your right-hand man again. So you're on your own tactically."

"This is a smash and grab, Pierre. We're in and out. I don't need an exec. I was just wondering."

"Agreed. The men in the other helo are technicians, a mix of MESMA and propulsion plant experts. The two with us are sonar operators to be trained under Antoine."

Jake reached out and shook hands with two young men wearing similar clothes to his – the beige pants with white cotton dress shirts that served as uniforms in Renard's fleet.

"Where'd you find them?" he asked.

"I had to go back to the well, so to speak. The French Navy. Terry took all the Australian recruits to the *Goliath*."

The helicopter climbed and banked, and Jake enjoyed the clear view of the stars. Moonlight shimmered in the waters, and the electric lights of the naval base became an ovular aura.

"There!" Renard said.

Jake followed the Frenchman's finger towards lights on the water. Moored to an anchored tanker, the *Goliath* revealed itself. Bathed under the fueling ship's deck lights, the *Specter's* transport ship appeared ominous.

"*Goliath*, for sure," Jake said. "Well named. That thing's almost as long as the tanker."

"Long enough to carry both the *Specter* and the *Wraith*, if ever needed."

"No shit?"

"It's a balancing act with parts of each submarine hanging over either edge of the cradle. The loading process is the key, getting each ship into precise position, noses practically touching each other and all the internal weight moved forward. It's tricky, but it's possible."

"You didn't think about bringing the *Wraith*?"

"Impractical. It would be a complex matter to divide the water around the *Kim* between the *Wraith* and the *Specter*. Plus, the time it would have taken to load the *Wraith* would have created an unacceptable delay. And worst of all, I can't recruit men fast enough to man all three ships. I'm afraid that the *Wraith* is orphaned, awaiting a loving commander and crew."

"Heck, we may have some South Korean defectors to your navy after we're done here," Jake said.

"Guard your arrogance," Renard said. "You've accomplished nothing yet in their eyes."

The words stung. A glance at his newest crewmen suggested that their own thoughts consumed them. He assumed his conversation took place on a private circuit and sharpened his tone.

"You've always appreciated my confidence. What's wrong with knowing that I'm good at what I do?"

"Overconfidence. Our clients failed to mention it at the briefing, but the *Gwansun* barely escaped the torpedo of a patrol craft. I know this because I am a participant in their operations center."

"It would have been nice to know this," Jake said. "I could use a study of my enemy's tactics."

"Our clients would never admit a near sinking of their front-line submarine by a North Korean gunboat to you publicly. They instead trusted that I would give you the details in private. The reconstruction of that exchange is loaded into the *Specter's* tactical system for your review."

"Face-saving jackasses. What if I needed to ask clarifying questions about South Korean evasion tactics and what the North Koreans know about them? That could have driven the way the gunboat attacked. That could drive how they attack me, if it comes down to it."

Renard shook his head.

"Don't be so quick to condemn our clients," he said. "They detest speaking of their weakness in public, but they are honest to a fault in private. They have provided me such information about their tactical doctrine and their intelligence on the North Korean understanding of said tactics. It's all loaded in the *Specter's* Subtics system. Henri will show you."

Jake leaned back in his seat and felt its shakiness.

"Fair enough," he said.

"The point I want you to remember is that the North Koreans may be armed with relics, but they have sent an armada staffed by capable, committed men. And they are willing to sink their own ships to achieve victory."

Jake glared at him.

"The *Gwansun* escaped by vectoring a threatening torpedo into a *Sango* class submarine," Renard said. "Granted, the shooting captain may not have known about a friendly submarine being nearby, but it's more likely that he was instructed not to care."

"And it proves that their anti-submarine tactics work."

"Agreed. Do not take them lightly."

"I won't," Jake said.

He reflected upon his mentor's comment about arrogance. The manifestations of a divine god in all the religions he studied abhorred hubris, and he considered it human nature to find arrogance repulsive. But he recognized that any successful submarine commander needed to ooze confidence.

Sensing his mind slipping into the abyss of a looping argument between the humility of human limits and a commander's need for perfection, he fidgeted. Then, clenching his teeth, he dissipated his frustration into his jaw muscles as he felt the aircraft stop and hover.

"You're first," Renard said.

Jake looked up and saw a crewman holding a harness and gesturing with his free glove for him to stand. He obeyed, and after a minute of contortions, he stared through the faceplate of a helmet at the bulge in his crotch. He yanked his groin straps and fumbled with his genitals until convinced of their safety.

The crewman reached, and the door crashed open, revealing darkness. Jake eased to the lip of the exit and slid his feet backward out of the helicopter until he felt the cable bear his weight. Releasing himself, he waved goodbye to Renard and slipped below the aircraft.

As he started twirling, he focused on the spinning black form of the *Specter* below. Happy he had kept an empty stomach, he tightened his abdomen on the way down.

When his vision paralleled the tanker's deck, he felt a hook latching onto his backside, and the spinning stopped. Moments later, he pressed his tennis shoes against steel and recognized the face of Claude LaFontaine, his longtime friend and the *Specter's* engineer. He kissed the air beside his cheeks and screamed over the rotor wash.

"Good to see you, Claude!"

"And you, Jake. Take off your harness and helmet and head below. You'll recognize much of the crew that's already aboard."

Beside LaFontaine stood a pair of Korean rescue swimmers. Trusting that his engineer and the hook-wielding helpers would get his newest crewmen to the submarine, he started towards the hatch.

But the view slowed him, and he stopped to take it in.

Like an enormous catamaran, the *Goliath* and its rakish bows extended into the night. Illuminated by internal lighting, the domed bridge sent checkered radiance into the sky. The forward sections appeared capable of slicing waves.

The sterns of both hulls also tapered upwards towards fantails to allow for surface-combat weaponry. He recognized the railguns and the radar system.

Submerged cylinders of equal girth to the *Specter* connected the customized bows and sterns of each hull. Fuel lines reached from the tanker to the *Goliath's* black arcs jutting above the dark waves. Taking in a final impression of the majestic transport ship, Jake scurried into his submarine.

Familiarity.

The ship he had commanded in protecting Taiwan and then the Falkland Islands felt safe and comforting, like a womb. Memory guided his walk to the control room.

He passed through a doorway and positioned himself behind the shiny railing of the elevated conning platform.

The metal casing that housed the consoles and monitors of the Subtics tactical system seemed shiny, and he realized that Renard had paid the Taiwanese maintenance crew to polish the interior.

Key familiar faces greeted him. To his left, before one of six dual-stacked Subtics panels, sat his sonar systems expert, Antoine Remy. Like all his aces, Remy had honed his skills in the French Navy prior to recruitment to Pierre Renard's mercenary fleet.

To his right, seated in front of panels and gauges that controlled the ship's skeletal and cardiovascular systems, the white-haired, sharp-featured Henri Lanier epitomized dignity in stature, appearance, and knowledge of any moving part of a submarine.

A few younger French-trained mercenaries, familiar from past missions spanning from the recapture of an Israeli submarine in the Atlantic Ocean to the defense of Philippine land in the Spratly Islands, sat in front of consoles.

"Did you miss us?" Henri asked.

Before Jake could answer, the smiling Frenchman crossed the deck plates, grabbed his shoulders, and kissed the air beside his jaw. Then Remy, his toad-like head appearing oversized for his body, joined Henri.

"It is good to see you, Jake," Remy said.

The younger sailors then greeted their commander.

"It's great to see you guys," Jake said. "I never thought we'd reunite for a mission on top of an armed, high-speed dry dock."

"It's so much more than that," Henri said. "At first, I argued with Pierre that it would be wiser to purchase a third submarine. But then he explained the *Goliath's* design. It has tactical merit far beyond that of a transport vessel."

"It's too loud and deaf for combat against submarines. I hope Terry recognizes this and keeps it out of my way."

Jake recalled having expressed prior concerns about his Australian colleague's abilities and having eaten his words.

"Terry has already proven himself," Henri said.

"I know," Jake said. "Any lesser of a commander, and I wouldn't be here. This rescue is going to tricky enough, even with the best people working it."

CHAPTER 10

Jake hid in the captain's stateroom, separating himself from fellow humans to face his parasitic demons.

The strange absence of pre-combat jitters created a void and let an unsettling sensation cloud his mind. He sought to frame the feeling but failed, leaning back in his chair like a zombie.

A broken home had skewed his childhood worldview. A malicious exchange of HIV-positive blood and subsequent wrongful expulsion from naval submarine duty had made him vengeful. He knew that people considered him an angry person, but something seemed different this time.

He felt angrier than normal, and this mission felt incomplete.

"What's wrong with me?"

From nowhere, the answer struck him – the lost anticipation of alcohol.

With the pill-driven death of his drinking desire, he lacked the expectancy of drowning himself in his usual post-mission hazy euphoria. Renard's intervention had broken his cycle of tasting fear, riding adrenaline through battle, and then returning home to douse his emotions.

He realized that if he survived rescuing the *Kim*, he would face the post-traumatic turmoil without his comforting chemical crutch. The demons of fear and anger dwelling inside him would rise unchecked, and the prospect of weathering such a storm scared him.

He rolled the chair forward, folded his elbows to his knees, and lowered his head to his hands.

"Shit," he said.

Philosophical sentiments rolled through his mind as he groped for solace. Randomly, the concept of Zen landed first in his thoughts.

Years of Buddhist studies had frustrated him, highlighting the strength of his demons and the weakness of his efforts to control them. Endless sitting meditations, readings, and discussions about denying desires to escape suffering had exhausted him, and he had abandoned the practice.

Buddhism would not fill the alcohol gap.

Taoism had crept into his awareness through his martial arts training, but after studying it, he considered it a temporary optimizing of harmony with nature's forces. But it failed to resolve any deep problems, such as keeping its practitioners from reaching their graves. He instead had tried going the other way of indulgence.

With his enormous net worth, he had explored materialism as his mechanism to decompress. Five star dinners, luxury hotel rooms, and travel to exotic destinations on a whim had garnered his attention for the early years of his wealth, but every effort to pamper himself had left him empty, questioning his purpose.

He couldn't buy a substitute for his escape into alcohol.

Violence – dominating others with his will – had held appeal in his past. Revenge had driven him to steal his Trident Missile submarine, killing dozens in the flight. His post-treason life had then centered around lethal submarine missions, and he had lost count of the hundreds of men he had doomed to watery graves. Anger had even compelled him to beat a man to death with his bare hands.

The result – guilt and emptiness.

Violence offered no sanctuary from the cauldron of his emotions, leaving him no shelter except alcohol.

He had considered other activities and ingestion addictions, but the logical endpoint for each was a circling back to its starting point. Excessive exercise, adrenaline sports, and martial arts provided temporary distractions, but they changed nothing about his philosophy. And new chemical indulgences seemed fruitless with their destructive effects and limited highs beyond that of alcohol.

Though temporary, cyclical, and damaging, alcohol had been his only reliable escape. But with the pills having removed his craving, he now faced the frightening void.

Knowing that nature abhors a vacuum, he predicted that anger, and the other dark emotions it masked, would consume the space that alcohol had relinquished.

He had forgotten a time when anger seemed distant. It lurked below the foreground, waiting to explode when his efforts to restrain it failed. Without the safe harbor of inebriation, he knew he would struggle harder to contain the rage.

But he found it odd that people considered him angry. The feeling seemed the normal, base human state. He wondered how anyone could examine the human condition and conclude anything beyond hopeless misery. Anyone who's paying attention to mankind's lot should be infuriated.

Why didn't this truth aggravate everyone? Did people ignore it? Were others angry but better at controlling it? Did they see a way around the impasse to which he was blind?

Seeking answers led him into a logical corner. Sampling and then rejecting the worldly philosophies and distractions had forced him to investigate the evidence underlying organized religions.

The endless controversy about the existence of an omniscient god suggested a need for the universe's uncreated creator that varied in essence from a random force to the personalized gods of Judaism, Christianity, and Islam. Regardless of the essence, every logical path he followed to understand a creator required a leap of faith beyond the known and knowable laws of nature.

That meant a need to account for the supernatural.

During his reflections, the possibility of the supernatural had cracked his defensive shell and had taken root in his mind. The seed planted, all spiritual doors swung open, and he doubted he could draw a conclusion if given a lifetime to examine the mountains of evidence behind the monotheistic beliefs, their countless offshoots, Hinduism, or any other school of religion.

The daunting task of exploring faith-based existences while racing the ticking clock of his life exacerbated his frustration. But at least, he realized as the *Specter's* deck rolled, it could fill a void.

"Interesting," he said.

He straightened his back as he acknowledged that he could divert his frustrations into research. Perhaps he could feed his mind the essential knowledge behind mankind's purpose to fill the void of alcohol and diffuse his anger. The thought offered him a chance at sanity after the mission.

It was the best he could fathom, and it kept his demons in check. But first, he had to survive rescuing the *Kim*.

The *Specter* heaved and redirected his thoughts to the pending dangers he faced off the North Korean coast. He stood, left his stateroom, and closed the door. After a quick walk to the control room, he grabbed the polished rail that encircled the raised conning platform.

The deck dipped and rebounded, knocking him off balance. He swore as he caught himself with the rail.

"God damn it!"

Henri gave him an inquisitive stare.

"Sorry," Jake said. "I'm a bit torqued, that's all."

"Indeed," Henri said. "You're not one to let the anticipation of combat consume you, but you've seemed on edge lately."

Jake appreciated the candor of his French accomplice. He counted on Henri to state his mind, and his directness had saved their lives in the past.

"Just not used to being rattled in this cage," he said. "Can it get any worse?"

"Sometimes," Henri said. "Such is life as the cargo of the *Goliath*."

"At least guys on the *Goliath* can take breaks and look out the window. This isn't right for guys stuck inside steel."

"I'm sure it's this bad on frigates," Henri said. "And imagine how it is on even smaller ships."

"No thanks. I did my first summer cruise at the academy on a cruiser. That was bad enough in the Atlantic. Then they made me ride a shitty little yard patrol craft for three days the following year. It was a puke fest. After that, I wised up, and it's been submarines ever since. Until now, sort of."

"I wouldn't worry about it, Jake. We're close to the drop off point."

Jake glanced at a navigational display showing fifteen minutes before he would detach from the transport ship.

"Where were you?" Henri asked. "You're not one to remain behind a locked door for long."

The question caught him off guard. He lied.

"I was just pondering some of the mission essentials. Trying to think if we forgot to analyze anything."

"Did you come up with anything?"

The Frenchman having called his bluff, Jake prepared to brush off the question with a negative response. But a random flash of inspiration shot through his mind.

"Yeah," he said. "I actually had an interesting idea. You can listen in while I run it by Terry."

He tapped a screen and waited for Cahill's voice to render over the loudspeaker.

"How are you, mate?"

"Good, Terry."

"What's on your mind?"

"I thought maybe you could create a diversion to get us in closer to the *Kim* and also cripple a few North Korean ships while you're at it."

"I'm listening. Go on."

"You have five hundred total rounds in your railgun magazines, right?"

"Right. Two-fifty per hull."

"What say you put two rounds into each engine room of the closest hundred ships to the *Gwansun*?"

The silent pause left Jake wondering if he had asked a stupid question.

"Brilliant!" Cahill said.

"I was afraid you'd call me an imbecile."

"I'm ashamed I didn't think of it meself. There's no way we're going to run out of ammo on this mission. I may as well make the area around the *Gwansun* appear like our destination by raining down hell there."

"Glad you like the idea."

"Like it? I love it. It'll take some heat off the *Gwansun*, focus the North Koreans' attention in that area, and give us more breathing room to maneuver in closer to the *Kim* before submerging. Who knows, I might even disable a few ships, like you said."

"You'll need to attack the ships while they're broadside to you, right? It's the only way you can get a clean shot at their engine rooms, despite the fact that a bow or stern shot rakes the ship and does more total damage. These railgun rounds just keep going through metal, like cannon shot through the old wooden ships."

"Indeed they do, mate. This forces us to think in ways that submarine officers don't normally think. Let me see what Liam says. That's what he's here for. Hold on a second."

Jake waited while Cahill consulted his surface warrior executive officer.

"Liam says to attack broadsides. It gives us a better chance of damaging propulsion plants. Given flight times of the projectiles, the targets may maneuver, but that's a chance we'll have to take."

"Makes sense," Jake said. "What's needed to get started? I've never operated a railgun."

"I've got it covered, mate. With their muzzle speeds, I'm already in range. I can use GPS satellites for guidance. Just give me a minute to warm up the cannons while you inform Pierre."

As the mission commander, Jake remembered that he needed to handle the communications with Renard.

"Good point. Can you patch me through?"

"Too lazy to raise your radio mast?"

"Why bother, since you're already connected?"

"Right. I was just kidding. I really like the equipment on this here cargo ship. Hold on. Okay, you're connected to Pierre."

The French accent came through the loudspeaker with digital clarity.

"Pierre, here. What's going on?" Renard asked.

"Terry and I want to try something."

He explained the tactic for attacking one hundred ships.

"Very well," Renard said. "I'll make sure you get updated targeting data from our supporting radar systems. I need a minute to verify it with our clients, but I see no reason they should disagree."

"I was concerned you may be against this for the cost," Jake said.

"Not to worry," Renard said. "The costs of each round are pass-through. Per contract, the South Korean Navy will pay for all consumables. But one beautiful factor about railgun rounds is their cost. They are quite cheap. I see no protest in expending two hundred of them to protect the *Gwansun* and give you a better chance of rescuing the *Kim*."

"Given the rate of fire, one round every five seconds for each cannon, we need almost nine minutes of continuous fire to get this done," Jake said.

"Get your cannons warmed up," Renard said. "Wait while I speak with our clients."

Renard's offline conversation took longer than Jake had hoped.

"What's keeping him, you think?" he asked.

"Fear, mate." Cahill said. "Koreans don't like to deviate from plans. Give Pierre time, though. He's a master negotiator."

"Well the way I see it, we were weapons free when we set sail. As far as I'm concerned, this is merely a courtesy."

"Right, mate. But remember who you're dealing with. It's a new client for Pierre, and they are the very definition of conservative."

"I'm back," Renard said.

"Well?" Jake asked.

"As a gesture of good faith, I had to agree to share the cost of the consumed rounds in your upcoming tactic."

"That's peanuts," Jake said. "Why did they even bother?"

"I still have much to teach you in the art of negotiation," Renard said. "Terry, you may fire when ready."

"I'm ready."

"Happy hunting," Renard said. "Show me what the *Goliath* can do."

CHAPTER 11

Terry Cahill wrestled with internal conflict. His targets served a narcissistic ruler and deserved to feel his wrath, but the railguns gave him an unfair advantage. He appreciated Liam Walker helping him retain his focus.

"The first fifty rounds are programmed into the system in splintering mode," Walker said. "I expect that targets will begin to scatter after the first fifty, and we'll need to adjust targets as their aspects change."

"Right," Cahill said.

It seemed cruel and unusual to kill from a distance ten times that of an adversary's counterpunch, and he felt uneasy, as if he teased karma.

"Terry?"

"Yes?"

"I await your order."

"Right," Cahill said. "Engaging targets pre-loaded into the tactical system, fire twenty-five rounds from each cannon. Set the rounds to splinter before impact."

Cahill felt confident that his decision to use the rounds' small internal detonators to break them into buckshot would inflict more damage to his prey's propulsion systems than would the deeper but singular puncture wounds of intact projectiles.

"Engaging targets pre-loaded into the tactical system, fire twenty-five splintering rounds from each cannon, aye." Walker said. "Firing each cannon."

The crack from the starboard railgun preceded that from the port hull's weapon. Flying at seven times the speed of sound, the rounds sought their victims.

Having aimed his first rounds at the farthest ships, Cahill hoped to synchronize the impacts. But with the first Mach 7 projectile requiring a minute to reach its target and with five seconds separating each shot, the initial impacts would provide warning to his later targets. He expected satellite tracking and targeting updates from South Korean aircraft to place his rounds on his alerted and fleeing prey.

"How are the cannons' parameters?" he asked.

"Barrel temperatures are normal for repeated firing," Walker said. "Recoil force is normal. Lube oil temperature is normal for repeated firing. Capacitors are cycling through the normal coulomb range for charge and discharge. Charge voltages and currents are normal. Wait."

"What?"

"Port cannon cooling water temperature is below the alarm threshold but high and rising."

Walker tapped his screen and barked into it.

"Port weapons bay, report cooling water pump speed!"

The voice squawking back seemed panicked and meek.

"Sorry, sir. It was on slow speed. I just shifted the pump to high speed."

"Very well," Walker said. "There's an obvious flaw in our software. Keep an eye on it."

"The system should have automatically shifted the pump," Cahill said.

"Agreed," Walker said.

"This is what happens when you press a ship into service too fast. You can't test everything. I just pray this is the worst glitch."

"We can only hope to be so lucky."

Cahill made a mental note to schedule a continuous fire training session with the weapons team, covering all weapon systems, prior to the next mission.

"First round time to impact, five seconds," Walker said.

Cahill lowered his gaze to his screen where he enjoyed the luxury of an American satellite's infrared overhead view of dozens of North Korean vessels. Like the leading edge of a heated hailstorm, his rounds trickled down on his adversaries.

"Rounds one and two have hit target one," Walker said.

"How do you know?" Cahill asked.

"I'm looking at the satellite imagery. You can see the heat cutting through the ship's engineering space."

"Really? It just looks like shades of blue to me."

"Rounds three and four have hit target two," Walker said. "You learn to interpret the visual data early in gunnery training as a surface warrior."

"I'll have to trust your judgment."

As hellish hail punctured his enemy, small plumes of azure grew in the after sections of targeted combatants. Cahill also noticed billows of soft turquoise as diesel engines began churning out maximum power.

"They're starting to accelerate," he said.

"Rounds five and six have hit target three," Walker said. "GPS guidance should still bring the rounds home, even as they attempt to evade."

"We shall see."

"Round seven – hit," Walker said. "Round eight has missed target four. Round eight splashed just wide."

"Unfortunate," Cahill said.

"GPS accuracy is measured in fractions of meters but not in inches. There's nothing we can do about it, unless you want to expend more rounds and trust the law of averages."

"No, I don't. I consider our cannons to be defensive weapons, and for good reason."

"What reason?"

He walked athwartships, stopped beside his executive officer, and aimed his index finger at his monitor.

"Because of this ship, this ship, this ship, that one, that one, that one, and possibly that one. They appear to be racing towards us."

"They already were racing towards us at flank speeds. We knew we were going to face a welcoming party unless we submerged before they intercepted us."

"But every ship within our operational area is taking evasive maneuvers in response to our cannons, except the welcoming party, so to speak."

"They're daring us to shoot them."

"Right," Cahill said. "So we shoot them. In defense, which means I need more information about them. What sort of ships are they? What sort of weapons are they carrying? What propulsion systems do they have? I need to know exactly where to lay down the cannon rounds to neutralize them."

The deck rolled as the *Goliath* turned thirty degrees to the right on a pre-programmed random submarine evasion course. Cahill appreciated the automation, knowing he would have forgotten the maneuver while studying the North Korean surface ships. A constant course would have offered a simple targeting solution for the torpedo of any lurking *Romeo*, *Sango*, or *Yono* submarine.

"I'm sending the tracking numbers of the so called welcoming party ships to Pierre for further evaluation," Walker said. "I've requested input from every available sensor."

"Very well."

"By the way, sixteen out of our last twenty cannon rounds were hits."

"Very well."

Cahill returned to his command console and observed the hornets' nest that his guns had stirred. Dozens of ships scrambled in haphazard directions at flank speeds, hitting evasive turns to avoid the kinetic energy weapons.

Per plan, his cannon rounds gave the *Gwansun* a reprieve from its hunters while hardening the enemy's focus farther from the stranded *Kim*. The only oddity that caught his attention was the undaunted trek of the seven-ship welcoming party that sped towards him with apparent disregard for their safety.

"The lead ship of the welcoming party is ten miles from South Korean-controlled airspace," he said. "Has Pierre acknowledged that our clients have a plan to engage them?"

"Four additional Fighting Eagle fighter aircraft have taken off to join the four already on patrol," Walker said. "That's more than enough to fend off the two pairs of North Korean MiGs and launch anti-ship missiles at the welcoming party."

"Then what are these mongrels doing?" Cahill asked. "They're on a suicide mission if they try to get within cannon or torpedo range of us."

"They could be attempting to launch anti-ship missiles."

"So what? That would be a waste of ordnance. They know that we could just submerge below their attack."

"Data coming in from Pierre identifies the welcoming party as two *Nampo* class frigates, two *Sariwan* class corvettes, and three

Taechong class gunboats. The frigates carry eight Kh-35 anti-ship missiles each. Those are Russian design with ranges up to seventy nautical miles. We're already within their strike range."

"Then they could have fired already," Cahill said. "The Kh-35 missiles are unguided, right?"

"Correct. That's exactly why they haven't fired yet, I assume. They want to get as close as we'll allow to reduce the time and distance we could flee before their missiles would arrive."

Cahill heard the boom of his railgun, followed by an extended silence. He looked to his screen and noticed that his guns had completed their fifty-round salvo. None of the twenty-five targets had fallen dead in the water, but Walker tagged nine of the ships as having been slowed by a partial loss of propulsion.

"You mentioned using our cannons against them in defense. Are you intending to fire?" Walker asked.

"Yes," Cahill said. "But it's going to take more than two rounds per ship to make a difference. For the welcoming party of seven ships, send six rounds at each ship's engine room. Aim three rounds at each ship's port and starboard main engine. Target the gunboats first."

"Not the frigates?" Walker asked. "They carry the only long-range weapons."

"You're thinking like a surface warrior. We're going to submerge before their missiles could hit. It's the anti-submarine ships with the most maneuverability that concern me. Gunboats first, then corvettes, then frigates. Six-round salvos per target."

"Setting solutions into the system," Walker said. "Track thirty-one, the nearest gunboat, is targeted. Ready to engage track thirty-one."

"Target track thirty-one with six rounds. Fire."

The guns rallied to life.

"Engaging track thirty-one," Walker said. "All remaining ships of the welcoming party are targeted, forty-two total rounds at seven ships in six-round salvos."

"Continue firing the forty-two round salvo."

As his cannon rounds became supersonic images on his display, Cahill noticed icons appearing in front of the North Korean frigates.

"Vampires!" Walker said.

Cahill's heart raced.

"Which sensors see them?"

"The patrolling Fighting Eagles. Separation is taking place now. I see ten distinct missiles, but I suspect we'll see more as they separate from each other in flight."

"They've called our bluff," Cahill said. "How long until their missiles could impact us?"

"Analyzing."

Assuming subsonic missiles flying at six hundred miles an hour, Cahill calculated that the farthest ones would cover their fifty mile trek in five minutes. He expected the closer weapons, launched from the frigate forty miles away, to veer off before turning towards him, extending their flight distance to fifty miles and allowing the salvos to overwhelm his defenses with simultaneous arrival.

"Arrival of the farthest group will take place in four minutes, thirty-eight seconds," Walker said. "The closer group is heading to the east but will likely turn towards us at a waypoint. They'll attempt to saturate us with all missiles arriving at the same time. All missiles have separated. They've launched half salvos of four and four from each frigate."

"Keep firing the cannons," Cahill said. "We'll have a full three minutes to submerge after our salvo is launched."

"You've got big brass ones, Terry. This doesn't make sense to me. I don't feel right without having point-defense missiles to fight back with."

"Trust me. I'm slowing us to eight knots. Shift propulsion to the MESMA systems."

"Propulsion is shifted to the MESMA systems."

"Secure the gas turbines."

"Both gas turbines are secured," he said. "All six MESMA systems are running normally, bearing the electric strain. Propulsion is running on air-independent power. Maintaining eight knots."

"Shut the head valves and recirculate internal air."

"Head valves are shut. Recirculating."

His cannons fired their final rounds and fell silent.

"Lower the weapons," Cahill said. "Prepare to dive."

"Lowering the weapons. Wait!"

Cahill glared at his screen and noticed four new icons rising from the east and flying at high subsonic speeds.

"What the hell?" he asked. "Are those aircraft or missiles?"

"No idea yet, but they're at low altitude."

"No matter," Cahill said. "Let's just dive under this mess and be done with it. Let me check with Jake, since it's technically his mission."

Slate's electrified voice filled the bridge.

"I concur," he said. "I've been listening. Get us underwater."

A familiar French accent crackled over the loudspeaker.

"I recommend an alternate course of action," Renard said.

"Great to hear from you, Pierre," Cahill said. "I didn't know you always listened so closely to our conversations."

"Whenever I can spare the time."

"I don't mean to be rude, but we need to keep this short."

"Perhaps not," Renard said. "The initial analysis is that those missiles to the east were launched by a submarine. There is no other possible launch asset. The ocean and air are empty to the east."

"So the North Koreans are getting skilled at launching missiles from submarines, or they're getting help from a friend," Cahill said.

"Based upon the analysis of the weapons' speeds, altitudes, and heat signatures, they appear to be Chinese CY-2 missiles."

"Chinese? Exported to the North Koreans or launched by a Chinese submarine working against us?"

"I have no idea, but I assure you there's a beehive of activity behind me trying to figure it out. But that's not important now. What is important is that those CY-2 missiles might be carrying anti-submarine torpedoes as warheads."

The realization struck Cahill like nails through his flesh.

"Damned if we submerge. Damned if we stay on the surface."

"Right," Renard said. "Our adversary has found the *Goliath's* weakness and has exploited it. Mediocrity in air defense. Mediocrity in sustaining an underwater torpedo evasion sprint."

Cahill's mind raced for an ad hoc answer to the undesired problem but found nothing. The silence from the brilliant minds in the conversation confirmed his fear. Nobody knew what to do.

His situation had flip-flopped from dominating to dire.

CHAPTER 12

Inspiration struck Cahill.

"We turn towards the CY-2s and engage with our laser. We could knock them out of the sky before they drop their torpedoes. Then submerge under the Kh-35s."

"It could work," Jake said. "If you can pull off that gnat's ass tight timing. But can you dump me off first? It would improve your maneuverability."

"Negative. There's too much friction on the support bed for me to just dump you. You'd be stuck if I tried to shake you or slide you off, and it would take too long to submerge and release you. I'm afraid you're coming along for the ride."

"I figured," Jake said. "Fair enough. But don't forget to use your cannons against the incoming CY-2s, too."

"That's like shooting a bullet with buckshot, mate."

"He's right, Terry," Walker said. "There's a chance of hitting, and we've nothing to lose except cheap rounds."

The familiar French accent crackled over the loudspeaker.

"Agreed," Renard said. "You have my permission to expend rounds as liberally as needed. I apologize for not having equipped you with simple point-defense missiles. I gravely miscalculated the odds of your ever needing them."

"I'll have to trust me laser and me cannons, then," Cahill said. "Shift propulsion to the gas turbines."

"Propulsion is shifted to the gas turbines," Walker said. "Ready to answer all bells."

"I'm securing automated anti-submarine legs and taking control of the ship. Coming to all ahead flank."

He tapped his screen, and a pop-up warning confirmed his manual control. Aiming towards the east, he sought to close the distance between the *Goliath* and the submarine-launched CY-2 missiles. As the deck rolled, a tenor of fear entered his executive officer's voice.

"What if this coordinated missile attack is a ruse to make us do exactly what we're doing?" Walker asked. "What if this takes us right over a submarine waiting to ambush us?"

A pit formed in Cahill's stomach. He had considered the risk but rejected it for mental self-preservation. If he gave the idea merit, it would consume him from inside.

"Look mate, if they're that coordinated against us and with that much foresight, they deserve to win the day. Let's stay focused on the crisis we know about."

"Don't you even want to consider anti-submarine evasion legs?"

"I can't risk the extra time for engaging the CY-2s with the laser. We need to knock them out of the sky and then submerge before the Kh-35s reach us."

"Let's get started, then. I'm targeting both cannons on the nearest CY-2."

"Very well, mate. Use maximum rate of fire. Target the nearest CY-2 and use continuous fire until the target is destroyed or until I say otherwise. Fire when ready."

The guns cracked, and airborne icons appeared on Cahill's screen. Forty-five nautical miles separated the *Goliath* from the salvo of four CY-2 missiles that a mystery submarine had launched. With the weapons closing at six hundred miles an hour and his projectiles intercepting them at seven times that speed, a Mach 8 net closure required thirty seconds to reach a conclusion.

Nobody spoke while the first cannon's round approached its target, shattered into buckshot, and failed to inflict damage.

"First round missed," Walker said. "Second round missed."

Five seconds later, the second pair of rounds missed. Then the next pair. Then the fourth.

"This doesn't look promising," Cahill said.

"The rain is making this more complex. But keep trying, Terry."

Cahill noticed the tapping of the drizzle on the windows.

"I'm wasting ordnance," he said. "I should wait until I can guide the rounds better when we're tracking the missiles on the phased array."

"You're thinking like a submarine officer. You have plenty of rounds, and they're cheap."

"Very well. Thanks for the reminder. Keep shooting."

Cahill questioned his decision as each round missed. But when the CY-2 salvo and the *Goliath* closed within twenty-five miles, Walker shared promising news.

"I'm tracking the closest CY-2 on our phased array."

"Good," Cahill said. "Shift guidance of cannon rounds from GPS to the phased array."

"Control of cannon rounds is shifted to the phased array. I'm hot-swapping terminal guidance of round twenty-five and all subsequent rounds to our phased array radar."

"Even with tighter lock on the missile positions, guiding rounds at Mach 7 is an inexact science."

"I wouldn't be so sure."

Walker glared at his monitor, compelling Cahill to do the same. The symbol of the nearest CY-2 veered to the northwest.

"Is that a hit?" he asked.

"I'm unsure," Walker said.

"Could it be some sort of evasive maneuver by the missile?"

"In theory, yes. But unlikely. If someone were guiding it or if it had its own evasion protocols, it would be dodging our every round."

"Then what just happened?"

Cahill watched the icon of the CY-2 missile recover its original course. His next eight rounds missed it by hundreds of yards as their tiny guidance fins proved incapable of chasing the displaced vampire.

"I conclude that round twenty-five was a hit," Walker said.

"Then why is that missile still coming at us?"

"I think we grazed it, and now it's wounded. Look. Its speed has dropped by ten knots. I think it's compensating for added drag caused by a cut to its skin."

"Damn, Liam. We wounded one. We may survive this."

"I wasted seven rounds when that vampire veered off course. I'm adjusting the cannons. Round thirty-three and beyond have a chance."

A few rounds missed, but then the nearest CY-2 missile veered again. This time, it stayed dead.

"Round thirty-eight is a hit!" Walker said. "Splash one vampire! Engaging the next closest CY-2."

"Very well, Liam. Keep it up."

"Rounds thirty-nine through forty-four are too far away in angular displacement to reach the new target, but rounds forty-five and beyond will be well placed."

Cahill watched the screen and noticed distances to the missiles dwindling. Assuming wise placement of the vampires' warheads, he expected the first shots to travel farthest west, boxing him in from behind. The last two weapons would attempt to enclose him from the east, meaning they could drop their payloads any second.

As he considered shifting his cannons to the trailing weapons, Walker spared him the decision.

"Round forty-eight is a hit! Splash Vampire Two. Shifting to Vampire Three. Rounds forty-nine through fifty-four are in flight beyond the angular reach of the new target. Targeting Vampire Three with rounds fifty-five and beyond."

Cahill slapped binoculars to his face and glared between rails of interlaced steel.

"Can you see it?" he asked. "Either of them? They should be cresting our horizon."

Walker raised his optics.

"Do you really want an answer?"

"I don't know."

"I see one. At least I think I do. It's just a spec."

"Better that I don't look."

"Eighteen seconds until the first missile overflies us."

Cahill glanced at his display and noticed that the missiles' paths aimed at his starboard bow.

"Forget the cannons," he said. "Coming to all stop. Coming hard to starboard."

"What are you doing?"

"Turning us ninety degrees to give our laser a clear view of the vampires."

He verified the status icon indicating that his laser was ready as he tapped in a rudder command. The *Goliath* creaked during its tight turn, and an alarm whined.

"You're overloading the hydraulic presses on the *Specter*," Walker said.

"Damn. Easing rudder to fifteen degrees."

"Torques have dropped below the limits on the hydraulic joints," Walker said.

"Very well."

"The laser is locked onto the nearest CY-2. Five seconds until the target is within laser range."

"Neither remaining CY-2 is behaving like it's trying to hit us, is it?"

"Agreed. No active seekers. They're flying a predetermined course to drop torpedoes in predetermined locations."

"Then we did the right thing coming for them," Cahill said.

"In range!" Walker said.

"Fire!"

"Laser is engaging!"

The rumble reminded Cahill of a rocket as the weapons sped across the windows framed by interlaced steel. He watched it bend, crumple, and then tumble into the water.

"Splash Vampire Three!" Walker said. "Targeting the last CY-2 with the laser. Laser is locked on. Five seconds remaining in cool down prior to engaging."

The final missile followed its predecessors towards the west, crossing the *Goliath's* bow.

"Hurry!" Cahill said.

"Engaging."

The weapon continued its flight.

"That thing's still in the air!" Cahill said.

"The laser hit it, I'm sure. It just didn't have time to inflict enough damage."

"It's going to drop a torpedo any second. Speed is our ally. Coming to ahead flank and turning left to open range to Vampire Four."

"I agree, Terry, but we won't have much time to run."

Walker nodded to the display.

"The frigate-launched vampires have turned towards us," he said. "We've given their seekers a high-speed target, and we couldn't escape their search area. Their seekers have acquired us, and they're coming for us."

"Then we need to submerge and pray that the CY-2 doesn't drop its torpedo for many miles to come."

"Vampire Four just splashed!" Walker said.

Cahill knew better than to ask why. He had either gotten lucky and destroyed the weapons with his laser's cut, or the missile had dropped its payload before committing suicide.

"Coming to all stop," he said.

"Terry?"

"To listen."

He tapped his screen to send his voice to the sonar room.

"Sonar team, listen for a torpedo in the water, bearing two-eight-five."

The response rang from the loudspeaker.

"The towed array isn't deployed."

"I know that. Use the hull array. If there's a torpedo seeker close enough to matter, you'll hear it."

"Nothing yet, sir."

"Keep listening."

"Inbound vampires will impact us in three minutes, Terry," Walker said. "We need to submerge."

"We may also need to run from a torpedo."

"I'm engaging the closest vampire with the cannons."

"Very well."

Walker's vocal pitch rose.

"You know this is pointless," he said. "I don't know how hard it is to beat a torpedo, but I guarantee you that we don't have enough firepower, chaff, or luck to escape eight vampires. We're dead men if you keep us on the surface."

Cahill agreed.

"Shift propulsion to the MESMA systems. Secure all weapons. Prepare to submerge."

"Weapons are secured," Walker said. "Lowering all weapons. Propulsion is shifted to the MESMA systems. All weapons are sealed. The ship is ready to submerge."

"Submerging the ship."

He tapped his screen and looked over his shoulder. Behind and below him, bubbles rose from the *Goliath's* submerged ballast tank vents under the starboard hull.

"I'm taking in water with the trim and drain pumps to make us heavy," he said.

"Ten meters," Walker said. "Eleven. Twelve."

Bubbles burst from the *Goliath's* central tanks under the *Specter*, and the seas reached the cargo submarine's beam. As aqua crests lapped the bridge windows, Cahill thought he had orchestrated his escape.

"The *Specter* is still exposed to the vampires," Walker said.

"We're coming down fast. Jake will be fine."

"I've lost communications. I've lost track of the vampires. Using the system solution and deduced reckoning, the first vampire will impact in forty seconds."

"We'll be under by then."

"I hope so," Walker said. "Fifteen meters,"

"We'll make it.

Water crept up the bridge windows, darkening the sunlight.

"Twenty meters," Walker said. "The ship is submerged. The cargo is also submerged."

A wavering voice from the *Goliath's* sonar team made Cahill shudder, but he remained calm.

"Torpedo in the water, bearing two-eight-zero."

"Get us out of here!" Walker said.

"Wait."

"We need to turn back to the east and run, Terry!"

"Just wait."

Cahill ran through his checklist of techniques for outsmarting an air-dropped, lightweight torpedo. Silence surfaced as the platinum option. He tapped his screen.

"All hands rig for ultra-quiet," he said. "Nobody move or touch anything."

The mission commander's assuring concurrence came as a soft semi-whisper in the loudspeaker. Despite the intentional low volume, the speaker sounded more angry than afraid.

"Good call, Terry," Jake said. "I agree. We'll stay quiet until we have the upper hand on these assholes again."

A world that railgun rounds, flowing water, and animated conversation had ruled gave way to the gentle hums of the bridge's circuitry.

"I don't get it," Walker said.

"A torpedo in the water doesn't mean it's coming for us," Cahill said. "Especially not one that was dropped that far away and searches in a circle."

Walker remained stone, revealing his discomfort with subsurface warfare, but his stiff frame slumped with the announcement from the sonar team.

"The torpedo is going in circles. No threat to us."

"Very well," Cahill said.

The dull roar of a turbo fan reverberated through the bridge, and the *Goliath's* sonar leader announced the obvious.

"The first Kh-35 missile has passed overhead. I hear another one arriving, but I won't be able to hear them all. It will depend how close they get."

"Very well," Cahill said.

"That's it, then?" Walker asked.

"Did you expect more, mate?"

"No. Just impressed with how quietly you can resolve things underwater."

"Keep learning," Cahill said. "You may have to make a decision underwater someday."

"I'm far from being able to do that."

"Regardless, keep learning. And draft a note to Pierre."

"Draft a note? Why not just talk to him when we surface?"

"I'm afraid that in me present frame of mind, I'll use an inappropriate tone with me boss."

"Got it. I'm listening."

"Tell him that the commander of the *Goliath* highly recommends an investment in point-defense missiles prior to the next mission, no matter what modifications are required. I have no intention of going through this again."

CHAPTER 13

Jake sensed his anger spiraling.

"I'm going to find that submarine and jam a torpedo up its ass."

"There's no time," Cahill said.

Wondering if ire tainted his perspective, he noticed that his Australian colleague's face seemed ugly in the display. His hair appeared dry, his jaw too wide, his skin rough, and his eyes beady.

"I'll be quick," Jake said.

"Quick means dead. You know better than that. Whatever submarine shot those CY-2s has the advantage. It's either long gone or waiting for you. You'd be at a tactical disadvantage, and sprinting towards it won't help anything."

"I'm better than the guy commanding that piece of shit."

The words sounded arrogant as they escaped him.

"I'm sure of that," Cahill said. "But that's not the point. Hunting down a submarine is outside our mission parameters."

"I'll use a slow-kill weapon."

Jake thought that using the special weapons designed for his mercenary work in Pierre Renard's fleet might placate his colleague. The slow-kill torpedo released small charges that clamped against a target's hull and then detonated in sequence, forcing the victim to emergency blow to the surface. The special weapons of Renard's fleet had helped him win battles while sparing lives.

"That's not what I meant," Cahill said. "I don't give a damn if those mongrels die. I mean we don't have the time, and we can't take the risk. This mission is about saving the *Kim* – not taking revenge on someone who almost killed us but didn't."

Jake stewed in silence and then looked to Henri. The Frenchman's purposeful disinterest in the conversation conveyed his disagreement.

Despite his team's resistance, he considered satiating his anger and giving the order to attack. For a decade, Renard had trusted him to lead his teams, and instincts played a key role in that trust.

His instincts craved aggression.

"If I give the order," he said, "we're going after that damned submarine."

"You're in command, Jake," Cahill said. "I know how to follow orders."

"Damned right," Jake said.

He wrestled with his demons, the call to violence dripping from his tongue. But a final glance at Henri, disgust casting shadows on the Frenchman's face, halted him.

"Wait," he said. "Hold on."

He extinguished the communications link to the *Goliath*.

"Henri!" he said.

The Frenchman crossed the *Specter's* control room and stood below Jake.

"Yes, my captain?"

"Why did you just call me your captain?"

"Because it is true. You are my captain. You have been so for me and my colleagues for many years and missions. Pierre may be our founder and grand patriarch, but you are our leader at sea."

"You're stating the obvious."

"Indeed I am. And I ask you to consider what other obvious facts I may be omitting."

"I didn't call you here to play semantics games."

"Then why did you call me here?"

A tide of understanding, carrying shame and humility, flowed through Jake, and he realized why his subconscious mind had compelled him to summon his wise colleague. He glanced at the deck plates, stepped backward, and fell back into his captain's chair.

He lowered his elbows to his knees and cradled his cheeks in his palms.

"Jake?" Henri asked.

"Yes, my friend?"

"Why did you just call me your friend?"

"Because it is true," Jake said. "And I needed a friend to set me straight, by highlighting the obvious."

"You see my point, then?"

"Yeah. Your captain is letting his anger cloud his judgment, and everyone except your captain could see it."

"The obvious."

"Right, the obvious."

"I'm always willing to help, Jake. Do I have my captain back?"

"Yes, you do. Now go back to your station and let me wallow in my shame."

"Don't wallow for long, Jake. Terry awaits your command."

Jake tapped his screen, invoking Cahill's image.

"Yes, Jake?"

"Forget the damned submarine. Let's get back to saving the *Kim*. We've got sixty miles to get there, and the closer we get, the more crap is going to get in our way. We've got some planning to do."

"I know, Jake. Let's think this through. We're only fifteen miles farther away than we had hoped to drop you off. I think you should stay attached at least for another ten to twenty miles."

He sensed Cahill's open-ended comment about distance as an invitation to continue calming himself by focusing on tactics. He deemed the Australian skilled at navigating the subtleties that dialed down his stress levels.

"We'll have the benefit of real-time secure communications until you drop me, which favors staying mated longer," Jake said. "But I'm more effective when I'm detached from you and separated from your ship's noise. No offense, but the *Goliath* isn't optimized for sound quieting like a true submarine."

"No offense taken. I still love me new ship, ugly and loud as it is. It's still quiet enough when slow."

"A Harley-Davidson is quiet enough when it's slow. My point still stands."

"So what's your decision, mate?"

"We'll detach me in ten miles. If there's a submerged welcoming party, it could be anywhere, and I don't want to push our luck. I need to be detached from you before we get detected."

"Course two-eight-one, speed eight knots?" Cahill asked.

"Perfect," Jake said. "And shift your mindset back to undersea warfare. We've already been surprised once by a submarine. One more time, and we may not make it home."

"Agreed. I'll deploy me towed array sonar line and feed you the data, as long as we're mated."

"Thanks. I'll keep mine stowed until I detach from you."

"Anything else?"

"No. Just keep your sonar team attentive."

He tapped the screen, and blackness replaced Cahill's face. "Antoine?"

As the toad-like head eased sideways, Jake realized that his sonar expert was engrossed in listening to the seas through the *Specter's* bow and hull arrays. Remy pulled down an earpiece to hear him.

"Yes, Jake?"

"Did you get that? We'll be using the *Goliath's* towed array."

Remy nodded and turned his head back to his visual display, seeking waterborne acoustic clues for adversarial assets.

Jake tapped his screen to call up a nautical chart. Stale data showed the movement of the swarm of North Korean ships where they had been ten minutes ago. The *Goliath's* railgun attack had created the desired effect of drawing surface combatants and aircraft towards the *Gwansun* and away from the *Kim*.

But isolated from radar input, the data decayed into shadows of guesses. With the *Goliath-Specter* tandem submerged, the open water held unwanted surprises.

"I'm getting data from the *Goliath's* towed array now."

"Thanks, Antoine. Do you see anything new?"

Jake expected the long line of hydrophones, receptive to lower frequencies and free of its host ship's noise, to hear sounds that hull-based sensors missed.

"Yes, as you might have guessed, I hear a lot of new sounds. I hear a shrimp bed, I hear whale calls, and I hear loud merchant ships in the transit lanes to the east."

"Right. Sorry. Finish your analysis and let me know if there's something that doesn't correlate to a known target."

"I will be surprised if there's something new out there."

"We'll all be. Try not to surprise me."

Remy's analysis had found nothing of interest, and Jake's anger of having been missile bait had receded during a quiet hour of transit.

"We're at the detachment point," Henri said.

Jake noticed the decreasing speed of the *Goliath-Specter* tandem as he invoked Cahill's image.

"Are you slowing us to detach me?" he asked.

"Right, mate. We can do this at speed, but I prefer to do it while we're at a crawl. It's safer."

"Sure."

He watched the speed meter glide to under a knot.

"Let's do it, Jake. Do you remember the procedure?"

"I do. You release the hydraulic presses and then I make the *Specter* light enough to drift up and away."

"That's right. You ready?"

"Yes. Commence detachment."

"Commencing detachment," Cahill said. "Releasing hydraulic presses."

The first step in the procedure was silent.

"I don't notice anything. How's it going?"

"Something's wrong," Cahill said.

The Australian's face disappeared, leaving Jake a view of the *Goliath's* control room. Cahill's voice and that of his executive officer emanated from the *Specter's* speakers.

"What's wrong with that press?" Cahill asked.

"I'm not getting positive indication of its position," Walker said. "I can't tell if it's pressing down on the *Specter*, locked in the open position, or somewhere in between."

"Can we get a visual with the rover?"

"Wait, you guys have a rover?" Jake asked.

Cahill's face returned.

"Well yeah, mate. We need to be able to inspect our cargoes from time to time. You know, in case something like this happens."

"What do you hope to find?"

"If the press is engaged or not."

"If it is?"

"Then you could rip it off its joint when you rise."

"What can you do to prevent that?"

"Since it's a starboard side press, I'd bring me starboard hull down a bit to place a tilt on you. That way, you'd slide up and to the left. That would reduce the stress on the press in question."

Jake visualized the maneuver.

"But it might make me bump into your port side presses."

"Not if you're light. You'd lift off while I tilt. But you're right, it's tricky timing."

"I'd rather not risk it if I don't have to. How long to get your rover out there?"

"It's fast and quiet. Just a few minutes. I need to know the state of the press anyway so that I know what I'm dealing with when engaging the *Kim.*"

"Go ahead."

Cahill looked away and nodded towards Walker.

"Liam's on it," he said. "I'll patch the video through to you."

Moments later, Jake watched dual conical light beams illuminating the *Specter's* bow. The sight of his own ship gave him an eerie feeling, like he was spying on himself.

The first starboard press came into view aft of the torpedo tubes. A number appeared on the hydraulic arm as it extended above its pivoting joint.

"Number one," he said. "Simplified for identification. Nice."

"Right," Cahill said. "Odds on the starboard side, evens on the left, as it should be."

"Which press is the one in question?"

"Eleven."

Twenty feet later, the rover's camera reached press three. Then it continued, passing between presses five, seven, and nine and the *Specter.* When it reached the next hydraulic appendage, the sight relieved Jake. The arm with the number eleven on it angled backward towards the *Goliath* like its siblings.

"That's good, right?" he asked.

"Right, mate. Let's make sure."

With respectable subtlety, the rover twisted and danced around the arm, giving visual evidence that it had withdrawn to its opened, latched position.

"It's latched," Cahill said. "It's just a problem with the indication. Probably an electrical short."

"So I'm free to go?"

"Yes. In fact, you should detach immediately. Liam is good at driving the rover, but you'll simplify his backtracking trip if you're out of his way."

"Ready to withdraw the communication link?"

Jake knew that a final, smaller press held electromagnetic transducers against his hull. Mounted opposite them, transducers within his control room exchanged magnetic oscillations, encoded with the audio and visual data that connected the transport ship and its cargo. He glanced at the temporary box of communications transducers bolted outboard his captain's chair and prepared for isolation from the outside world.

"Ready," Cahill said. "Good luck, Jake."

"Good luck to you, Terry. Withdraw communications."

The screen went black.

Alone, as a submarine commander prefers, Jake ordered the *Specter* lifted from its perch and driven forward to hunt those who stood between him and the *Kim*.

CHAPTER 14

Lieutenant Yoon leaned into his crutches and tolerated the throbbing in his belly. Below him, Senior Chief Nang tapped keys and entered data into the *Kim's* tactical system.

"How slow can you make them run?" Yoon asked.

"Twenty-five knots by design. I'm not sure how to set it through the system, though. This isn't my normal job, sir."

"I know. Press the settings icon. That's right. Now the transit speed. Set it to minimum."

"Done, sir."

"How far does that extend the range?"

"You're pushing the maximum range for a SeaHake torpedo," Nang said. "That's twenty-eight nautical miles per the manual. I can't promise that you'll hit anything, though. That's an hour of run time, and the whole world will change position up there before the weapon gets there."

"That's fine," Yoon said. "Leave that up to me and our data feed. There will be plenty of targets in the vicinity, and we'll hit several. When this is done, fewer ships will remain to threaten us and the *Gwansun*."

The display next to Nang showed the swarm of North Korean vessels buzzing around his countrymen's submarine in response to a friendly vessel's long-range rounds. With the bulk of the threat concentrated away from him, he felt safer. But he'd be damned if he'd sit idle and let his colleagues die in his stead without fighting back.

"Don't mind me asking, sir. But are you sure you want to risk this? The noise of a launch, I mean?"

"This ship is designed for optimal quieting, including minimizing torpedo launch transient noise."

"It's still unnecessary noise."

"I consider it necessary to retain my dignity. The *Gwansun* is risking everything for us. I will do what I can to assist her."

"Okay, sir. I hope it works. Bearing and speed are set for each weapon in tubes one through four."

"Report all the weapon settings."

"All four weapons are set on bearing three-three-zero, speed twenty-five knots. Seekers will awake at twenty-two miles. Weapons are set in passive search mode. Nobody will hear them unless they drive right over an enemy submarine."

"Are they set for surface mode?"

"Yes, sir. If the weapons happen to end up anywhere near the *Gwansun*, they'll only engage surfaced vessels."

"Very well. Do you have a qualified man on station in the torpedo room? There's a lot of activity about to happen."

"Seaman Hong is there, sir."

"But is he qualified? Can he operate a torpedo tube, backhaul, and reload?"

"He's the best we have who's still alive. He's not qualified yet, but he was close enough that I'll trust him. He's a bright kid."

Yoon assumed that Nang embellished the youngster's abilities, but he appreciated the optimism.

"Very well," he said. "Shoot tube one."

A pneumatic system whined from the torpedo room, and Yoon's ears popped.

"Tube one, normal launch," Nang said.

"Very well. Launch tube two."

Minutes later, Yoon watched the icons of his four torpedoes moving towards the constellation of enemy warships.

"The weapons are going in the right direction, and at the right speeds," he said.

"It appears so, sir. Depending what ship you target and how they all move around, you've got at least thirty minutes before you hit anything."

"The longer the better. I want these to detonate as far from us as possible. I've still got wire control of all four of them, and I expect I'll be able to guide them towards whatever target I need."

"What if the wires break?"

"Then they hit what they hit," Yoon said. "I'll tend to them as long as I have the wires. Thanks for your help, but there's not a lot of button pressing left to be done. I can handle it from here. Head to the torpedo room and help Seaman Hong with reloads. And remember, above all, to keep things quiet."

Thirty minutes later, Yoon arched his back into the seat to lessen his stomach pain while relieving his armpits from their abrasions. He watched the icons representing enemy shipping slip across the screen as data from a floating antenna wire on the water's surface carried the latest positional updates from his fleet to the *Kim's* tactical system.

Over this shoulder, he saw Nang enter the control room.

"Tubes one through four are reloaded with SeaHake Mod 4 torpedoes, sir."

"Very well. Good job keeping it quiet. There's no sign that any enemy assets heard any of your work."

"How close are we to taking out a target?"

"I could engage a target now if I wished, but there's enough fuel left in the salvo to keep the weapons running longer."

He felt Nang studying him.

"Have you gotten any sleep recently, sir?"

"I took a nap."

"A nap. You mind if I ask how long?"

"A few hours."

"You look like it was more like a few minutes. You sure you're alright, sir?"

Fatigue's fog covered Yoon's mind, and he knew that he suffered from sleep deprivation.

"I don't have much choice, Senior Chief. There's nobody else who can keep this ship behaving like a weapon system."

"It's more important that we remain a quiet hole in the ocean. We're doing fine with that."

"You're not trying to talk me out of using my torpedoes are you? They're half way to finding targets."

"Well, maybe. I mean, why give the enemy any reason to suspect that they're hunting more than one submarine?"

"I'm not. The risky part is done. Given that we survived the launch noises and that no hostile submarines have backtracked our torpedoes back to us, we've already survived, and our ruse is assured. The victims will credit the *Gwansun* with the attack."

"If you say so, sir. Then the only trick left is hitting four targets simultaneously, right? When you hit the first, the others start running away in random directions?"

"It's a challenge to make the weapons arrive at the same time, though there is a measure of leeway that the torpedo can compensate for with its speed. But you're right. If the detonations aren't timed, the first explosion gives the other victims more time to flee."

He visualized the four weapons branching out after the closest targets. If he accelerated two of them, he could synchronize the salvo's timing on targets.

"Is that why the *Gwansun* is attacking only one ship at a time?" Nang asked. "That seems to be its pattern."

"Probably. It needs to reposition itself frequently to avoid detection. That puts it at higher risk of breaking the wires to its torpedoes and gives it less time to coordinate salvo attacks."

"I see. But we don't have that problem, so to speak."

"Right. Therefore, it's our duty to start taking out some of the adversary. And I've just got it figured out. I'm going to shift torpedoes two and three to search mode now. They'll speed up, and this should work out."

"Anything I can do to help, sir?"

"Not really. Not here anyway. You can head to the engineering space and make sure the shaft isn't sliding out the back of the ship."

"I check it a few times an hour, just out of paranoia. I've also got a man back there at all times watching it."

As he tapped keys to accelerate two of his torpedoes, Yoon thought of his next steps. His fleet had told him that a mysterious savior ship would pluck him from the sea and carry him home. He wanted to believe in his deliverance by *deus ex machina*, but pride and logic precluded his hopes in a fairy tale.

"Then maybe you can look at the shaft for another reason."

"What's on your mind?"

"I noticed that you were unusually reserved when I mentioned the latest iteration of our rescue plan."

"Well, yes, sir. I'm half questioning if this underwater transport ship isn't fake intelligence to test if someone hasn't cracked our communications security. It's just crazy. I told the guys, and nobody else believes such a ship exists."

"I was thinking the same thing," Yoon said. "Of course, it's possible, but I question the existence of such a ship, although the long-range rounds are an enigma. We have no cannon with such a range in our arsenal. Only railguns can reach that far with ballistic flight from a muzzle."

"I've heard of those railguns. They've got them on the latest class of American destroyers."

"Regardless, I suspect that it's one of the fleet's combatants masquerading as a rescue transport ship, probably to draw the enemy's ships, especially its submarines, away from us. The railgun is a nice touch, if that's what they've really used. It's crippled enemy shipping and diverted the enemy."

"It all sounds good, sir, but they can't protect us forever like this."

"Neither can the *Gwansun*. And neither can we protect ourselves forever, even if I unloaded every weapon in our arsenal against the enemy. They're too numerous, and they won't cease until they've accomplished their mission."

"I hate to say it, but if they get the *Gwansun*, they may think they've done what they needed to do. They may think that the *Gwansun* is us and then head home. They really don't have evidence that there are two of our submarines out here."

"Since you hate to say it, never say it again."

Yoon wiggled to shift the location of the sting in his abdomen and to stretch stiffness from his back.

"Sorry, sir. It's just that... you're right. I won't say it again, and I'll make sure the guys don't either."

"That's an order."

"Aye aye, sir."

"We need to face facts, Senior Chief. The only way out of here is on our own power."

"You know what you're saying?"

"I'm saying that you need to strengthen the weld at the shaft, risk a ton of noise from the shaft and weld when I order us to attempt propulsion, and pray that nobody will hear us before we can slip away with at most three to four knots of speed."

"You want me to add to the weld now?"

"Yes. Add pieces in a spiral pattern so that they're lateral to the stress when the shaft is under the torque of propulsion."

"I see what you mean, sir, but I'm out of welding material, unless I start cannibalizing systems."

Yoon kept his eyes on his tactical screen and steered one of his torpedoes towards its target.

"Cannibalize which systems, for example?" he asked.

"I could use pipes from the refrigeration system."

"Good idea, but no," Yoon said. "We'd soon be choking on the toxins of our deceased shipmates' carcasses. We need to keep the freezer operational. Not to mention food in the refrigerator in case we end up staying out here for weeks."

"You're right, sir. I also assume that if I use piping material, it should probably only be material from high-pressure systems."

"I think you're right."

"I could use hydraulic lines from the trash disposal system. We can get by without it, especially with so few of us making trash."

"Agreed, but that's not a lot of metal."

"No, sir, but it's a start."

Yoon analyzed the torpedoes and decided that they followed optimum courses for acquiring four targets. He let them do their jobs and reflected upon the construction of the *Kim*, certain that some system wouldn't require usage before he could return home.

"How about stern plane hydraulics?" he asked. "This ship won't reach speeds high enough to require stern planes."

"I guess you're right, sir. That should give me enough metal to at least give propulsion a try."

"Even two knots would make a difference. Anything is better than nothing."

"This is going to take a while, sir. I'll need to isolate the hydraulic systems we just talked about and then drain them."

"I know. I'll double check your isolation plan to make sure you don't kill yourself with hydraulic oil. I'm concerned about the noise, too, while you're working."

"I can cut through with my welding torch. That's not as loud as hacking or scraping."

"True. But make sure to cut the seaward side of the piping first so that the second cuts are sound-isolated from reaching the hull."

"I will, sir."

Yoon glanced at the lower half of his display, diverting his attention from his torpedoes to his own ship. The *Kim* appeared in the safety of isolation, the nearest enemy combatant steaming away from him at a range of sixteen nautical miles.

"God willing, it won't matter. The only concern is the unknown of how many submarines are within hearing distance."

"That's where our fake rescue ship comes in, sir. Hopefully, all the hostile submarines are going in its direction."

"Hopefully, but that's a destiny we don't control. What we do control is our last gasp chance at driving ourselves to safety. Start with cannibalizing the trash disposal system."

As Nang departed, Yoon watched his torpedoes achieve their destinies. Though beyond the *Kim's* sensor range, the first explosion became evident as the weapon fed its data back to him.

With airborne radar systems feeding targeting data to the *Kim's* tactical system, Yoon gave his weapons easy targets. Within minutes of energizing their sensors, each seeker had heard the damning noises of its prey.

Each weapon had then accelerated to terminal homing speed, and then the first weapon returned a signal annotating that it sensed a ship's keel above it, prior to its algorithms authorizing the final command of detonation.

Two more weapons followed suit, condemning cracked keels to the abyss.

As the final weapon strayed, Yoon frowned. But like playing a video game, he steered the weapon with rudder commands, and it circled back towards the fleeing target. Equipped with radar-quality information, he succeeded in bringing his adversary to his weapon.

His attack complete, he felt his adrenaline subside and his guilt rise. The simplicity had been unfair.

But four fewer anti-submarine surface combatants hunted him – four enemies that he knew would have shown him no mercy.

CHAPTER 15

Kye shut the bridge wing door behind him, shook off droplets, and peeled his parka hood behind his neck. He walked to his executive officer and tapped him on the shoulder.

"Yes, sir?"

"Secure the lookout watches. The rain is too heavy and visibility too poor for them to be of any use."

The executive officer acknowledged the order, and Kye left a trail of puddles as he stepped to the navigation table. A lieutenant lowered his smart phone and looked up.

"The Internet connection remains strong, sir. I'm receiving satellite weather updates every five minutes."

"Show me on the chart," Kye said.

"Here, sir. This rainstorm will continue moving east by northeast. We'll reach its southwestern tip in twenty minutes if we maintain course and speed."

"The weather radar information from our enemy's meteorological association is quite useful. They try to help their merchant fleets with accurate and frequent weather updates in these waters, but they inadvertently are helping us outsmart them."

"Agreed, sir. But only to a point. This storm won't provide enough coverage to bring us into waters controlled by the enemy."

Kye eyed the chart and noticed a penciled cloud.

"You've drawn another storm there to the southeast that's moving away from land. It can provide us cover to approach the enemy's controlled sea."

"But we'll have to travel at least fifty nautical miles without rain coverage to get there, sir. We'll be exposed to enemy sensors. We'll have to guard our speed and maneuvering to avoid revealing our status as a warship."

Kye appreciated that the lieutenant had spoken about possibilities to overcome dangers instead of voicing excuses to turn back. His men had learned about his expectations of courage.

"So be it," he said. "Chart me one course at the maximum speed of our escort trawler, and another at three knots."

The lieutenant gave a quizzical look.

"Three knots?"

"A worst case scenario in case we need to slow and pretend that we are throwing fishing nets over the side. Chart it."

As the young officer angled dividers across the paper, Kye glanced at the penciled icon showing his escort trawler. The fishing vessel followed him at a distance of half a nautical mile.

Unsure if he would need the trawler's service, he considered it an insurance policy. Per his plan, if his adversary approached him, he would offer the trawler as a decoy. The permutations of how such a scenario might play out had danced in his mind since deploying, and he had convinced himself that he had considered the gamut of possibilities. He was ready for the unknown, although all outcomes were a crapshoot.

"Sir," the lieutenant said. "The storm is moving at ten knots on course zero-six-one. We can't intercept it at three knots."

"What minimum speed do we need?"

"Six knots, sir."

"Very well. Then just chart the course for the trawler's maximum speed of fourteen knots, but have us arrive at the storm's leading edge."

The lieutenant dipped his head, opened dividers, and walked the instrument across the paper.

"Course one-three-eight, sir."

"Very well."

Kye hailed his executive officer.

"Yes, sir?"

"Slow to five knots and bring the trawler to one hundred meters aft of our stern and fifty meters off our port quarter."

Fifteen minutes later, with his ship's radars dark to avoid revealing himself as a combatant, Kye had no information about his proximity to his escort ship.

"Get me a report from the trawler," he said.

"I will contact it now, sir," the executive officer said.

Kye pressed his palms into the navigation chart.

"The trawler has a radar fix on us," the executive officer said. "It is at the ordered relative position, one hundred meters abaft of our stern, fifty meters off our port quarter."

"Very well," Kye said. "Now set task force course to one-three-eight, speed fourteen knots."

"Course one-three-eight, speed fourteen, aye, sir. I will inform the trawler."

Kye felt *Taechong Twelve* roll into the undulating swells. After thirty minutes, sunlight cracked through the clouds. Ten minutes later, the rain stopped. Keeping his active radar systems secure for stealth, he stepped to the Electronic Support Measures display and queried its operator.

"What do you see?" he asked.

"Grumman scanned array radar," the operator said. "There's a Boeing airborne early warning aircraft bearing two-two-three."

"What's the signal strength?"

"Level three, sir. Strong enough for us to be tracked, but no signs that our enemy is devoting any extra energy to following us."

"They have all they need to vector aircraft towards us or to launch missiles if they so choose," Kye said. "But this is expected. We knew that the enemy would be monitoring the air and sea. This is where we blend in with merchant shipping."

"Sir, there's also an intermittent AN/APG-67 radar ranging from low signal strength to imperceptible. It's bearing zero-six-six now. Probable enemy Fighting Eagle combat aircraft."

"Agreed," Kye said. "That's the combat air patrol. They'll be flying in unpredictable patterns and aiming their radar in unpredictable directions. Ignore that radar unless you get a strong signal strength."

As he walked to the port bridge wing, he addressed his second in command.

"Keep our ship's radars dark, but get me a full radar sweep of surrounding shipping from the trawler."

"Yes, sir. It's a dark and stormy night. Minimal moonlight. Visibility is poor, even under the clearest sky. I would say no more than twelve miles, as long as we remain at darkened ship."

"Agreed, but remain attentive. The last thing we need is to stumble upon an enemy fisherman. Listen for local radio traffic about updates to fishing locations. Watch where the trawlers are attempting to find their catches."

After the executive officer acknowledged, Kye walked to the bridge wing. Behind him, he saw navigation lights as the trawler emerged from the storm's wall. The fishing ship's proximity highlighted its immensity, and he estimated that the vessel displaced ten times the water displaced by *Taechong Twelve*.

He returned to the bridge, and his executive officer yelled to him.

"Sir, we've just crossed into contested waters."

"Very well. Re-station the lookouts. Also, station two Igla Missile teams on our fantail."

"I'll see to it, sir."

"Have the trawler maintain course and speed," Kye said. "I have the conn."

The executive officer shouted.

"The captain has the conn."

"Helm, all stop," Kye said.

He then stepped out to the port bridge wing where a young sailor was slipping sound-powered phones over his head. Leaning into the railing, Kye felt wetness on his palms as the trawler's white and green running lights bobbed in the swells and approached his port beam.

Darkness then swallowed the waterborne reflections of starlight as the trawler's length eclipsed Kye's view.

"All ahead standard," he said. "Make turns for fourteen knots."

The lookout repeated his order into his phones, and the gunboat pushed forward.

During an hour of transit, Kye gave a dozen small rudder commands to prevent a collision with the massive fishing vessel. The vigilance wearied him.

"Sir," the lookout said. "The executive officer reports that we have crossed into enemy waters."

"Very well. Have him come here."

Moments later, his second in command stepped through the bridge door.

"Sir?"

"Do you have an officer on staff you trust to keep us within fifty meters of the trawler?"

"Yes, sir. Lieutenant Park is skilled in ship handling."

"Bring him out here and have him take the conn. There are matters to which I must attend."

After relinquishing control of the gunboat's maneuvering, Kye returned inside, grabbed a short-range bridge-to-bridge radio, and hailed the trawler.

"This is Kye, get me your captain."

The underling who handled the trawler's radio followed orders, and moments later, Kye heard the voice he wanted.

"This is the captain."

"We're in enemy waters," Kye said. "Be ready to be approached or hailed."

"I remember your instructions on how to respond to enemy challenges. I am ready."

"Good. There may be moments where we cannot risk communicating between ourselves, even on a bridge-to-bridge radio channel."

"Your idea of feigning that you are a watch stander on my forecastle should prevent any listener from questioning the presence of a second ship with me."

"To minimize suspicion, I will call myself the forecastle watch hereafter," Kye said. "Regardless, from here forward, my crew will request updates from you as needed. You will not initiate communications with my ship. Understood?"

"Understood, sir."

"Also, if I begin erratic maneuvering, you will maintain course and speed, even if a collision between our ships is imminent. From here forward, you must appear to be a solitary fishing vessel, and the burden of concealing my ship rests entirely with me, unless I order you otherwise. Understood?"

"Understood, sir."

"You've shown great bravery coming with me this far. Continue it, and I assure you that your courage will be relayed upward through my fleet's channels. Kye, out."

The Electronic Support Measures operator cried out.

"AN/APG-67 radar – high signal strength! Bearing zero-four-two. Probable enemy Fighting Eagle combat aircraft."

"There's nothing probable about it," Kye said. "It's the combat air patrol. They've finally taken note of us. Remain calm. This is expected."

The executive officer moved beside him and whispered.

"Expected, sir. But now what? If attacked, we can't shoot back outside a range of three miles. And even if we engage successfully in combat, we sacrifice the stealthy progress we've made infiltrating enemy waters."

"It's quite simple," Kye said. "We hide in plain sight. Bring us within twenty meters of the trawler."

"Twenty meters? The low-pressure water between us will risk drawing our hulls together."

"What of it? The aircraft won't hear such a collision. I'll take bumps and scrapes to my hull before letting airborne radar systems see the separation between my ship and the trawler. But you make a good point. This will be difficult maneuvering. Join the lieutenant on the bridge to oversee his ship handling."

The executive officer departed, and Kye watched him and the lieutenant glaring at the ominous darkness of the trawler. Then he heard the rudder order from the lookout emanate from the bridge's loudspeaker.

Three degrees left rudder.

Kye concurred and let his officers continue with the tricky maneuver. As the trawler's blackness spanned a wider section of his bridge windows, he heard the rudder shifted to three degrees to the right. Then the rudder went amidships, followed by fine corrections to manage oscillations in the gunboat's course.

Content that high-flying aircraft would mistake the trawler-gunboat tandem for a single fishing vessel in the night, Kye lifted the bridge-to-bridge radio to his mouth.

"Bridge, forecastle watch," he said. "Over."

"Forecastle, this is the bridge," the trawler's captain said. "Go ahead. Over."

"Do you see any aircraft with your night vision, bearing zero-four-two?"

"No, but I haven't looked. Give me a moment."

Kye realized that the trawler lacked the sensors to recognize the increased power of his adversary's airborne radar system. He felt his heart begin to pound when the trawler captain's voice came back in a higher pitch.

"Forecastle, bridge. Low-flying aircraft, bearing zero-four-two. I see two of them, coming right towards us."

"How low?"

"I'm just now picking them up on surface search radar, if that tells you how low. Speed two hundred and fifty knots. They're coming for us, low and slow."

"When do you expect them to overfly us?"

"I'm checking now... Three minutes."

While Kye ran mental calculations on his next moves, a voice squawked over the loudspeaker asking the trawler to identify itself. As he hoped, the trawler's captain followed his instructions to ignore the request.

"Seal the bridge windows," he said.

Sailors began affixing covers to the windows, blinding them to the outside but preventing the red light from escaping to watchful airborne eyes. He went to the port bridge wing.

"I have the conn," he said. "You two, head to the starboard bridge wing. I need skilled eyes on both sides of the ship."

As his executive officer passed him, he grabbed his arm.

"I'm going to place us on the other side of the trawler as the aircraft pass over us. When I'm blinded on this side, I will pass the conn back to you. When I do, you will push us back up the trawler's starboard side as fast as possible so that the pilots can't see us, if they happen to look over their shoulders. Nighttime or not, I don't trust the darkness to hide us from their night vision."

Kye barked to his lookout.

"All stop! All engines back full!"

The trawler began to slide ahead of the gunboat.

A look sternward revealed his fantail jutting behind the fishing ship.

"All stop!"

Silencing his propellers removed the damning visual evidence of churning water, and he expected his stern's unlit smallness relative to the fishing vessel to pass unnoticed.

The increasing whine of flying engines rose to a crescendo overhead, and he felt two aircraft overfly him.

"All back full!"

With his steering control made erratic with a backing bell, he watched his bow gravitate towards the trawler. The impact was unavoidable, and a thump echoed throughout *Taechong Twelve's* hull. The bow lurched from the impact, but suction dragged it into the escort vessel a second time before the gunboat cleared.

As his forecastle slid behind the whitened churning foam below the looming wall of the trawler's stern, he considered his exposure maximized – a condition he wished to minimize.

"All ahead flank! Left full rudder!"

The trawler walked to his starboard bow and began to glide down his starboard side. He lost sight of the distance separating the ships.

"Shift the conn to the executive officer!"

He entered the bridge and felt confined within its red light and shadows. Blinded to the trawler's position, he had to trust his officers on the starboard bridge wing. As he crossed to his gunboat's other side, he heard the expected order to shift the rudder to starboard, angling his bow back in line with the fishing ship.

Reaching the starboard bridge wing, he regained his sight of the trawler. After easing the rudder amidships, his executive officer had positioned the ship within meters of its escort.

"Keep the conn," Kye said. "You've done well, but learn from my mistake and open range to avoid another collision."

"Do you think it worked, sir? Do you think they saw us?"

"Time will tell."

Minutes passed as Kye's heart rate receded, but the lack of further harassment irked him.

"They're gone, sir," the executive officer said.

"That's a problem. They must have taken photographs of the trawler for identification purposes. Someone will come for us again when they realize we are not part of their fishing fleet."

Kye returned to the darkened room.

"Secure from sealed bridge," he said.

The window coverings came down, and his temporary claustrophobia waned. He risked the bridge-to-bridge radio.

"Bridge, forecastle. Over."

"Forecastle, bridge. Over," the trawler's captain said.

"Do you see the aircraft? Do you have any abnormal radar activity?"

"I've lost the aircraft on radar and visual, and they are no longer hailing us. However, there's a ship moving towards us, leading us, actually, on an intercept course. It's in the west moving at almost thirty knots."

"Enemy frigate," Kye said. "I need its location."

"Bearing two-six-one, range twenty-two miles."

Kye placed the radio on the navigation table and watched a lieutenant scribble the adversarial combatant's data onto the trace paper.

"If we turn to intercept the storm at its closest point, how long until we reach its edge?"

"Fifty minutes, sir."

"And how long until the frigate reaches us on that geometry?"

"Just over an hour, but it'll be in weapons range before we reach the storm."

"This will be tight, but it will work out."

Half an hour later, the trawler reported seeing the frigate, and Kye had grown weary of the enemy combatant's repeated, unanswered hails to the fishing ship.

"Seal the bridge," he said.

Exiting the darkness, he stepped onto the starboard bridge wing. The angle of approach to the frigate required that he move closer to the trawler's bow to hide behind the escort ship's bulk.

"Make turns for sixteen knots," he said.

When his bow paralleled that of his escort, he slowed to fourteen knots, keeping pace with the giant vessel.

Droplets began dancing on the deck plates, and he lifted night vision optics to his face. Ahead, a wall of darkness marked the rainstorm he sought.

As he returned inside to eavesdrop upon the frigate's calls to the trawler, the threat of a warning shot concerned him. He realized that a shot across his escort's bow could become a shot landing on his.

Fifteen minutes passed, and the threats became grave. Then both lookouts reported that a gun round had exploded a half mile in front of him. He grabbed the radio.

"Maintain course and speed," he said.

"I will," the trawler captain said. "The frigate will not stop firing, though, until I turn back."

"We're almost in the storm," Kye said. "In fact, radar return for the frigate is likely already murky. That's why it's becoming impatient and threatening you with its cannon."

The lookouts reported that another round had landed closer to the bow. But they also brought good news that rain covered the ship. Kye pulled his parka hood over his head and darted to the starboard wing.

Visibility had worsened, and the storm appeared to half-swallow the trawler. A boom got his attention, and he turned to see the frigate's latest round shooting a stream of liquid into the air. The cascade crested, dipped, and then landed on his bow.

The next warning would be a hit, and he considered the facade complete. The rainstorm would have to protect him.

He entered the darkened bridge and grabbed the radio.

"It's time to concede," he said. "This is far enough."

"Understood," the trawler captain said.

Kye listened as the trawler captain responded to the frigate and identified himself as a North Korean fishing vessel. After an angry exchange, the fishing captain blamed his first mate for a clerical error in charting his ship's position, apologized for the mistake, and offered to reverse course.

By the time the trawler veered away, Kye had positioned *Taechong Twelve* within the storm's protection. With the frigate's interest focused on the contrite trawler, he sighed and felt his blood pressure fall.

Exhausted, he hoped that his risk would pay off by bringing him the enemy submarine, his nation's captive admiral, and the strange, meddling transport ship.

CHAPTER 16

As the *Specter* crawled at three knots, Jake stood over the shoulder of a young Frenchman who sat beside Antoine Remy.

"I've seen it happen before, but only with the best of the best," he said "Can Julien really handle both drones?"

"No need to take my word for it," Remy said. "Ask him yourself."

"Well?" Jake asked.

"Yes, I can," Julien said. "They behave just like they did in the trainer, and I practiced handling two drones all the time."

"The trainer?" Jake asked. "How realistic is it?"

Remy turned his toad-head and replied.

"I verified its realism. I was the consultant to the software team that Pierre employed to create it."

"Okay, then. Good enough for me. I imagine I should stop doubting that warfare has gone halfway to video gaming."

"The drones have traveled ten miles each on courses of forty-five degrees relative to port and starboard," Julien said. "There's a ten mile spread between them. We've made an equilateral triangle with our drones."

"Very well," Jake said.

He looked over the young man's shoulder and saw the drones' inverted semicircular icons.

"Prepare for active search, semicircular pattern starting at zero-nine-zero relative and ending at two-seven-zero relative, fifteen-degree search increments. Middle frequency, half power."

The sailor tapped his screen.

"I'm ready," he said.

"Bring the drones to all stop."

"Done," Julien said.

"Henri," Jake said. "Bring us to all stop."

"We're at all stop, Jake."

"Transmit active, both drones."

Lines of acoustic energy walked up two halves of a split monitor. Then second traces grew fifteen degrees left of each original swath, followed by the third traces displaced another fifteen degrees. When the twelfth and final line extended from each drone, Jake saw no returns.

"Okay," he said. "The water's empty a good six miles in front of each drone. We'll reposition ourselves five miles forward from here. Julien, bring the drones to eight knots."

"Drones are accelerating to eight knots."

"Henri," Jake said. "All ahead two-thirds, make turns for eight knots."

"Making turns for eight knots," Henri said.

"Join me by the navigation table," Jake said.

He pressed a palm into the table and pointed as the Frenchman approached.

"Best estimate of the *Goliath* is here," he said. "I had Terry drop behind and to the side of us so that we'd have good quality data on him, instead of having him straight in our baffles."

"It's a good estimate," Henri said. "Antoine can hear him just fine. His ship isn't built for sound quieting, and I fear for him."

"That's why we're here for protection," Jake said. "And it's time to start protecting."

"You've already committed to an active search from the drones."

"I mean to boost my active search to include the *Specter's* bow sonar. There's no time to be cautious. If I screw around and take my time, Terry's going to drive up my ass, and I won't be able to protect him. This is going to be an aggressive search with everything we've got."

"You're going to keep our active search secure, though, are you not? No need to blare out an announcement of our location."

"Of course, I'll use secure active, starting with the shortest duration pings and using longer pings only if I have to. With the micro-pings, the old technology on the bad guys' ships won't be able to tell us apart from clicking shrimp if they're lucky enough to hear us at all."

Henri's voice assumed the patriarchal tone that warned Jake that he might be behaving like an errant child.

"There's a fine line between arrogance and confidence. Guard your location on that line."

"Trust me," Jake said.

"I always have – except when you're dead wrong and about to kill us."

"Am I dead wrong now?"

"No," Henri said. "You're fine at the moment. But I'll be watching you."

"I consider that business as usual."

Half an hour later, Jake stood beside Remy.

"So... nothing?"

"I haven't heard a thing for five miles," Remy said.

"Julien," Jake said, "bring the drones to all stop. Henri, bring the ship to all stop."

After the triad of the *Specter* and its drones drifted to motionlessness, Jake looked to Remy.

"Still nothing? Even when we're at dead stop?"

The toad-head shook.

"They're quiet, if they're out there at all," Remy said.

"They're out there. They had to be watching us ride in on the *Goliath*. They know we're coming. They're just being super quiet and waiting for us to pass by them fast enough to be heard."

"Regardless. I can't hear them, which means they're making no noise."

"So be it," Jake said. "More active searching it is. Line up the ship's sonar for secure active, highest frequency, shortest pulse length. Half power. One hundred and eighty degrees."

Remy acknowledged the order and tapped his screen while Jake turned to Julien.

"Prepare for active search, semicircular pattern starting at zero-nine-zero relative and ending at two-seven-zero relative, fifteen-degree search increments. Middle frequency, half power."

Jake watched the active transmissions from the *Specter* and its drones. On the fourth emission from the starboard drone, the young operator buried his finger into the display.

"There!" Julien said.

"We got one," Jake said.

He tapped the shoulder of the sonar apprentice seated on Remy's other side.

"Designate the new contact as target Master One. Set range to thirteen thousand, two hundred yards. Speed zero."

"Zero?" the apprentice asked.

"Yes. That's a submarine with a smart and patient captain. He's waiting in silent ambush for us because that's the only way he can win. Speed zero. Bearing zero-one-two."

"The bearing is uncertain with a drone," Julien said. "It doesn't have the hydrophone spread we have on our hull."

Jake forgave the newbie for stating the obvious.

"Agreed," he said. "But it's good enough for me. I'm shooting at Master One on that bearing. Antoine, set the solution into the slow-kill weapon in tube one. We'll refine the targeting solution and steer the weapon as needed."

"The solution is set in tube one," Remy said.

"Maximum transit speed?" Jake asked.

"No. I set it to medium to reduce the chance of our weapon being heard too early."

"Set maximum transit speed," Jake said. "Trust me. Do it."

"Tube one is set at maximum transit speed," Remy said.

"Shoot tube one."

The torpedo tube's pneumatic whine filled the control room, and the rapid pressure change popped Jake's ears.

"Tube one, normal launch," Henri said.

"Keep an eye on Master One," Jake said. "He's not going to just sit there after being painted by our drone."

"Launch transients, Master One!" Remy said. "Master One is also accelerating."

"Jake!" Julien said.

"What?"

"I just picked up another submerged target from our other drone. Range twelve thousand, four hundred yards. Bearing three-three-nine."

Jake noticed the hunched shoulders of the young men. Their tennis shoes tapped the deck plates, and their fingers fidgeted below their displays, seeking outlets for nervous energy.

He crouched.

"You three, look at me," Jake said. "That includes you, Antoine."

The toad-head rotated on its thick neck.

"The new target is Master Two. Antoine, get tube two ready for Master Two. Also, take control of drone two for tracking Master Two."

Remy turned to his screen, and Jake faced the sonar apprentice.

"You stay with Master One. Take control of drone one, use it to track Master One, and steer weapon one into it. Got it?"

"Yes."

"Also, listen for Master One's torpedo and make sure it's heading for our drone and not for us. Master One thinks our drone is a submarine, and that's what I'm betting he shot at, unless he's the luckiest captain in the world, which he's not. You can handle this."

The apprentice nodded and turned back to his screen while Jake continued the discourse with Julien.

"You've got good sonar training, don't you?"

"Yes, of course. I was a sonar operator on the *Casablanca*."

"Good, you're now our defense. You're listening to the water around our ship, and you're using the secure active to make sure nobody is near enough to shoot us. We just made launch transients, and you're going to make sure nobody heard us. Got it?"

"Got it."

"Don't worry," Jake said. "If anyone is coming for us, they'll be loud. The system would probably flag the noise for you automatically, but someone needs to pay attention. That's you. Make sure drone control has shifted to the other guys."

"I've shifted drone control to the others."

"Good. Start listening."

"Tube two is ready, Jake," Remy said. "Target is Master Two, maximum transit speed."

"Very well, Antoine. Shoot tube two."

After the whine and ear popping, Jake realized that one of his targets had withheld its reactive counter-strike.

"No signs of a weapon from Master Two?" he asked.

"No," Remy said. "The captain is showing some maturity. I'll be sure to watch his every move."

"Maturity won't help him, given the advantage we have."

His torpedoes seeking his targets, Jake turned his thoughts towards defense. He walked to the elevated conning platform and studied his personal tactical display.

Master One's weapon chased after his first drone, and the worst case estimate of the hostile weapon's movement showed it passing miles in front of the *Specter*.

He noticed that the *Goliath* was creeping up beside him and into possible danger, if he believed the system's estimate of Cahill's location.

"Julien, do you hear the *Goliath*?" he asked.

"Hold on, let me check. I haven't been listening."

"See if you can hear it. I'll wait."

"No, nothing, Jake."

"Good. That means Terry heard our launch transients and figured out we're in combat. He was smart enough to go to all stop. I'll reset the system with him at zero speed."

He tapped buttons to update his best guess of the *Goliath's* position as it drifted off his starboard flank. He then exercised the learned patience of a veteran submariner as ten minutes passed before the first torpedo's seeker came to life.

Within seconds of blasting its condemning acoustic energy into the water, the seeker acquired Master One. The North Korean submarine's limited speed and aged technology made its countermeasures useless and its attempt at flight pitiable.

The apprentice announced the fate.

"Weapon one has detonated under Master One. Submunitions are deploying. Submunitions are now attaching."

"Weapon two's seeker is awake and has acquired Master Two," Remy said.

"Very well, Antoine. Belay your reports on weapon two unless you notice something wrong."

Remy nodded as Jake walked to the sonar team and crouched between them.

"Submunitions are detonating," the apprentice said. "Two of them."

"How many did you hear attach to the hull?"

"Twelve, at least. It's hard to tell. Some of them attached at the same time."

"That's at least half of them. That's more than plenty to get the job done. Do you hear Master One heading to the surface yet?"

The young sailor became animated as he pressed his speaker to his ear.

"I hear high-pressure air. Master One is blowing to the surface! I hear hull popping, too."

"Any more detonations?"

"Yes. Two more submunitions have detonated."

"Perfect," Jake said. "Just like it's designed. The initial detonations force the surfacing and let the crew escape, and then the staggered delayed detonations make sure the ship goes back down for good."

"Three more detonations," Julien said.

"Very well, Julien. Belay your reports unless you hear anything except ongoing detonations and Master One heading back down to the bottom of the sea."

"I will, Jake."

He pointed his nose at Remy.

"Report status of Master Two."

"Our weapon detonated under its hull, but I counted only seven submunitions attached."

"Seven. That should still be enough. How many have detonated?"

"Just one. Wait. Now two more."

"That should be enough to force a surfacing."

"Launch transients!" Remy said. "Multiple launches. Master Two just shot from both its tubes."

"And no signs of surfacing?"

"No."

"That captain has balls."

"Yes, and he also had the sense to wait until he heard our torpedo before shooting back at us."

Jake stood.

"Torpedo evasion!"

"I don't have a solution to the weapons yet," Remy said.

"I'm not waiting. And this is a slow evasion. We have plenty of distance between us and the torpedoes, and I don't want to make unnecessary noise or lose my drones. Henri, make turns for ten knots. Come right to course zero-six-one."

Henri acknowledged the order, and the deck tilted. Jake placed his hands on the shoulders of Remy and his apprentice for balance and to get their attention.

"Guys, accelerate the drones to ten knots and send them on course zero-six-one."

As men carried out his orders, Jake reminded himself to breathe and think. He remembered the *Goliath*.

"Antoine, do you have solutions on those incoming torpedoes yet?"

"Preliminary. I'm entering them into the system now."

Jake disliked what he saw. One weapon would threaten his ship if he stayed in his position. Though he expected to drive out of the incoming seeker's acquisition cone, he noticed the *Goliath* awaiting the torpedo near the end of its fuel range.

"Shit," he said. "Time to risk underwater comms. Henri, line me up in the direction of the *Goliath*. One-quarter power."

Jake trotted to the conning platform and reached for a microphone.

"You're lined up at one-quarter power in the direction of the Goliath," Henri said.

"Torpedo evasion," Jake said. "Course zero-six-one. Ten knots. Torpedo evasion. Course zero-six-one. Ten knots. Torpedo evasion. Course zero-six-one. Ten knots."

He lowered the microphone.

"Are you hearing this Antoine?"

"Yes, it's going out clearly."

"Double the power, Henri."

"Power is doubled."

"Torpedo evasion," Jake said. "Course zero-six-one. Ten knots. Torpedo evasion. Course zero-six-one. Ten knots. Torpedo evasion. Course zero-six-one. Ten knots."

Cahill's garbled, echoing response shot from the control room's loudspeaker.

"Evading on zero-six-one. Ten knots."

Jake sighed and reached for his foldout captain's chair. As he sat, he pondered his victims' fates.

"Antoine, what's going on with Master Two?"

"All the submunitions have detonated."

"And?"

"Fighting for its life," Remy said. "I hear high-pressure air as part of an emergency surfacing. I hear an attempt at maximum propulsion to drive upwards, and I hear the drain pump pushing as much water overboard as possible. It's on the way up."

"Holy shit," Jake said. "Are you telling me I hit a North Korean submarine with a slow-kill, the entire payload has detonated, and the captain still has control of his ship?"

"I think our weapon detonated too far forward. Most of the submunitions missed, and a few probably attached and detonated in the free flood area of the bow. I'm thinking only three or four of the detonations broke through the pressure hull."

"That should still be enough damage to doom a ship of that size."

"Give it time, Jake. Its torpedo tubes are empty, and it's taking on too much water for even the largest ship in the North Korean arsenal."

Jake found himself hoping that his enemy reached the surface and escaped before his ship flooded.

"I hear hull popping," Remy said.

"On the way up?"

"At the moment. But I hear no more propulsion noise."

"If our weapon hit forward, driving to the surface is impossible. The flooding is forcing a down angle. Shit. This could be a death blow with no survivors."

"And it is," Remy said. "I hear hull popping. I think it's on the way down now."

Jake pictured his enemy's horror while sinking in a cold, confining, crushing coffin.

Their captain had responded to the mercy of his slow-kill weapon by retaliating with a counter strike that had placed both the *Specter* and the *Goliath* at risk. One man's stubborn refusal of clemency had led to fifteen men suffering mortal terror prior to their ship collapsing around them and the pressures of the deep vaporizing them like the stroke of a diesel engine.

Rapid thoughts of religion shot through his mind, finding hard earth in their attempt to take root. He reckoned that no god could have designed a world this cruel. With his conscious intent, he would have to prevent the recurrence of such a catastrophe.

"Henri," he said, "reload tubes one and two with heavyweight torpedoes."

"Heavyweights? Are you sure? You just allowed one crew to live."

"No, I'm not sure. But do it anyway. If I change my mind later, so be it. But I'm not going through this shit again."

CHAPTER 17

The *Specter* and *Goliath* had evaded the North Korean retaliatory salvo and slowed to motionlessness. Jake stooped over the navigation table and dragged a cursor to a location a thousand yards behind the *Specter's* flank. He scribbled the coordinates onto a scratchpad and then stepped to the conning platform.

"Am I still lined up?" he asked.

"Yes, half power," Henri said.

Jake grabbed the underwater communications microphone.

"Prepare for new trailing coordinates. Over."

Seawater transformed Cahill's voice into a garbled echo.

"Ready for coordinates. Over."

Jake read from his scratchpad, and then Cahill read the numbers back.

"Make ten knots. Over," Jake said.

"Roger, ten knots. Over."

"I will contact you with new orders soon. Out," Jake said.

He stepped back and sat in his chair.

"Antoine, listen for the *Goliath*. Get me as much understanding of its noise signature as you can. I need to figure out how bad the risk is of being heard as we go faster."

"I've got the sound cuts from our measurement of *Goliath's* noise at varied speeds," Remy said. "I've also got the calculations of how far *Goliath's* noise travels in these waters, given our latest temperature profile."

"Good, listen anyway. Verify what you think you know."

Jake leaned forward and dropped his head to his knees. The stretch in his back sent a tingle up his spine as blood coursed through tight muscles.

He sighed and leaned back into his chair.

"Julien," he said.

"I just let him take a break," Remy said. "He's using the head and grabbing a bite to eat."

Jake looked at a clock. Above him the sun was rising, and his crew hungered for breakfast.

"I've arranged for silent breakfast," Henri said. "Paper plates, plastic utensils. The usual."

"Great," Jake said. "Good thinking. Is there a plan for everyone to get what they need?"

"Food and use of the facilities, yes," Henri said. "Rest is another issue. I recommend using the next six hours to give each man three hours of sleep. Few men slept last night."

"Agreed. Let's make use of the quiet time. This is a good time to get some depth separation with Terry, just in case our paths accidentally cross in two-dimensional space."

"Terry's limited to one hundred meters," Henri said. "I recommend we go deep."

"But not too deep. I want to stay in the same acoustic layer as him so that we can communicate. Make your depth one hundred and fifty meters."

"Can I have speed, please?"

"Sure, make turns for three knots. Come left to course two-eight-one."

"Coming left to course two-eight-one," Henri said. "Descending to one hundred and fifty meters."

The deck dipped and tilted as Julien entered the compartment through the door behind Jake.

"I heard you were looking for me?"

"I was going to have you start moving the drones again, but now I'm thinking it's better to have you train our other newbie."

Jake looked to the sonar apprentice seated beside Remy. The apprentice who had experienced combat had departed, yielding his seat to his rested counterpart.

"I don't remember his name," Jake said.

"Leroux," Julien said. "Noah Leroux."

"Thanks. Get with Noah and drive the drones on course two-eight-one at three knots. Here's the kicker. I want you to put the drones on a continuous two hundred and seventy-degree active back and forth sweeping search, fifteen-degree swaths, full power."

"Full power? You might be announcing our arrival."

"The one thing I realized after the last exchange is that there are probably thirty pissed off little submarines swarming in our direction. Not to mention, three times that many surface ships."

"You think that the *Gwansun's* distraction is no longer working?"

"The *Gwansun's* distraction fell apart once I started leaving a trail of broken hulls pointing in a different direction. I think they know we're here, and they'll have a pretty good idea of where we're going soon, if they don't already."

"I see what you mean."

Jake nodded towards Leroux.

"Let him control one of the drones until he's got the hang of it. It should take him no more than fifteen minutes. Then Remy can watch over him and handle the other drone."

"Steady on course two-eight-one," Henri said. "Steady on depth one hundred fifty meters."

"Very well, Henri. Join me at the navigation table."

Jake approached the chart and leaned into it beside the French mechanic.

"I just explained this to Julien, but I need to explain it to you. You can clue Antoine in later, since I don't want to bother him now."

"I can hear everything you say all the time no matter where you are," Remy said. "I hear you breathe when you sleep across the ocean from me, and you should be thankful that I do. You bet your life on my hearing, and it's quite a safe bet."

"Fine. I'll explain it to Henri, to you, and to anyone else with superhuman hearing who cares to listen. I'm taking us and the *Goliath* to ten knots. The *Goliath* will be in our hip pocket for protection and so that we can talk to Terry at low power."

"Aggressive," Henri said.

"Yeah, we lost an hour round trip with that torpedo evasion. I need to make up time. Plus, I assume that we've invited the North Korean armada to hunt for us after sinking two of its submarines."

"So be it," Henri said. "We will assume an aggressive posture. What's your plan?"

"We'll keep the triangle formation with the drones, but I want them on continuous active search on a two hundred and seventy-degree back and forth sweep and at full power."

"Aggressive, indeed."

"But necessary, due to time constraints and the *Goliath's* noise. Antoine, how loud is Terry?"

The toad-head swiveled on its tree trunk neck.

"Worse than I had hoped. The average sonar operator could hear him out to eleven thousand yards at this speed."

"And I suppose you could hear him at twice that range because you're superhuman?"

"No, because his worst vulnerability is the broadband noise. All those jagged edges. It's just babbling, high-frequency, flow noise. Anyone can hear it if they're listening. You either need to slow him down or be ready to deal with him being heard out to almost six miles."

"That's still suicidal range for North Korean submarines, even if they're waiting in silent ambush," Jake said. "Their launch transients are loud enough for me to shoot at them, and they're too slow to evade our counter-strikes."

Henri's deep sigh and glance towards the deck reminded him that his enemy considered suicide an acceptable tactic.

"Right," Jake said. "They don't appear to care about dying. So we need to find them first, which is business as usual, except that we're escorting a noise farm behind us, our enemy welcomes death, and we're in a hurry to save a helpless ship. Did I summarize this mess correctly?"

"You did," Henri said.

"So keeping the drones on constant full-power active and our bow sonar on constant secure active is the best course of action."

"Agreed, for lack of anything more insightful."

"I think we cleared out a good chunk of ocean with our last attacks, but nature abhors a vacuum. More bad guys will come. I figure we've got about an hour and a half before we could run into any unwanted company."

"This is your time to rest."

"And Antoine's," Jake said. "And yours. The entire A-team needs to sleep."

"My understudy is competent in handling the ship's control station. However, I don't trust him to drive the ship as you trust me. Is there a man you trust to drive this ship in your absence and mine?"

"Yeah," Jake said. "Him."

He pointed at Julien.

"A sonar technician with drone training and no ship navigation experience whatsoever?"

"If he can drive two drones, he can drive one submarine for three hours. The kid is sharp."

"Why not have Claude drive? He's capable."

"He's also exhausted. When I leave here, I'm going to drag him from the engineering spaces myself and toss him in his rack before I go to sleep in mine."

"Then you'd have Remy's understudy with one apprentice listening on sonar, my understudy on the ship's control panel, and a sharp kid driving while you, Antoine, Claude, and I sleep?"

"Yep. If we run into company, our watch team will be attentive enough to wake up the right people."

"Decisions like this are why you're in command."

Jake turned to Julien.

"Come here."

"I heard what you're saying. I think I can handle it."

As the young sailor stood over the chart, Jake spread open mechanical dividers from the icon that marked the *Specter.*

"When the *Goliath* reaches this point behind us, take the ship and our drones to ten knots. There's nothing else you need to do unless you find a hostile contact, or unless Terry calls for help. If you detect a hostile contact, slow us and the drones to five knots, tell Terry to do the same, and secure all active transmissions."

"Okay, I got it. Ten knots once the Goliath reaches here. If I hear a hostile contact, slow everyone to five knots, and secure all active transmissions."

"Right. And if Terry calls for help, wake me."

"May I, Jake?" Henri asked.

"Have I ever stopped you?"

"Perhaps Julien should wake me instead if Terry calls. You're the one who needs the sharpest mind once we enter combat. Your rest is paramount to our survival."

"But I... Shit. Okay. Wake Henri if Terry needs help."

As Jake reclined into the coffin-sized rack in his stateroom, sleep overcame him.

In his dream, he soared over the ocean, and North Korean submarines fidgeted like helpless insects trapped on flypaper below him. He dropped bombs, each one finding a target from an infinite inventory of his munitions. Invulnerability pulsed through him, until he noticed that his enemy's swarm grew faster than he could kill it.

The infernal infestation of black steel insect-hulls filled the sea, consuming helpless prey that Jake discerned as the *Kim*, the *Goliath*, and the *Specter*. His bombs useless and his colleagues dead, he sought higher altitudes to escape the rising mound of buzzing metal darkness.

Unsure what weapons awaited him as he failed to outpace the cloud of countless killers, he sensed his inevitable doom. A demonic North Korean submarine would catch him, crush him, consume him, or somehow condemn him, no matter how fast or high he climbed.

Death grasped him, rolled him onto his back, and recited his doom. He heard the growing rhythmic chop of approaching submarine screws that sliced through a water spout that crashed through him on the way to the stratosphere.

As he braced for his end, he reappeared on the ground, his pistol pointed at a captured crew of a North Korean submarine. Their arms bound behind them, they knelt in the dirt, staring at the earth in preparation for death.

A North Korean commando stood beside him.

"Kill them."

"I'm one of them."

"No, you didn't run your submarine aground and sacrifice the mission. You're better than them. Kill them."

"I almost got my crew killed years ago. If it wasn't for Henri that one time, I hate to think..."

Jake counted the crew. Eleven.

"What day is it?" he asked.

"September eighteenth. Kill them."

"What year?"

"Nineteen ninety-six. Kill them."

"They ran their *Sango* submarine aground off the coast of Gangnueng in enemy territory, didn't they?"

"Yes, and they must pay. Kill them."

"How can you judge them?"

"Somebody must. Kill them."

"What about mercy?"

"You've exhausted your mercy. Kill them."

"I'm not God. I'm not playing God."

The commando dug the cold barrel of a pistol into Jake's temple.

"You will, or I will. If not, then someone else. Their fate is sealed. Kill them."

Jake leveled his weapon at the back of the nearest head, pulled the trigger, and waited for the recoil.

A loud thump rousted him from his sleep. He tasted a putrid mix of stale breath and fear as he twisted his torso and opened his eyes. Henri's white hair cracked through the door.

"What is it?"

"Submerged contact."

"I'll be right there. Make sure Antoine gets a weapon ready."

He rolled to the deck, walked to the sink, and gulped a swig of mouthwash. As he wiggled into the stinking, unwashed white dress shirt, he leaned over and spat. Then he trotted to the control room and stooped over Remy.

"How'd you beat me here, Antoine?"

"I told you. I hear everything. My body knew to wake up and come here."

"What is it?"

"Submerged contact. Bearing three-four-nine. Range thirteen thousand yards. Drone one had active return, but it's now in passive mode, as you ordered. All sonar systems are in passive mode. And we're at five knots, as are the drones and the *Goliath*."

"Tell me what you hear."

The toad-head pointed its nose at the display, and Remy lifted his finger before pressing his muffs into his ears. Jake recognized his sonar guru's command for silence and glared around the room to share his understanding. As men stopped breathing, he thought he heard heartbeats.

"From drone one, I hear a five-bladed screw."

"Do you have blade rate?"

The finger went up again, and Jake bit his lip.

"I have blade rate. For a *Sango* class, the propeller speed correlates to nine knots."

"Could it be a *Yono, Sinpo*, or something else?"

"No, it's a *Sango*."

"Whatever the heck it is, it's too close and it's making maximum speed. Designate the contact as Master Three. Do you have a weapon ready?"

"Tube one. Maximum transit speed. Ready to fire."

"Jake!" Julien said.

"You just stopped me from launching. You better have a damned good reason."

"Submerged contact, bearing either zero-two-one or one-eight-one on the towed array sonar. I hear a fifty-hertz tone."

Jake felt a compulsion to shoot Master Three while analyzing the new contact, but he realized that making launch noises with a nearby submarine could be fatal.

"How do you know it's submerged?" he asked.

"I don't. I'm guessing. But I don't hear any other noise, and anything from the North Korean surface fleet would be loud. Plus I don't see any surface ships on the chart near here."

"Surface ships move fast, and our data on the chart is stale," Jake said. "But I'll spot you this one. Designate the contact on the towed array as Master Four. Give Master Four a range of eight thousand yards, speed zero, and assign it to tube two."

"Eight thousand yards?" Henri asked. "Dear God, Jake. That's close enough for us to be heard, not to say that the *Goliath* is even more vulnerable."

"There's a skilled or lucky captain coming for us. Either way, it's time for some old school submarining."

"You mean target motion analysis?"

"Since the towed array sonar can't tell its left from its right, I'll turn and see if Master Four walks up or down the array. Then I'll know which side he's on."

"And then what?"

"And then you'll see some decisive shit," Jake said. "Unfortunately, I think you'll see it from both sides of this argument."

CHAPTER 18

Jake glared at Remy's display, waiting for the Subtics system to integrate the incoming sound. Having turned thirty degrees to the right to force an answer for Master Four's location, he expected his sonar ace to disambiguate the bearing faster than the computer. But since he couldn't stand in helpless silence, he had to watch the integrating algorithm make its attempt.

"`Master Four is to the starboard," Remy said.

"Very well," Jake said "Get ready for simultaneous launch, Master Three and Master Four. I'm not making two sets of launch transients."

"Tubes one and two are ready for Master Three and Master Four respectively," Remy said.

"Shoot tubes one and two."

"Tube one, normal launch," Henri said. "Tube two, normal launch."

"Very well, Henri, make turns for twenty knots. Come left to course two-eight-one."

"Twenty knots, two-eight-one, aye. We will deplete our battery in eighteen minutes at this speed."

"That's enough time, Henri. Julien, bring the drones to ten knots, course two-eight-one. Don't tell me that we're going to overrun them. I already know that, and I'll deal with it if it happens."

Jake trotted to the conning platform and grabbed the microphone to hail Terry.

"Torpedo evasion. Speed twenty knots. Course two-eight-one. Torpedo evasion. Speed twenty knots. Course two-eight-one."

"You know that you're gifting a high bearing rate to the enemy crew," Henri said. "If they can hear us, you're making their targeting solution much easier. If they can't hear us, you're making sure they do with our speed."

"I think we're within four and a half miles of Master Four and that it's all academic at this range."

Cahill's echoing voice reverberated through the water.

"Roger, torpedo evasion. Speed twenty knots. Course two-eight-one. I can sustain this speed for thirteen minutes. Over."

"Understand. Go shallow. Prepare to surface and sprint. Over."

"Roger, going shallow. Preparing to surface and sprint. Over."

"Very well. Out."

Jake looked to Henri and saw the disapproving expression that dug a pit in his stomach. He wondered if he had just erred and doomed his team with his aggressiveness.

Demons inside him clawed at his mind, craving the self-destruction of second guessing. But he had stared them down before and survived.

"Nothing yet, Antoine?" he asked. "No counter-fire?"

"No, nothing yet. But be patient. Master Four is close and will launch soon. It's a *Yono* class submarine."

"How can you tell?"

"I can practically hear the crew breathing. You need to take this torpedo evasion as seriously as any one you've ever undertaken."

"I am. What about Master Three?"

"We're opening range. Every second it doesn't shoot is a second in our favor that we may get lucky and escape it unheard."

"But Master Four?"

"Torpedo in the water! Master Four just shot!"

"Be calm," Jake said. "We knew this was coming. We're already on the proper evasion course."

"Another torpedo from the *Yono*!"

"That's all it has. It only has two tubes. Stay calm. Antoine, track them. Noah, take control of weapon one. Julien, take control of weapon two."

"My wire broke," Julien said. "I have no control over weapon one."

"That's fine," Jake said. "Master Four is a sitting duck at this range anyway."

"I have solutions to the incoming torpedoes," Remy said.

Jake looked over his sonar expert's shoulder. The first weapon vectored ahead of him while the second boxed him in from behind.

"Shit."

"I'm estimating an optimum evasion course," Remy said. "I don't like what I see."

"Just recommend it."

"We need to stay where we are on course two-eight-one. It keeps us away from the incoming weapon to the north, and it puts us thirty degrees off a tail chase from the weapon to the south."

"Perfect. Thirty degrees opens range while sliding us out of the weapon's seeker cone. We'll stay on this course."

"The incoming weapon is a Russian Type 53K. I can tell by its blades and its seeker, which just went active. I estimate that it's four miles behind us, or, rather behind the *Goliath*. It's a coin toss which one of us the weapon will acquire."

"Weapon speed?"

"Forty-five knots."

"That's twenty-five knots of net closure to cover four miles," Jake said. "More than seven minutes before it would catch us. That's enough time to take action."

"But not enough time to exhaust the weapon's fuel," Remy said. "The weapon has an expected range of ten and a half miles. The Subtics system says that the weapon will have more than three miles of range remaining when it reaches us."

"We're not optimized in this evasion. We can do better. We can make more speed, as can the *Goliath*. What's our system say for our optimum evasion speed?"

"Exactly all out," Remy said. "Twenty-five knots. If our MESMA system stays up and running, we can get twelve minutes of sprinting out of the battery. And twelve minutes is when the torpedo would catch us. Accelerating to twenty-five knots would also reduce the torpedo's margin to a mile and a half, but it would still reach us."

"What if Terry goes to twenty-five knots?"

Remy tapped buttons to pull up the *Goliath's* technical data.

"His batteries are much smaller, and his ship is much larger. So even with his extra MESMA systems, he's at a disadvantage. His batteries will die in ten minutes."

"That's fine."

"You would sacrifice him?" Henri asked.

Jake had a desperate plan, but he realized that all his plans appeared desperate until they worked. He kept his deepest thoughts to himself while orchestrating the two-ship evasion. He faced his French mechanic.

"Just trust me. I've got a plan. Make sure I'm lined up at full power to talk to Terry."

"You have full power."

Jake trotted to the conning platform and grabbed the microphone.

"Make turns for twenty-five knots. That's two-fiver knots. Over."

"Making turns for twenty-five knots. Time on the battery is ten minutes. Over."

"Understand ten minutes. Out."

Jake slammed the handset back into its cradle.

"Henri, make turns for twenty-five knots."

"Making turns for twenty-five knots. Get ready for Claude to complain."

"Talk to him. If the limit on our speed is shaft torque, that's fine. If he complains about anything else, I want to know."

Jake moved to the navigation plot to give himself a larger field of view of the scenario.

"You were right," Henri said. "Claude says the shaft torque is at its maximum design limit. You can't go any faster without risking it cracking."

"We're going fast enough," Jake said. "I trust the system's recommendation. It makes sense. Now the trick is to outsmart this old weapon. It can be fooled. Get gaseous countermeasures ready."

"Gaseous countermeasures are now armed and ready for deployment," Henri said.

"Deploy gaseous countermeasures!"

Explosive gas hammered the hull as launchers spat canisters into the sea. Pressing his palm into the navigation chart, Jake tapped the display to mark the location for reference.

For a moment of ignorant bliss, effervescent water masked the *Specter* from the torpedo.

"How's the *Goliath* doing?" Jake asked.

"I track it at twenty-five knots, right behind and above us," Remy said.

"Above. He's shallow. Any hull popping?"

"I might have heard some, but it's not what I'm paying attention to, to be honest."

"I'll assume Terry's shallow. So was the submarine that shot at us. I'm assuming the weapon is shallow, too."

"All reasonable assumptions," Remy said. "Where are you going with this?"

"Deep," Jake said. "Deep enough to escape the incoming torpedo seeker's acquisition cone vertically. Normally, I'd expect the weapon to follow us, but in this case, I think it'll stay on Terry. And when I tell him, Terry will hit the surface, turn on his gas turbines, and leave the weapon in his dust."

"Perhaps," Henri said.

Jake cringed at the Frenchman's stern paternal tone.

"But you might be sending him to the wolves," Henri said. "You don't know what's on the surface out there. You don't know how many more submarines may be around him."

"The *Goliath* is built to fight, and Terry knows how. Let's just get away from this torpedo first and debate Terry's surface tactics next. Antoine, how long until the torpedo reaches our countermeasures?"

"Two minutes and ten seconds."

"Now's the time to dive, while it's blinded to us."

"Agreed," Remy said.

"Henri, announce to the crew to brace for a steep angle. Then make your depth three hundred meters, smartly."

As the deck dipped twenty-five degrees downward, Jake hiked up to the conning platform, stuck his tennis shoe onto the railing for balance, and grabbed the microphone.

"Comms check. Over."

"Comms check, satisfactory. Over," Cahill said.

"Perform comms check with me every thirty seconds. Over."

"Roger, comms check with you every thirty seconds. Over."

"If comms check fails, surface and sprint to twelve miles separation from shooting submarine. Over."

"Roger, surface and sprint to twelve miles separation from shooting submarine. Over."

"Will find you on radio after evasion. Over."

"God willing, if we're still alive. Over," Cahill said.

"We'll make it. Out."

Henri leveled the deck.

"On depth, three hundred meters," he said.

"Very well. Slow us down. Make turns for ten knots."

"Making turns for ten knots."

"Come right to course three-two-zero."

"The weapon has passed through our countermeasures," Remy said. "I must inform you that course three-two-zero is too broad to the weapon to be an evasion course."

"I know. Ten knots is also a shitty speed for evading the torpedo, but I'm not evading it. I'm slowing and drifting off the line between it and the *Goliath*. I assume the weapon will follow the *Goliath*, and I want to slip quietly out of its way."

"Time and bearings will tell," Remy said.

"Comms check. Over," Cahill said.

"Comms check, satisfactory. Out," Jake said.

He stowed the microphone.

"Are you seeing bearing rate on that torpedo yet?" he asked.

"Perhaps a half a degree per minute," Remy said. "It's too soon to tell."

Jake glared at his tactical display, wishing the direction of the incoming torpedo's sounds to drift behind the *Specter*.

"Comms check. Over," Cahill said.

"Comms check, satisfactory. Out," Jake said.

He kept the handset in his palm, knowing he'd need it again.

"The torpedo is showing a bearing rate of three quarters of a degree per minute to the right," Remy said. "It's drawing aft of us and maintaining its track towards the *Goliath*."

"Good. That's what needed to happen."

"You're going to have to set Terry free soon," Remy said. "He can't outrun the torpedo if it gets too close."

"I will as soon as I'm convinced the torpedo is locked on him and not us. Are you sure yet?"

"No. It's probable, but it's not yet certain."

"Comms check. Over," Cahill said.

Jake lifted his microphone.

"Comms check, satisfactory. Out," he said.

"Loud explosion on the bearing of Master Four," Remy said. "You've taken out the submarine that shot at us."

"Very well. Bearing rate to the torpedo?"

"Just over one degree per minute. It's moving into our baffles. It's locked onto the *Goliath*."

"You'd bet your life on that?"

The toad-head nodded.

"Comms check. Over," Cahill said.

Jake hesitated.

"Comms check. Over," Cahill said.

"Surface and sprint," Jake said. "Surface and sprint. Over."

"Roger, surface and sprint. Out."

"What do you hear, Antoine?"

"The *Goliath* sounds like what you'd expect - two submarines surfacing with more broadband flow noise than a tornado and the loud spinning up of gas turbines."

"What about the torpedo?"

"Drifting into our baffles and crossing to our port quarter."

"Let's recover from this mess, then. Henri, come left to course two-eight-one. Make your depth one hundred meters."

The deck rolled and rose.

"Julien, can you get the drones back into a triangular pattern?" Jake asked.

"Yes. We got lucky. You drove towards them during the evasion, and you didn't snap the control lines. They're fine."

"Send the drones on course two-eight-one at ten knots."

As Julien acknowledged, Remy turned his head.

"Loud explosion. We just hit Master Three."

"Very well," Jake said. "Master Three is gone."

He walked to his sonar expert and stooped beside him.

"You are tracking the *Goliath* at thirty-plus knots, right?"

"It's a difficult geometry for me to estimate his speed, but I'm rather confident that Terry will be okay. You did it again. You got us out of another hostile encounter."

"I hope so," Jake said. "The problem is, I can only wonder what sort of welcome Terry's finding up there. God knows how many surface combatants are rushing into the area now. I can only pray that I didn't just order him to his death."

CHAPTER 19

Cahill digested the onslaught of information. Long-range South Korean radar systems fed the *Goliath's* starving tactical system, and the transport ship's organic phased array radar detected ships nearby.

"Let's identify the closest threats," he said. "As long as we're pinned up here running from that damned torpedo, we may as well rid ourselves of some unwanted company."

"Shall I make ready the railguns?" Walker asked.

"Yes. The highest priority targets will be any airborne combatants I can find."

"It's less cluttered up here than I had feared. The activity still seems concentrated around the *Gwansun*."

"But the armada is heading our way," Cahill said. "Look at the speed leaders on these icons. Half the damned ships are pointing right at us. They'll reach us before we can reach the *Kim*."

"And from the looks of it, some of them might overrun the *Kim*. I fear that our latest skirmishes have made our mission more challenging."

"But not impossible."

Pierre Renard's voice filled the space.

"Gentlemen, please inform me of your status."

"Surfaced and still sprinting from a torpedo."

"Is everyone alright?"

"Yes," Cahill said. "Jake sank four submarines already, but one of them got off a good shot in our direction."

"You're surfaced in enemy territory during the day," Renard said. "I hold you twenty-two miles from the nearest enemy warship, but I have no insight into the submarine situation."

"I will have safely outrun the torpedo in another three miles. At that point, I'll slow and submerge and listen for submerged contacts."

"I dislike this. You're at best at parity on your own against submerged adversaries. You'll be limited to slow speed to avoid placing yourself at an acoustic disadvantage."

"I'm aware that this predicament sucks without Jake's escort, but nonetheless, here I am. Can we at least get some cannon fire into any aircraft that might be a threat to me or into the engine rooms of any surface combatants headed in me direction?"

"Right. Allow me a moment."

For a fleeting instant, Cahill pondered turning back to South Korea. Saving strangers from a distant country seemed unworthy of him risking his life. Then he recalled his commitment to adventure and to facing danger to right wrongs.

"Bogeys Five and Six are maritime patrol aircraft," Renard said. "They've been flying in sonobuoy deployment patterns around the *Gwansun*, and now they're headed for you. I recommend four splintering rounds into each and then assessing damage. GPS guidance is available to you if needed."

"I'm ready to fire now," Cahill said.

"Go ahead."

"Liam, prepare four splintering railgun rounds to intercept Bogey Five and four rounds to intercept Bogey Six."

"Four splintering railgun rounds each are ready for Bogey Five and Bogey Six," Walker said.

"Fire the cannons."

The boom from the starboard railgun preceded the port hull's weapon, and the rounds entered ballistic flight.

"What about surface combatants?" Cahill asked. "I'm more concerned about the *Kim* than meself."

"I understand your selfless concern," Renard said. "But you have a ruse to uphold. You must behave as if the *Kim* doesn't exist, lest you attract attention in its vicinity. The North Koreans have you on radar, and you must first attack ships that appear a threat to you."

"I don't like that logic, mate. It doesn't sit right. But I don't see a way to refute it."

"Based upon your prior attacks on engine rooms, I recommend four splintering rounds into the five closest ships. I've tagged them for you in the tactical data feed."

Cahill glanced at his display and saw pulsating red flags atop the icons of speeding enemy warships.

"You heard him, Liam. Four splintering rounds into each. Keep the cannons firing until you've sent out twenty rounds at the five targets Pierre flagged."

"I've set the cannons to continue firing," Walker said.

A new voice filled the bridge.

"This is *Specter*," Jake said.

"What the bloody hell are you doing shallow?"

"Helping you out," Jake said. "The hostile torpedo is out of fuel. You should stop running now."

"Thanks, mate. Slowing to five knots."

The undulations under Cahill's feet waned, but the rough waves signaled an approaching storm as they tossed the *Goliath*.

"I'm sending a tactical feed to you, Pierre," Jake said. "You'll have a history of what we just went through."

"I'll incorporate it into my ongoing feed to you and Terry," Renard said. "Terry's first rounds just downed a maritime aircraft. His subsequent rounds failed to stop the other aircraft, however."

Cahill's screen showed the removal of Bogey Five while Bogey Six flew towards him."

"Prepare four splintering rounds for Bogey Six," he said.

"Four splintering rounds are ready," Walker said. "Rounds eighty-nine through ninety-two."

"Very well," Cahill said. "Continue firing through round ninety-two."

"Your rounds are proving well-placed against the warships," Renard said. "Three of them have slowed already and appear to have suffered damage to their main engines. Fires have broken out on the other ships, and I expect they will soon slow."

Moments of silence slipped by during which a microphone clicked but nobody spoke. An icy suspicion crawled up Cahill's spine. A submarine commanding officer's conditioned reaction overcame him.

"Take the bridge, Liam."

He darted down the stairs, through the door, and into the tactical control room. His sonar supervisor stooped over an operator who stared wide-eyed at his monitor.

The supervisor looked at his captain.

"Just confirmed, sir. Torpedo in the water."

Cahill bent towards the sonar display and noted the bearing of the new torpedo's sound. The *Goliath's* towed array hydrophones heard the weapon, but the ship's self-noise prevented the conformal array from providing data.

He grabbed the nearest microphone.

"All ahead flank," he said. "Come right to course three-four-one."

A loudspeaker announced Walker's response.

"Coming to ahead flank, course three-four-one. What the hell's going on, Terry?"

"Torpedo in the water. I'm taking us to flank to outrun it. I'm turning us sixty degrees to resolve ambiguity on the towed array."

The deck plates lurched under Cahill, and he steadied himself against a sonar console. He watched his sonar operator scrunch his eyelids to listen to the torpedo while wishing it away. Then the operator's tight throat spat out the words Cahill needed.

"The bearings to the torpedo are walking forward up the array. We just turned towards the torpedo."

"The torpedo bears zero-zero-nine," Cahill said. "Snapshot, tube two, bearing zero-zero-nine."

As the sonar supervisor acknowledged the order to send a retaliatory torpedo down the bearing of the incoming weapon, Cahill grabbed the microphone.

"Continue right to course one-five-nine for evasion."

"Continuing right to one-five-nine," Walker said.

"Snapshot ready," the supervisor said.

"Shoot tube two."

"Tube two, normal launch," the supervisor said.

The nothingness of the *Goliath's* weapon launch struck Cahill as alien. With his port-side torpedo tubes in a different hull, his senses lacked tangible feedback of his counter-strike. But he trusted his sensors and his team.

"Very well. Is there any sign of the launch platform?"

"No, sir."

"Any sign of a second incoming weapon?"

"No, sir."

"Damn. That means the shooter had confidence in his single shot. And why wouldn't he? We were making flank speed, tons of noise, and gifting him a high bearing rate. We sprinted right into this."

"But we can sprint right out, too, can't we? We have the speed."

"It all depends on the distance to the weapon. Keep listening. Assume a speed of forty-five knots and resolve the weapon's course and distance."

"I'm patching Jake and Pierre through to the tactical control room," Walker said.

"Go ahead."

"Have you been attacked?" Renard asked.

"Yes. Single torpedo. I think I've got the jump on me evasion, but only because Jake was smart enough to tell me to stop running from the last torpedo."

"Have you identified the shooter?"

"No. I'm moving too fast. But I did get off a snapshot. So I'll at least distract the mongrel, and maybe I'll get lucky and hit him."

"Leave that to me," Jake said. "I'm going to head below the layer and take care of it. But before I do, I've got your incoming torpedo on my towed array. I just sent the bearing histories. You can use them to get yourself a tighter solution."

Cahill looked at a tactical display on the *Goliath's* Subtics system as it accepted Jake's updates.

"Thank God," he said. "I should outpace it long enough to exhaust its fuel, but I could be running into another trap. These mongrels' submarines are everywhere."

"But they're probably not in the water between you and me that you just sprinted through. Come back the way you came, and you should be fine."

"Right. Liam, continue right to course one-nine-one."

"Continuing to one-nine-one."

"What about you, Jake?" Cahill asked. "I'm bringing a torpedo right towards you?"

"Don't worry about me. I've snorkeled enough to head deep for a while, as long as I don't need to sprint. I'll get out of the way and hunt down whoever shot at you."

"Your batteries are at what? Thirty percent?"

"Thirty-five. But I can make enough speed on MESMA."

"How the hell are you going to chase somebody down at a sustained MESMA speed?"

He heard Jake's sardonic laugh.

"Because your snapshot has already made the bastard run. I heard him for a bit, before he went under the layer. I only need another minute of data on him to get a firing solution."

"Happy hunting, mate."

"Just make sure you think twice before launching a torpedo at a submerged contact," Jake said. "Make sure it's not me."

"Wouldn't think of it."

"I'll keep an eye out for hostile assets in your path, too," Jake said. "I'll be in a good position to do so. You just keep running. *Specter*, out."

"Everything's on the razor's edge but seems under our control at the moment," Renard said. "You may as well take advantage of your time on the surface to use more of your railguns. In fact, a warship just emerged from a storm and appears to be headed dangerously close the *Kim*. I've tagged it for you."

"Do you see it, Liam?"

"Yes, and I've prepared the cannons with four splintering rounds."

"Shoot four splintering rounds. I'll be right up."

On the bridge, Cahill harmonized his body's kinesthetic sensations with the sight of the growing waves. As the storm grew from the west, he feared that the water's undulations would slow his evasion.

Walker's greeting revealed to Cahill that he had let his face show his emotions.

"Easy, Terry. It looks ugly, and it tosses us about, but we can still make enough speed to evade. I've been through worse in a frigate."

Thirty seconds later, the *Goliath's* four rounds impacted the target, and Cahill awaited the assessment.

"Modest damage at best," Renard said. "The ship has hardly slowed. I recommend four more rounds."

Four rounds and a minute later, the enemy combatant near the *Kim* fell dead in the water.

"That's good enough for that target," Renard said. "Your data feed tells me that you just launched your one hundredth round. You have plenty more and should make use of them."

"I'd like to keep at least a hundred for me exit."

"Of course, but that gives you three hundred to use now. That could hobble more than half the surface combatants that stand against you."

"Fine," Cahill said. "It looks like a plague of locusts from me perspective. You'll have to tell me where to send me rounds."

"That poses no problem," Renard said. "In fact, if you'll allow, I'll take control of your cannon."

"I was half afraid you'd say that, and half hoping. It'll feel weird, but it's your ship and you have the bird's eye view. Go ahead, mate. It's all yours."

Every five seconds, each railgun obeyed Renard's wireless will and spat out a round. The prolonged attack became hypnotic until a gun fell silent.

"Port cannon is jammed," Walker said.

"Is our port weapons bay watch on it?"

"He says he sees the problem. It was with the feeder. He's clearing it now."

Three minutes later, the port railgun sprang to life.

"That took too long," Cahill said. "I don't want to consider what three minutes without a cannon would mean in a defensive struggle. Make note in the deck log to investigate the failure mode and come up with a quicker way to resolve it next time."

Jake surprised him with his voice.

"Good news. Your incoming torpedo is out of fuel. You should stop running."

"Slowing to five knots," Cahill said.

He tapped the icon to slow the *Goliath*, and the roller coaster ride subsided.

"What are you doing shallow again?" he asked.

"I already took care of business."

"I didn't hear an explosion."

"Be patient."

"I hate to interrupt the reunion," Renard said. "But Terry needs to submerge, and you two need to rendezvous to continue the mission. The cannons have inflicted enough damage for now. I don't expect that you'll experience challenges from surface ships any time in the near future."

"Right," Jake said. "I'll snorkel towards you, Terry, and you come towards me at five knots. We'll reconnect, right about, here."

"Where?"

"I'm tapping my navigation chart. The coordinates will be in your system soon."

"Got them," Cahill said. "I agree, I'm submerging now."

He tapped symbols to shift propulsion power to his MESMA plants, spin down his gas turbines, and close his head valves. Then he energized his huge, high-displacement, centrifugal trim and drain pumps to suck water into the *Goliath's* tanks.

As he pointed the transport vessel towards Jake, the deck rolled and bounced in the seas. He braced himself against a console and shouted up towards the microphone.

"This is a great plan," he said, "as long as you're sure there are no more submarines in the area. How's it look down there? Are you sure we control the water?"

His sonar operator announced a loud explosion to the northwest and concluded that the *Specter* had sunk the ship that had shot at him.

"That was a *Romeo* class submarine that shot at you," Jake said. "And now it's a tomb. Yeah, Terry, we control the water. Get down here with me, and let's save the *Kim*."

CHAPTER 20

Jake drifted on the edge of consciousness as he reclined in the captain's chair.

"Battery charge is complete," Henri said.

"Secure snorkeling."

"Snorkeling is secured." Henri said.

"Make your depth one hundred and fifty meters."

The deck dipped while Henri sent the submarine downward.

When the ship leveled, Jake stepped down to the navigation table and surveyed his location relative to the globe and to Cahill. The *Goliath* drove at five knots above him, a mile off his starboard quarter, and the *Specter* pushed through the water twenty miles east of the best estimate of the *Kim's* location.

"Now the hard part begins," he said.

"Best to let Terry know about your intentions," Henri said.

"He'll be along just for the ride, but you're right."

Jake leaned into the elevated conning platform's rail and twisted his arm up to the underwater communication handset. He tugged it from the cradle and pulled it down to his lips.

"Commencing search pattern alpha, course two-seven-zero, base speed five knots. Over."

"Roger, search pattern alpha. Over," Cahill said.

"*Specter*, out."

"Search pattern, alpha?" Henri asked. "Is there a search pattern beta?"

"Sort of. There's only one search pattern, but alpha means it's our first search leg. If I change my mind and search for the *Kim* on a different base course, it's pattern beta, and so on."

"I hope we don't need a beta."

"Me neither," Jake said. "We're going to make ten knots sixty degrees off base course to the left until we've covered ten miles sideways. Then back sixty degrees to the right until we've covered ten miles sideways to the other side. We're on secure active with the drones ahead of us in a triangular search, and we'll repeat the pattern until we find the *Kim*."

"God willing, the *Kim* is all we find."

"We must have broken through and depleted the North Korean defenses by now. We've run into enough hostile submarines for one day. We deserve a break and a peaceful conclusion to this."

"Let's get started, then. Course two-one-zero?"

"Course two-one-zero," Jake said.

The deck rolled, and Jake walked back to his seat.

Ninety minutes later, fatigue and random thoughts began to invade his mind when Julien surprised him.

"Active return from drone one."

"Secure all active transmissions," Jake said. "Let's see it."

The icon appeared on his display thirteen miles from his ship.

"That's a little further downstream of the ocean current than expected, but it's reasonable," he said. "Sweet. We deserved to get lucky."

"Are you sure the *Kim's* crew is expecting us?" Henri asked.

"They are, but there's nothing they need to do."

"I mean I don't want them shooting at us."

"They know we're coming," Jake said. "They know our sonar frequencies, and they'll respect our safety for sticking our necks out to save them. But I doubt they'll even hear anything until the *Goliath* is right underneath them, and by then they'll have no option but to enjoy the ride."

"I'm sure Pierre has seen to it."

The doubt in Henri's tone irked him, but Jake ignored it as an annoying trait of his French friend. He allowed himself to feel the relief of finding the *Kim*.

"He has," he said. "If they're hearing our drone's sonar, which is by no means a given with their staffing situation, they're probably celebrating their rescue. This is a good thing. This is the pot at the end of the rainbow we've been fighting to get to."

"Should I confirm their location?" Julien asked.

"Not yet," Jake said. "Give it ten minutes. Let's make sure this resourceful Korean crew didn't figure out a way to regain propulsion. We already know from the data link that they managed to take out surface combatants to help the *Gwansun*. These guys are scrappy."

"I think I would hear their propeller," Julien said.

Jake looked to the youngster and then to the toad-head seated beside him. The sonar guru wiggled his wrist and shrugged.

"Maybe," Remy said. "With a drone's limited hydrophones, it's a coin toss, and it depends on the ship's speed. I agree with Jake that it's best to wait and use the drone's active sonar to verify that our colleagues aren't moving."

"Ten minutes will go fast," Jake said.

They did, and Julien's verification proved that the prize Jake sought remained motionless.

"I need to clue Terry in on the location," he said.

He returned to the navigation chart and plotted an intercept course to the *Goliath*, which Cahill kept on a baseline course and speed to allow predictability of his location.

Jake ordered the triangle of the *Specter* and its drones aimed down the shortest distance between himself and Cahill's path. Then he waited until closure between the ships allowed communications at the lowest power.

"Line me up for underwater comms, lowest power, aimed at the *Goliath*."

"I've lined you up with underwater comms, lowest power, aimed at the *Goliath*," Henri said.

"Target found, prepare for coordinates. Over," Jake said.

"Roger, target found," Cahill said. "Awaiting coordinates. Over."

Jake recited the numbers, and Cahill repeated them for verification.

"Commencing spiral out defensive search. Over."

"Roger, spiral out defensive search. I will pick up our cargo. Great job finding her. Over."

"Good luck loading her. Out."

He returned the handset to the cradle.

"Spiral out?" Henri asked.

"An old defensive tactic to get away from a bad guy. I'm using the pattern to make sure there's nobody around to bother Terry while he works. Join me by the chart."

He moved to the navigation chart and felt Henri beside him. He tapped the location of the *Specter* and then the *Kim*.

"We backtracked to catch up with Terry. So now we're sixteen miles from the *Kim*. I'm going to head towards it directly until I'm five miles away. Then I'm going to drive an ever widening circle around her."

Jake fingered a spiral around the Korean submarine.

"Not a true spiral, I trust?"

"No, more like an expanding octagon. It's pretty simple, and you don't have to get it perfect, especially with the drones out in front. I'm hoping it's just a precaution, but Terry's going to be making noise, and I need to cover his back."

"This could take hours."

"I figure six to eight hours. In fact, this is predictable. I'll enter the future turns into the system and see what it says."

He grabbed a stylus for precision and tapped icons to bring up a menu to enter the *Specter's* track. Drawing the future as a series of turns, he stopped and frowned at the mishmash of canted lines.

"That was ugly," Henri said.

"I never was an artist. Here, you draw it."

The Frenchman took the stylus and etched a better course.

"Nice," Jake said. "That's what we'll follow. Seven hours of hunting and hoping we prove there's nothing out there."

"I think you should rest during the early hours," Henri said. "The chances of something hostile being close to the *Kim* are low, and you'll need to be fresh when you lead us out of here."

"Fair enough. Bring in the understudies for three hours?"

"Right. Remember that they're backups from our perspective, but each man was a top talent in the French Navy before joining us. You've trusted them, and they've lived up to that trust thus far."

"Okay, bring in the backups."

"I will. Are you going to sleep?"

"I don't think I can yet. Maybe in about half an hour. Too much coffee."

"Me too. Join me in the wardroom for some food?"

Realizing that the stress of combat had left him hungry, Jake salivated at the thought.

In the tiny galley space, he withdrew a paper plate of ravioli from a microwave oven, pushed through the door into the wardroom, and set the food before Henri. He then retraced his steps to a crock pot and ladled pasta-covered meat chunks onto his plate.

After heating his food, he carried his lunch to the captain's chair and sat. The first bite burned his mouth, and he cooled it with a swig of apple juice.

"Something's bothering you," Henri said.

Jake ignored the comment until he chewed and swallowed.

"You always think there's something bothering me."

"Yes, but I'm always right about it. I've known you too long for your moods to escape me."

"Okay. So I'm always bothered and you're always right about it. What are we going to do with this laser-guided insight?"

"Talking it through seems to help."

Jake downed a huge mouthful and wiped his mouth.

"Well, I may as well let you know that Linda forced me to see a shrink to deal with my anger."

"A shrink?"

"A psychologist."

"She forced you?"

"More or less."

Henri grunted and jabbed a fork into his food.

"Well, shit. Don't go all silent on me just because I shared something personal with you."

"I'm impressed, I admit."

Jake studied Henri while he chewed.

"Holy shit. You're not jealous are you?"

Henri stared back at him.

"Why would I be jealous? I'm hardly a certified talk-therapy professional. That statement was paranoid."

Jake let Henri ingest several bites before jabbing back.

"Paranoid, but accurate. You don't want anyone probing my head but you, do you?"

The Frenchman aimed a fork of ravioli at Jake's nose.

"I support you, and I admit to taking pride in safeguarding your well-being. If you can benefit from professional support at home, that's great. But out here, nobody can look after you like I do. I keep this ship in one piece, and I keep you sane so that you can lead us to success and home again."

"No offense intended. I get it."

He let Henri fill his mouth before continuing.

"Mom."

The Frenchman looked away, and Jake thought he noticed him suppressing a smile while he swigged apple juice.

"Call me what you want. You still haven't answered my question. What's bothering you?"

"It doesn't take a genius. I just sank five submarines. How many more men did I just kill?"

"*Yonos* only carry a crew of two."

"Still, I sent down *Sangos* with crews of fifteen and a *Romeo* with fifty. And the crew of that *Sango* that refused to surface - they got to listen to their submarine creak and groan all the way to the bottom. Do you know how horrific that is? Can you think of a worse way to die?"

"Crucifixion, perhaps?"

"Oh for God's sake, don't throw Jesus at me now."

"I won't. But in fairness it was a defensible answer to your question. The ancient Romans perfected the arts of torture and death, and crucifixion was considered the epitome of agony. It was so bad that they wrote laws preventing its use on Roman citizens."

"So Jesus suffered. I get it. But I'm suffering now, and I don't see anyone helping me."

"I'm helping you."

"Really? How?"

Jake jammed the remnants of his lunch into his mouth. Henri took advantage of the break to eat a bite.

"Talk therapy," Henri said. "And you don't have to pay me."

"My net worth is stupid big. The money isn't a concern."

"But I am making progress with you."

"Really? Do tell."

"Your stress isn't just from killing. It's from the decisions of killing and sparing. People who kill experience the stress. People who save lives do as well. That's obvious. What's worse is the decision. Nobody should have to make life and death decisions for other people, but you're subject to it constantly."

"Okay. So it sucks. That's my life. You're not exactly cheering me up."

"But at least you know a problem you need to address."

Jake gulped his juice.

"You mean that humans aren't made for this."

"Precisely. But it's a reality, isn't it?"

"Yeah. Your point?"

"It's a reality which humans must face but which no human can be equipped for."

"You mean I'm playing God. I get that. I've always gotten that. I don't like it, and pointing it out without a solution doesn't help anything."

"There is only one logical conclusion. There's a need for a god, and such a deity must exist. And it's not you. When you realize that and follow the logic through to its conclusion, you'll note a change in your demeanor."

Jake pondered Henri's words as he reclined into his rack. He planned a short nap, hoping to finish one rapid-eye-movement sleep cycle. When his alarm went off two hours later, sleep's sneaky claws fought his effort to roll from his rack.

But he found his way to his personal plumbing. Avoiding the risk of shower noises, he ran baby wipes over his naked body and donned clean clothes. Though feeling his fatigue, he knew that the rest had benefited him.

He reached the elevated conning platform, and a glance at his display showed him seven miles behind the *Kim*, searching in a clockwise spiral. Deduced reckoning of the *Goliath's* position showed the transport ship thirty minutes from its destination.

Wanting to believe that Cahill would make the rescue and egress look easy, he accepted that his vigilant search for hostile company played a vital role in preserving their victory.

He walked to the navigation chart, more to stimulate blood flow than to improve his tactical view. Bending, he allowed his head to drop and his fingers to reach the dusty deck plates. The stretch brought him back to reality in time for Julien's report.

"Active return from drone two."

The surprise elevated Jake's awareness.

"Secure all active transmissions," he said. "All stop. Bring the drones to all stop. Designate drone two's new contact as Master Six. Get Master Six on the chart."

The icon appeared on his display twelve miles from his ship. The triangle between the *Specter*, the *Kim*, and Master Six placed seventeen miles between the new threat and Cahill's future work site.

"Shit," Jake said. "I've got a decision to make."

Henri's understudy looked at him from the ship's control station and shrugged.

"I need to decide whether to sink Master Six and risk that the noise attracts unwanted attention, stay here and police Master Six to make sure it doesn't hear Terry when he's working, or trust that Master Six won't hear Terry and keep looking for other bad guys."

"I don't envy your captain's job. Should I get Henri?"

"Yeah, get him," Jake said. "This is one of those moments where I appreciate the old codger's advice."

CHAPTER 21

Cahill glared at the *Goliath's* short-range, side-scan sonar. His eyes burned, and he looked away and blinked.

"Still nothing," Walker said.

"Submarine warfare requires patience," Cahill said. "Apparently so does submarine rescue."

"We could turn the power up on our scanning radar."

"Not when we're trying to maintain our stealth."

"Right," Walker said. "I get it. I don't like it, but I get it. At least in surface warfare, it's definitive."

"How do you mean?"

"I mean when you light up your radar, you expect to get a return from your target, but you also expect that you're announcing your presence to the enemy. Down here, it's a coin toss. We use our active sonar, and we may get the return we want, and we don't know if our enemy hears us searching, even with this short-range high-precision scanning sonar. It just adds to the willies of the blindness."

Cahill looked out the window at the pitch blackness and then shifted his eyes back to the sonar display.

"You get used to it."

"I may never," Walker said. "Jake placed us within a mile of her, but it's still as invisible as if it didn't exist."

"We'll find her. This search pattern will reveal her. We just need to be diligent."

"Maybe not," Walker said. "We may have just found what we're looking for. Could that be it?"

An oblong shape took form on the display.

"We'll know soon. Give it a moment."

The significance of the image's outline became undeniable.

"Securing the scanning sonar," Cahill said. "We've got it. Let the crew know where it is and have them prepare for loading operations."

"I'll let the crew know," Walker said. "It's supposed to be waiting for us at fifty meters of depth. It looks more like sixty, but I won't complain. We can handle that no problem."

"Its crew probably had trouble getting it to a neutral trim. It's a challenge to give a submarine an exact equal weight to the water around it so that you're not sinking or rising with a level deck. I'll give them a silver medal for getting it done within ten meters of the depth Pierre requested."

"But it's easy for us on the *Goliath*."

"Yeah, because we're built for it," Cahill said. "You're spoiled and you don't know it. We have huge automated trim and drain pumps that are made to push high volumes of water for tight depth control when shallow. But true submarines are usually moving and can use their planes and ship's angle to compensate for minor imperfections in their trim. And they need to go deeper than our pumps work. So no need and no use for the oversized, high-volume pumps."

"But the *Kim* is getting no value from its planes or ship's angle because it's stranded."

"Right."

"Its heading appears to be about one-one-zero, based upon its hull length and trigonometry."

"That's a good estimate. I'll position us behind it on that heading and drive us under it. Stand by for some more patient ship handling. This will be delicate."

Cahill took thirty careful minutes to maneuver the *Goliath* behind and below its mark. The forward scanning sonar placed the *Kim* three hundred yards away.

"Slowing to three knots," he said. "Securing the forward scanning sonar. Turning on the exterior lights."

Lights turned the blackness before him into an ugly pale gray. He looked over his shoulder at the cargo bed to orient his eyes on a tangible target beyond his bridge windows. Illumination from his ship's port side kept the invisible far hull in darkness.

"This is spooky," Walker said.

"I spent me entire career underwater, and I can't argue you with you one whit."

The surreal surroundings became less unsettling and then familiar in the quiet minutes during which Cahill approached his prize.

"Slowing to one knot," he said. "Energizing upward scanning sonar."

He was exhilarated when the tactical system's integration algorithms transformed the acoustic return from his scanning sonar into the form of the *Kim's* stern.

"Slowing to half a knot," he said.

"It's left of center, Terry. Its stern is too far to our port side."

"We'll compensate with the outboards."

"Right. Agreed."

The *Kim's* shape grew and walked aft on the sonar display.

"This is a good enough picture," Cahill said. "It's only off a few degrees to the right. We can adjust visually once it's in view. Securing the upward scanning sonar."

"I'd bump me head on it if I broke through the glass and swam towards it, but I still can't see a damned thing."

"Yeah, it's close. Close enough. Slowing to all stop. Deploy all four outboards."

"I'm deploying all four outboards. Outboards are deployed. Are you sure you don't want constant upward scanning sonar?"

"I'm sure. We're close enough. No sense risking it. Bring us to all stop with the outboards."

Walker tapped keys, and four small outboard motors with propellers located under each corner of the *Goliath* nudged the ship's mass to motionlessness.

"Now twist us six degrees to the left."

"Twisting left. Two degrees. Now four. Slowing our twist. And, the outboards have twisted us six degrees to the left."

"Very well. Now mark your depth."

"Steady at eighty meters."

"Very well. Mark distance from the bed to cargo's keel."

"System-calculated distance from the bed to the cargo's keel is eighteen meters."

"Very well. Shift trim control to automatic loading mode, verify setting of two meters per minute rise rate."

"Trim control is in automatic loading mode, set at two meters per minute rise rate."

"Very well. Now keep your eyes glued to the system and make sure it behaves. One false bump and scrape, and we announce our location for miles in every direction."

Cahill shot periodic glances at the display to double-check Walker's double-checking. Instead of seeing the errors he feared, he admired the *Goliath's* delicate computerized dance of shuffling water fore and aft to keep itself level while shedding water overboard to gain levity.

Much as the screens before him highlighted the automated grace of the transport vessel's cargo loading routine, Cahill ignored the technical spectacle in favor of the view he sought through his window.

"Depth is seventy meters," Walker said.

"Slow the system to one meter per minute rise rate."

Cahill reminded himself of the virtue of patience as he awaited his quarry. Then the sailor in the port weapons bay rewarded him by reporting the first sighting.

"This is the port weapons bay. I have visual on the cargo. I see its screw."

Before Cahill could respond, the bow came into his view. His heart raced, but something – an indiscernible feeling of incongruity – crept up his spine, dampening his initial elation.

"Do you see it?" Walker asked.

"Yeah."

"I'll have to watch the video replay later, unless you want me to take me eye off the loading procedure."

"Keep your focus. You'll have to watch the replay later. Get me a secure loading."

Breathless, he absorbed the illusion of the *Kim* falling through translucent molasses into the *Goliath's* waiting cradle.

"Per protocol, the system is stopping the ascent to allow us to assess the need for manual adjustments," Walker said.

Mesmerized, Cahill studied his pending cargo. The abnormality that had clawed at his spine took root in the recesses of his mind. Then the thought became a clear recognition of a wrinkle that would require a modification of his plan.

"Terry?"

"No, continue loading."

"I shall continuing loading. Shall I use the loading sonar to mark the cargo's final position?"

"No. Do it visually. Use the cameras."

"Terry? The chance of error goes up."

"Visually. Trust me."

Cahill became cold stone as he watched the *Goliath's* retracted hydraulic presses climb up the cargo's side like mechanical fingers.

"We're askew in azimuth half a degree," Walker said. "I'm adjusting manually."

Cahill ignored him.

"Terry, I'm adjusting manually."

"Very well."

"Slowing to half a meter per minute."

"Very well."

"Contact!"

"Engage the presses!" Cahill said.

"By procedure we're supposed to wait until we're sure of complete contact."

"I don't care. Engage the presses now."

"Done. Presses are engaged."

The presses rotated and pinned down the submarine.

"Bold call, Terry, but we got her. Can we head home now?"

"No. I have control of the ship."

He tapped icons.

"Emergency surfacing and preparing the cannons for manual targeting."

"Terry! We're planning a submerged egress. Why would you surface?"

"I know what I'm doing."

"If you're planning on sprinting out of here, Jake won't be able to patrol ahead of us. We'll be exposed to enemy submarines."

"I said, I know what I'm doing."

"But the cannons? Manual? Why?"

He ignored Walker.

"Terry, explain yourself. For God's sake, you at least owe me that."

He kept his eyes aimed out the glass, drew in a deep breath, and sighed it out.

"What the hell's going on? What's wrong?" Walker asked.

Cahill looked to the deck as he failed to suppress a sardonic smile. He then raised his eyes over his shoulder to Walker and responded with the confidence he believed he needed to convey to his executive officer.

"That's not the *Kim*."

CHAPTER 22

Walker raced across the bridge and became stone beside Cahill.

"Dear God," he said.

"Stay calm," Cahill said.

The *Goliath* began to rock as it approached the stormy surface.

"What is it?"

"It's a *Romeo*. Similar dimensions as the *Kim*. It was an easy mistake."

"Mistake? How the hell did we load an enemy submarine by mistake? Why the hell didn't it shoot at us?"

"The crew probably mistook our sonar for an echo sounder or for what it really is – sonar equipment to find fish. They wouldn't very well reveal their position by shooting at a fishing ship. They had no idea we were coming until we grabbed them."

"They're not afraid of death. They're practically suicidal. Why didn't they shoot a weapon and have it come back and kill us all? How do we know that's not what they're about to do?"

"Easy, mate. The two most important safeguards on a torpedo are keeping it from exploding in your torpedo room and keeping it from swimming back at you when you shoot it. Every torpedo on the planet has an anti-circular run feature to keep it from killing the ship that launched it. Trust me, they're as helpless as a bug in our spider web."

Cahill kept his eyes on the *Romeo* he had pinned down on his cargo bed. Its antiquated rakish shape allowed it better speed on the surface than submerged, and the red paint climbing high up its sides appeared sanguine in the water.

"Ugly and old, but still dangerous," he said. "I have to give the captain credit for picking a good ambush position. He was in the right place and just got unlucky that we were extremely careful with our speed of approach."

"Why didn't he shoot Jake when he found him with his drones?"

"You assume that his crew heard the drones. His ship's hydrophones and processing equipment are old. Jake's drones aren't as secure as the *Specter* when transmitting active, but they still can use very short duration bursts. They're not exactly easy to notice."

"Okay, but why didn't you abort the loading when you saw that we had the wrong ship?"

"I thought about it, but I judged the risk of trying to slip away unnoticed too dangerous. One false sound, and we would've been an easy target. And even if I could have gotten us out of here quietly and shot at them, they would've had a good chance of hearing the launch. Then we would've faced a one-for-one exchange. I decided to keep them in me cargo bed."

"Maybe, but now they know something's wrong. We've grabbed their ship and are manhandling them to the surface. Why aren't they doing anything?"

Both weapons bay watchmen shouted reports that trampled each other, but Cahill understood their redundant meanings – both men reported seeing the *Romeo* spinning up its propeller.

"There you have it, mate," he said. "They're trying something. They're trying to escape."

"Lateral stress on the hydraulic presses is rising."

The darkness above the *Goliath* turned gray as the surface's light approached.

"They won't make it out of our bed," Cahill said. "Our presses will hold, and we'll be surfaced before they can break free."

"Lateral stress is at the alarm point."

"They'll hold. I'm energizing the laser."

"What the hell's the laser going to do?"

"Cut pinholes in its forward ballast tanks. Maybe. I don't know. It can't hurt to try."

"I see," Walker said. "Do you want me to keep our radar dark when we surface?"

"Yes. God willing, we'll be up here for hardly a minute, and if we get lucky, we'll submerge again before anyone notices."

"Wishful thinking."

"I know. One crisis at a time. Let's get rid of this *Romeo* and then worry about who might hunt us."

Cahill tapped an icon.

"Port and starboard weapons bays, when we surface, I want you to aim the cannons manually three quarters up the side of the cargo vessel. In case you haven't noticed, we accidentally loaded an enemy submarine. You'll be putting holes through it hull high enough so that your rounds travel over the *Goliath* when they pass through. Acknowledge that you understand."

Both watchmen responded.

"Five rounds from each of you. Start just aft of its conning tower and then walk each shot back five degrees, maximum rate of fire. Then you're each going to put one round just below each ballast tank vent that you can see. Acknowledge that you understand."

The *Goliath* rocked hard and then broke the surface as the men responded. Rain pelted the windows, and gray drizzle separated Cahill from the *Romeo*.

In the distance, he saw the dark gray forms of his railguns rising atop his stern sections.

"Commence fire!" he said.

The first rounds punctured the *Romeo's* skin, created the horrific shriek of avulsed steel, and continued into the gray oblivion.

"The laser, Liam."

"Aiming. Firing."

"Did you hit?"

"I can't tell in this infernal rain."

The deck lurched in the swells, and Cahill grabbed a console for support.

"Keep shooting," he said. "Pinholes could make a difference."

As the next railgun rounds gored the *Romeo*, Cahill saw the submarine raise its antenna.

"Calling for help," he said. "That's not a concern. Keep shooting the ballast tanks."

Motion atop the submarine caught his attention.

"Cease fire! Aim cannons at the top of the conning tower."

Human forms took shape on the cargo's apex, and Cahill thought he discerned a shoulder-launched weapon tube beside a man's ear.

"Aim the cannons at their waists."

"I can't see anyone," the starboard bay watchman said.

"Can you see the conning tower's top?"

"Yes."

"Aim for it. Fire!"

The rounds sliced holes in steel. Cahill thought the human forms crouched in a startle response, but he hoped they fell to their deck without legs.

"Keep firing."

Two more rounds from each railgun proved that the men atop the *Romeo's* conning tower were motionless.

"Cease fire!" he said. "Aim the cannons at its propeller. Shoot off the blades. Commence fire!"

Three rounds from each gun erupted.

"The propeller is wrecked," the port bay watchman said.

"I concur. It's useless," the starboard bay watchman said.

"Aim at the after torpedo tubes. Disable those weapons."

Two rounds from each cannon fired, and the watchmen reported that they had impaled the *Romeo's* two rearward-looking torpedoes.

"Cease fire, all weapons. Secure all weapons. Submerging the ship."

He tapped an icon that ordered the *Goliath* to inhale the sea into its trim tanks.

"We're under," Walker said. "The *Romeo* is still above."

"Not for long."

Abated by depth, the rocking became gentle.

"It's under now, too," Cahill said.

"How deep do you want to go?"

"I don't. Stop us here."

"Steadying at twenty-five meters."

A report from his tactical control room filled the bridge.

"The *Romeo* is blowing its ballast tanks. High-pressure air is escaping from its rear tanks and mid-line tanks."

"That means the forward tank is holding air," Cahill said. "It'll rip free from the forward presses if we stay under."

"Then what the hell do we do?" Walker asked. "Shall we surface and pummel it more with our cannons?"

"No. I've got a better idea. We'll pin it down. Watch."

He tapped icons.

"Coming to thirteen knots. Coming to full dive on the stern planes."

The deck dipped, and Cahill reached to a console for balance.

"Axial stress on the forward presses is rising through the alarm point."

"Come on, *Goliath*. Give me speed."

"We're at six knots," Walker said. "Now seven. Ship's angle is fifteen degrees down. Now twenty. Passing fifty meters."

Cahill envisioned emergency air filling the *Romeo's* forward ballast tanks, converting them into submerged steel balloons. Against its upward force, his presses strained and seawater from his ship's motion pushed down.

"Nine knots," Walker said. "Twenty-two-degrees down angle. Passing seventy meters."

Alarm lights illuminated and a buzzer heightened Cahill's anxiety.

"Silence that."

"It's silenced," Walker said. "Ten knots. Eighty-five meters. We're approaching design test depth."

"We have plenty of margin on our depth. We can go deeper than one hundred meters."

"Terry, the presses are going to rip off!"

"Damn it! Very well. If we need to rise nose up, we'll rise nose up. Leveling the deck. Pumping water from forward to after trim tanks. Coming to zero degrees on the stern planes."

"Axial stress on forward presses is falling, but axial stress on rear presses is rising."

"There's still a huge air pocket inside that submarine's pressure hull. They're shoring up the holes, fighting for their lives. Coming to full rise on the stern planes."

"Depth is steadying at ninety-two meters. Ship's angle is down five degrees and rising. Speed eleven and a half knots."

Cahill thought of reaching the surface and wondered if his adversary would attempt to escape through the conning tower. He wondered how much water weight the *Romeo* carried in its pressure hull and if the *Goliath* could support the entire ship above water. He wondered if the North Korean crew would surrender if given a chance. The permutations of possibilities perplexed him.

"Doctor Tan, lay to the bridge," he said. "All hands help Doctor Tan find his way to the bridge."

"Making thirteen knots," Walker said. "Ship's angle is ten degrees up. Depth is seventy meters and rising. Stress on all hydraulic presses is below alarm levels."

"Very well."

"What happens on the surface, Terry? I'm not sure I see your plan, or if I do, I don't like what I'm seeing."

"I fight to hold that *Romeo* in our bed, nose up in the air as high as I can get it while holding its ass underwater."

"I got that part. I still don't see a good outcome. It's going to become too heavy, and it'll backslide off our bed. If there's one person left alive within it, some guy who was smart enough to stay alive by breathing forced air, he could shoot any or all of those six torpedoes out of the forward tubes on his way down."

"That's the plan, mate. If it backslides, it backslides, and I'll ride it down and take me chances. But it may not."

The shallow depths rocked the *Goliath*, and blackness yielded to gray. Then the bridge cracked the surface, and rain pelted the windows.

"I'm keeping our stern planes on full rise to keep our stern down," Cahill said. "Weapons bays, mark your local depths."

"Starboard weapons bay reads twenty-four meters."

"Port weapons bay reads twenty-three and a half meters."

"Sonar, do you still hear water rushing into the *Romeo*?"

"Yes, sir. Water's going in the holes we shot through its pressure hull and air's coming out the holes we shot in its ballast tanks. It'll take a long time for it to empty its high-pressure air tanks through the holes."

"I'm only concerned about the water flowing in. Let me know if you hear it stop."

"It's getting heavy, Terry," Walker said. "Lateral stresses are rising on all hydraulic presses."

The bridge door clicked open, and a small man with black hair and thick glasses appeared below Cahill.

"Do you need me?"

"Sorry, Doctor Tan," Cahill said. "False alarm. I don't expect to be communicating with any survivors after all."

The translator nodded, turned, and departed.

"Hydraulic presses are at the alarm point," Walker said.

"Damn it. All stop," Cahill said. "We'll backslide with her. I'm flooding into the central trim tanks, maximum pump speed."

Rough waves slapped the windows as seas climbed up the domed glass. The pelting of droplets gave way to the silence of the subsurface world.

"We're at twenty meters," Walker said. "That's for the bridge. The weapons bays are twenty-five meters deeper at this steep angle."

"Right. Let's see if I can level us off. I'm pumping water from aft to forward trim tanks."

"Our up angle is lowering. We're at fifteen degrees up. Now fourteen. Keep it going, Terry. The presses are handling the stress."

"I'm going two degrees up on our stern planes."

"Up?"

"Because we're falling backward."

"Right. I'm still learning these underwater concepts. Our angle is down to ten degrees up. Depth is fifty meters at the bow, sixty-four at the weapons bays. We're descending at twenty meters per minute."

Cahill looked at the stress levels on the hydraulic presses and saw them holding at tolerable levels. Then the sonar supervisor announced that the water flow into the *Romeo* had subsided.

"That's it, then," Walker said. "We've flooded its entire pressure hull. The only possible survivors are men lucky enough to be breathing forced air."

"Increasing stern plane angle to five degrees up."

"Ship's angle is four degrees up," Walker said. "Now three."

"We've got this now," Cahill said. "I'm accelerating to five knots to get better control of me ship."

"Two knots," Walker said. "Three knots. Rate of descent is dropping to ten meters per minute. The deck is level."

"That's good enough. I'm going to let the system handle this now automatically."

He tapped icons and entered parameters. Speed five knots, ship's angle level, depth sixty-five meters. The *Goliath* obeyed his wishes by pumping water overboard from its central trim tanks.

The lowered stresses on the hydraulic presses revealed that the *Romeo's* living space had been flooded, offsetting the rising forces of its dry forward ballast tanks.

"We've got control, Terry. Now what?"

"Now we crush any survivors. I'm coming to one hundred and ten meters."

"One hundred and ten?"

"Permissible with captain's orders, and I'm the captain."

He tapped keys, and the *Goliath* drove downward with a gentle angle.

"That's good enough. That's a whit more than ten atmospheres on any survivors."

"Divers can endure that, at least for short periods, I think."

"True, but let's see how they deal with a rapid ascent. God knows what tortures I'm putting any survivors through, but I'm taking no chances."

"I won't argue."

"Coming to thirteen knots, full rise on the stern planes. Let's make one more trip to the surface and see if anyone is trying to talk to us. I'm sure Pierre has learned that we've exposed ourselves to radar by now."

The deck rose as Walker tapped keys.

"Indeed he has. He's been hailing us with the low-bandwidth communications for the last ten minutes."

Gray opaqueness supplanted pitch blackness and then gave way to pelting rain as the *Goliath's* bows shot through the surface. The prows crashed back down, and the stern sections nudged through the waves.

"Link me with Pierre."

"Done."

"Are you alright?" Renard asked.

"We're fine."

"What are you up to, man? You're exposing yourself and you're shooting your cannons at a target I don't see."

"Long story, mate. Short version is I picked up the wrong submarine. I've got a *Romeo* in me cargo bed. I shot holes in it and dragged it under. It's completely flooded, but I'm not taking chances with survivors. So I took meself to one hundred and ten meters and then back up shallow again to cycle pressures on survivors."

"Dear God, man. That's gruesome. But it's good thinking."

Cahill watched the tactical display absorb input from a data feed. The remnants of the North Korean armada drove towards him at flank speeds – or the best speeds possible for those his guns had hobbled.

"But now I've got bigger problems. We're back to having no *Kim* and no chance of drawing away the enemy with another distraction. They know where I am, they can speculate me intention, and they're coming. We're out of bloody time. Perhaps you can rally Jake and the *Gwansun* to join me in a three ships verses the world scenario? Put them in a semi-circle around me, and let me use me cannons."

"No need," Renard said. "Jake's at snorkel depth and has shared the location of an enemy submarine he found drifting with the current. But now that you've told me your cargo was a *Romeo*, I'm certain that Jake's discovery is the *Kim*."

"You'll let him know?"

"I've already sent out the data feed. You'll have the *Kim's* coordinates, too. You'll be happy to know that the *Gwansun* is also coming to help. It'll have your back, so to speak, while Jake has your front and sides, during loading and egress."

"So what now?"

"Cycle your depth a few times en route to the *Kim* to compound the stress on any survivors on your *Romeo*. Then dump the *Romeo*, grab the *Kim,* and bring it home."

CHAPTER 23

Jake paced behind his sonar team.

"How many contacts now?" he asked.

"I've lost count," Remy said.

The *Specter* and its drones patrolled in a horseshoe pattern in front of the *Kim* as the *Goliath* approached it. Numerous North Korean warships gathered around him.

"Some have stopped," Remy said. "Some are still coming. I've never seen anything like this. None are close enough for high-percentage torpedo shots."

"Enough guessing," Jake said. "If they're far away, I can risk exposing my antenna. Let's see what Pierre sees. Henri, bring us to periscope depth."

He walked to the conning platform and sat in his chair as Henri angled the deck upward. The ship rocked in the shallows as the French mechanic verified the connection with Jake's mentor.

"They're concentrating their forces," Renard said. "I predict that they'll soon make a run at you. They may release their slower ships first, or they may make a common slower speed, but it's obvious that they're working together, finding strength in numbers. I am concerned."

Jake studied the tactical display. Two dozen ships formed a line to the south, and three times that many formed a wall to the north.

"If they're going to go all out to sink any submarine they find, that means one of two things."

"Either there are no more enemy submarines in the area," Renard said, "or they just don't care about killing their own."

"Can't Terry just blow his way out?"

"If there are no remaining enemy submarines, then yes. But that's a bold assumption. If there are any, he'll race right into their torpedoes."

"Let me sweep ahead. Now, before Terry's loaded the *Kim*. No North Korean submarine can make good speed without making noise. You don't need me protecting the loading operation. The *Gwansun* can protect him."

Jake glared at the display in silence.

"Pierre?"

"I'm thinking. You've made a good point. Two additional South Korean submarines have deployed and have swept a corridor under friendly airspace for Terry. He's got about ninety nautical miles to cover to reach safety. That's less than three hours at his best surfaced speed."

After performing mental calculations, Jake refined the plan.

"He could outrun the western half of the ships. He could also outrun the eastern half that he's already damaged. Can't he just shoot anything that shows threatening speed and power his way out?"

"Indeed he could, as long as you keep submarines out of his way."

"Then let's do it. I need to get started."

"Very well. Let me explain what I was thinking about when you noticed my silence."

"I'm listening."

"Start with a twenty-mile wide search, forty-five degrees off the egress course. Tighten your search to fifteen miles on your second pass, and then to ten thereafter. Terry should have the *Kim* loaded in an hour, and he'll catch you by your third or fourth ten-mile wide search. At that point, I will want you to do something quite unconventional."

"What's that?"

"When Terry overruns you, you'll launch three torpedoes. You'll set one right down the middle and then one each forty-five degrees to either side of the egress course. When the angled shots reach three miles wide off course, you'll turn them parallel to the others. You'll set a ceiling of twenty meters on all weapons so that you don't hit Terry."

"Insurance policies? They'll hit anything in his way for the remainder of his sprint to friendly waters."

"Right."

"You'll let the South Korean submarines in friendly airspace know to stay out of range?"

"Of course."

"And I shoot any submarine I run into?"

"Correct. And shoot any surface combatant as well. In fact, shoot anything that you remotely suspect may be a warship. Be liberal with your munitions in clearing the way."

Henri called out.

"Shall I set us on course?"

"Yes. You heard the search pattern. Forty-five degrees left of egress course, which is one-zero-zero."

"So course zero-five-five?"

"Yes. Get it started, and I'll check on you in a minute."

"Keep an eye on your low-bandwidth communications," Renard said. "The way this mission has gone, we may yet need to chat before you get home, and I'll give you updates about Terry."

"I will. I know the drill from here."

"I'm sure you do. Good luck, my friend."

Jake aimed his nose at Remy.

"Where's the acoustic layer, Antoine?"

"Too deep to matter for *Sangos* and *Yonos*. One hundred and sixty meters if you want to hunt *Romeos*."

"I need to hunt everything," Jake said. "We'll porpoise between one hundred fifty and one hundred seventy meters during this search. Henri, can you handle that, every ten minutes?"

"Of course."

"This goes for the drones, too. Until I say otherwise, every depth order I give to Henri is also an order for drone depth. Got it, Julien?"

"Got it."

"Henri, make your depth one hundred and fifty meters."

Henri drove the *Specter* downward and leveled it on Jake's ordered depth, speed ten knots, course zero-five-five.

Towards the end of the first leg, Julien announced a target.

"I've got a contact on drone two bearing zero-two-two, range twelve miles from our ship."

Expecting excessive action, Jake had reloaded his tubes.

"Designate the contact on drone two as Master Seven. Prepare tube one to engage Master Seven, maximum transit speed."

"Would you like a ceiling or a floor?" Remy asked.

"No. Anything that gets hit out here deserves to be hit, even a fishing ship. Nobody in these waters is innocent."

"Tube one is ready," Remy said.

"Henri, take us to one hundred and seventy meters. I'll shoot from below the layer to mask my sounds from the target."

The deck dipped and leveled.

"Shoot tube one."

"Tube one, normal launch," Henri said.

"Very well. We'll continue searching on this depth for the rest of this leg. We'll come above the layer when we turn to the right."

During the next search leg, Henri announced that Renard had sent a low-bandwidth update stating that Terry had loaded the *Kim* and was sprinting home on the surface.

"Right on schedule," Jake said.

"Torpedo one is in terminal homing," Remy said.

"Very well."

"Torpedo one has detonated."

"Can you hear sounds of Master Seven sinking?"

"No, the distance is too great. But I'm sure you hit something."

"I'm not being selective."

Jake considered himself to be in undersea warfare's blood lust equivalent of running through a hostile jungle with his rifle at his hip. He would break anything in his way.

"Would you like me to have the team backhaul tube one and reload it with a heavyweight torpedo?" Henri asked.

"Not yet. Wait until we're below the layer."

"It's time to head deep now anyway," Henri said.

"Make your depth one hundred and seventy meters."

"Steady on depth one hundred and seventy meters," Henri said. "Shall I backhaul and reload tube one?"

"Yes, backhaul and reload tube one."

"I've got a contact on drone one bearing one-nine-nine, range eleven miles from our ship," Julien said.

"Henri, secure from backhauling and reloading tube one."

The Frenchman handled Jake's request, minimizing the chance of the *Specter* creating metallic noises.

"Designate the contact on drone one as Master Eight," Jake said. "Prepare tube two to engage Master Eight, maximum transit speed."

"Would you like a ceiling or a floor?" Remy asked.

"No. I can infer from its position below the layer that the contact is a *Romeo*, but it can evade to any depth."

"Tube two is ready," Remy said.

"Henri, take us back up to one hundred and fifty meters. I'll shoot from above the layer."

The deck rose.

"Steady on depth one hundred and fifty meters."

"Shoot tube two."

The second weapon chased its prey while its launch platform continued scanning the water for North Korean targets. At the end of the leg, Jake ordered the *Specter* back to course zero-five-five.

"I've received an update on the *Goliath's* position from Pierre," Henri said. "Shall I read off the coordinates?"

"Yes."

Jake grabbed a pencil and scratchpad. When he had the numbers, he headed to the navigation table and tapped them into the system. A line from the *Kim's* loading coordinates to the update of Cahill's position showed the *Goliath* on course and on schedule to overrun Jake within an hour.

He stared at the navigation chart, hoping that Cahill's chances of bringing the *Kim* home increased with each mile the *Goliath* closed towards friendly water.

"It's time to go deep," Henri said.

Jake agreed, and the ship settled below the layer.

"I can hear our torpedo running now," Remy said. "Its seeker just went active, and I can hear it."

"Is Master Seven running yet?"

"No. Wait! Yes. Just now."

"Track it and have your apprentice steer the weapon."

"Our torpedo has acquired Master Eight," Remy said. "No need for steering. The weapon will handle it from here."

"You've got them on the run, Jake," Henri said. "Shall I continue backhauling and reloading tube one?"

"Yes. Continue backhauling and reloading tube one."

The destruction of Master Eight seemed businesslike to Jake.

When he found and destroyed Master Nine on a subsequent search leg, he looked at his trail of broken hulls and dead bodies as a cleansing operation. The macabre weight of wasted humanity bypassed his awareness and sank deep into his subconscious mind.

During several legs, he had reloaded his tubes and charted Pierre's updates about the *Goliath's* movements.

"I've got another update from Pierre," Henri said.

"Read it off."

Jake tapped the coordinates into the navigation chart.

"Antoine, you should be able to hear the *Goliath* soon."

"Wouldn't you rather have me searching for bad guys?"

"Fine. Just let me know when you can't help but hear her. There will be a point where I'm no further use to Terry."

"Of course, I will," Remy said.

"You haven't heard anything for a while."

"I think we're in the clear, to be honest. The North Koreans couldn't have predicted our exact route home, and they had to spread their submarines out to cover all the angles. I think we've taken care of everything in Terry's way already."

"I hope you're right. Keep looking. We've got ten minutes before he overtakes us."

Henri hailed Jake.

"You should prepare the three escort weapons."

"It's a bit early, but it can't hurt to get started."

He wrote down numbers on his scratchpad to simplify his communications task with his team. Reconsidering the complexity of his intent, he decided to handle it with his own fingertips.

"Antoine, I'm taking control of tubes one through three."

He tapped in the courses of the three weapons, and he ordered their ceilings of twenty meters. He chose a medium transit speed to give his heavyweight Black Shark torpedoes a slight speed advantage over the *Goliath* while extending their range.

Julien surprised him with his announcement.

"I've got a contact on drone two bearing three-five-two, range thirteen miles from our ship."

"Designate the contact on drone two as Master Ten," Jake said. "Prepare tube four to engage Master Ten, maximum transit speed. No ceiling. No floor."

"Tube four is ready," Remy said.

"Jake," Henri said.

"What? I'm shooting a weapon."

"Given the low speed of our adversaries and the distance, Master Ten will be no threat to the *Goliath*."

"That's a good observation, but I disagree. Anyone can get lucky. Antoine, shoot tube four."

"I've shot tube four."

"What's the torpedo room say, Henri?"

"I'll check."

He could tell he had upset the Frenchman by shooting, but he knew he had carried out Renard's intent by being aggressive.

"Tube four, normal launch."

"Very well. Cut the wire to tube four. Backhaul and reload tube four with a heavyweight torpedo."

Jake refocused his attention on the three torpedoes he would control. The *Goliath* reached three miles behind him.

"Antoine, give me a no-shit listen to the *Goliath*. I'd like to know that you hear Terry before I shoot weapons in front of him."

"I hear the *Goliath*," Remy said. "The bearing matches the solution in the system."

"Shooting tube three," Jake said.

"Tube three, normal launch," Henri said.

"Shooting tube one," Jake said.

"Tube one, normal launch," Henri said.

Jake counted down thirty seconds to allow the weapons to travel to the right and in front of Cahill respectively. Then he launched tube two to travel on the left of the *Goliath's* track.

The weapons reached out beyond the transport vessel, and Jake inserted steers into their programming that turned them on the egress course.

"That's it," he said. "Let's position ourselves behind Terry and drive a straight line behind him."

When Remy announced the explosion from the direction of Master Ten, the walls behind which Jake had stuffed his killing crumbled, and he fell back into his chair, exhausted.

CHAPTER 24

Cahill watched droplets splash against the windows.

"I still can't believe Jake took out four ships," he said. "And only one was a submarine. He was on a rampage, killing anything and everything. He even took out a fishing trawler."

"He was just following Pierre's orders. I don't know that you can blame him."

"But still, it's not like him. I expected him to be more – what's the word I'm looking for?"

"Merciful."

"Right."

Indulging himself in another look over his shoulder, he admired the view of the *Kim* riding in his cargo bay. Its steel plates bowing inward between its ribs, it appeared like an inverted caterpillar. He judged that the surviving crew's proximity to death had been razor sharp.

He then returned his attention to the threatening warships. Based upon his organic phased array radar and the surveillance that the entire South Korean military provided him, nothing stood between him and a successful return to a friendly port.

Submarines still concerned him, but Jake's torpedoes raced ahead to bridge the gap between his position and the boundary of safe waters.

"It's weird being escorted by torpedoes," he said.

"Weird isn't the word. I'd say crazy. But somehow it seems to make sense."

"Okay, that's enough."

"Sorry?"

"I mean the cannons. We've shot everything we needed to shoot. I'll keep them and the lasers readied as a precaution, but I'll conserve me ammunition."

"For what target? We're practically home."

Cahill considered reminding Walker to refrain from jinxing the mission, but no predictable threats remained. He let the comment float unanswered.

"I can't wait to get onto dry land and breathe dry air."

"Agreed, mate," Walker said. "It hasn't let up in days."

Cahill tapped his screen to overlay weather radar information over his tactical scene. A storm loomed ahead.

"Well that explains the rough seas."

"We should be able to beat it, though," Walker said. "I think we can cut around its eastern edge and avoid having to drive through a torrential downpour."

"Yes, if the storm holds its shape, course, and speed."

After several minutes of silent railguns, Cahill noticed a human form appear atop the *Kim's* sail.

"There's our first sign of life," he said. "Get Doctor Tan up here."

Cahill glared at the man on the *Kim* until the sailor made eye contact. He waved, smiled, and held up his palms to compel the man to stay where he was. Somehow, the crewman understood and waited, hunched over in the rain.

When Doctor Tan reached the bridge, Cahill handed him a microphone.

"The exterior loudspeakers will reach the *Kim*, but he obviously has no way to speak back to us. Just let him know that we've been employed by his government to rescue him and that he can check all his facts with his command via radio."

Tan rattled off the message in Korean, and then the man raised a thumb before disappearing into the submarine.

Moments later, Renard's voice filled the cabin.

"That's a very cautious crew you've saved. They were listening to all the broadcasts, but since they could hear the cannon fire, they decided against transmitting to avoid any confirmation of their identity to the enemy. But now, you've got an open channel. You can say whatever you want to the *Kim's* acting commanding officer, a Lieutenant Yoon. You'll need your translator, though, since he speaks no English."

"Right. How should I identify meself?"

"He knows who you are. Just tell him you're Terry Cahill."

"First things first. How's his crew? Does anyone need medical attention?"

"Yes. Him. But he refused evacuation by helicopter when offered. He wants to stay with his men all the way to home port."

"Admirable. Doctor Tan, please tell Lieutenant Yoon that Terry Cahill is honored to have him and his ship aboard the *Goliath* as me guest and that I promise to get him home safe."

The doctor translated, and Cahill heard a response from the *Kim's* young de facto captain. Tan rendered the translation.

"He says that he's most grateful and looks forward to meeting you in person. He and his crew cannot adequately express their appreciation for your courage and your support."

"Alright. Let's not make this a group hug."

Tan lifted the microphone.

"No, don't translate that. Just tell him that I'm at his service and that I'll keep the line of communication open."

Ten minutes later, the rain storm morphed in the direction least favorable for Cahill's avoiding it.

"Well, shit, Liam. Get ready to be tossed about."

Binoculars at his face, Walker ignored him.

"What's got your attention, Liam?"

"That storm. The leading edge. It doesn't look right."

"How can a storm be wrong, or right for that matter?"

"That's what I'm trying to figure out. The edge closest to us doesn't look nearly as dark as the rest."

Wanting to dismiss the issue, Cahill instead offered advice.

"Have a look through infrared on an exterior camera, then."

"Right. I'll call it up."

Cahill wondered if he should submerge below the storm and enjoy a quiet return trip, but then he opted to maintain speed and deal with the discomfort, deciding that everyone on his ship and the *Kim* wanted to get home in time for a late dinner.

"That's a ship, Terry! That's an accursed warship. I think it's North Korean."

"Shit! Doctor Tan, hail it. Warn it that I'm going to blow it out of the water if it doesn't contact fleet headquarters immediately and prove that it's friendly."

While the doctor spoke, Cahill warmed up his torpedoes and had Walker ready the railguns.

"I've locked on with our phased array. It took concentrated power because that bastard's hiding under chaff. Range, nine miles."

"Chaff? Damn. It's hostile. Open fire."

"Starting with the engineering spaces?"

"No. Start with any torpedo launchers you can hit. Set the rounds to splinter. Now!"

The railguns erupted.

"Based on dimensions and visual analysis, that's a *Taechong* class patrol boat," Walker said. "They normally don't carry anti-ship missiles. The main armament is an eighty-five millimeter cannon and six lightweight torpedoes, three per side, no reloads."

"Lightweight or not, I'm assuming there's a few coming our way. I'm coming hard left to open range."

A whistle traced an arc above the windows, and an explosion erupted on the *Kim's* conning tower.

"Holy shit, it hit us!" Cahill said.

"We're barely within its cannon range."

"Not for long."

The *Goliath* lurched into the crashing waves. Cahill and Walker braced themselves while Doctor Tan toppled against a bulkhead. Another round hit the *Kim's* tower, followed by a third before the *Goliath's* evasive maneuvers forced the rounds to fall wide.

"Preparing tube one in surface mode," Cahill said. "It's warming. It's ready. Shooting tube one."

"Our cannon rounds have taken out its port side torpedo tubes."

"Target the engineering spaces. But if you get a clear shot at the starboard torpedo tubes, take them out."

"Targeting engineering spaces. Our torpedo is away, and we have wire control."

"What's going on?" Renard asked.

"We're under attack. The *Kim's* been hit. Has the crew reported any damage to you?"

"There's been no report received here yet."

A voice in Korean filled the net.

"He says they're fine," Doctor Tan said.

"Let him know I'll have them out of cannon range soon, if not already."

After the doctor translated, Cahill reported to Renard.

"I just encountered a hostile *Taechong* class patrol boat coming out of a rain storm. I'm going to send it back to hell with me cannons and a torpedo for good measure, but I'd really like to know if there are torpedoes coming at me without having to slow and listen for meself. I took out three of its tubes, but I couldn't get at the ones on its far side."

"At least one of your escort submarines should hear what's going on. Keep running until I get data from them. I'm sending helicopters your way, too."

"What for?"

The pause in Renard's response confirmed his mortal danger.

"To evacuate your crew and that of the *Kim* if necessary."

As the *Goliath* raced from its adversary, Cahill considered how to squeeze every knot from his ship.

"Pierre?"

"I'm here."

"If I want to go faster, what's the limit?"

"The motors' internal torque. They're already enhanced from the standard submarine design. I'm afraid you're already sustaining your top speed."

"What about an unsustainable top speed?"

"Not worth the risk for an extra half knot. You'd likely lose propulsion completely if you pushed the limit."

"Damn. I'm maxed out then."

The Frenchman's voice rose half an octave.

"I've got confirmation from your nearest submarine escort. Three torpedoes are in the water."

"Tell me that they have good solutions on them and that I can escape them all."

"They have solutions on them all, and they're fanning out. One was aimed at you, one ahead, and one behind, to cover all your evasion options. I'm sorry. The best you can do is escape two of the three."

"Am I on a good course?"

"Yes. You're evading the lead and center torpedo. The lagging torpedo is seven and a half miles behind you, coming at you with fifteen knots of closure. The torpedo is active and appears to have acquired you."

Cahill's sonar supervisor announced that he heard the incoming weapon's seeker.

"Agreed. It's acquired me. So what do I do for half an hour before a torpedo blows up under me ass?"

"May I recommend an evacuation? Get your crew and the *Kim's* onto rafts. I've equipped your ship with the best inflatable life rafts available, and helicopters will be there before you could be overcome by the weather."

"But not before we get hit."

"No. I'm sorry."

Cahill's mind raced for solutions and found nothing. He then sought a means to mitigate the destruction.

"It's a lightweight torpedo coming at a pretty damned large ship," he said. "The *Goliath* isn't necessarily lost, you know."

"I've been considering this," Renard said. "I agree."

"I'll have all watertight compartments closed. One hull should be intact, and if the other has any sort of buoyancy after impact, we may just have a salvageable ship."

"Perhaps. You'll have to release the presses on the *Kim*, however, just to assure that you don't drag it down, if it comes to it."

Fifteen minutes later, the crew from the *Goliath's* port hull had crawled to the starboard side, and Cahill heard the report from his starboard weapons bay.

"The *Kim's* crew is gathered on its fantail and crawling over to the *Goliath* using the hydraulic presses. There's a guy with a belly wound that's getting help from his crew, but I'm not sure he's going to make it."

"He'll make it," Cahill said. "I'll give him credit that he's too tough not to."

"There's also some older guy that's got to be almost fifty years old."

"That's the guy this mess is all about. How's he looking?"

"Fine, I guess. Spooked like everyone else. Now that I notice it, he's getting a lot more attention and a lot more hands on him than the average crewman."

"That's because he's the most likely candidate to jump overboard and try to drown himself. It's a good thing that they're not allowing that."

The watchman's pause suggested that he was absorbing the desperation of the prisoner.

"What about me crew?" Cahill asked.

"We're on the starboard fantail with the life rafts. Everyone is snapped to tethering lines so that they don't get swept overboard."

"Let me know when everyone is ready to jump. Then I'll give you a few minutes to join them."

"You're planning on staying?" Walker asked.

"I'm the captain, mate."

"Then I'm staying, too. I didn't come this far to abandon you."

"Don't be a fool. You could get yourself killed."

"Then why should I let you be a fool?"

"As I said, I'm the captain. I'll be a fool if I wish."

"You don't have some crazy plan to evade this torpedo, do you?"

"No, just a plan to see what I can do to minimize the damage."

"Then why can't I stay with you?"

"Because it's your duty to lead the evacuation. God knows what sort of dangers they'll face in the water. They need a leader."

"Terry!"

"I'll be fine. There's practically more danger getting them into the water and looking after them than there is here on the bridge. Get off me damned ship, Liam. That's an order."

"Alright then. Good luck, mate."

Cahill shook Walker's hand and dismissed him.

Minutes later, the starboard bay's watchman announced that the executive officer had joined the crew top side. Cahill ordered his final crewman to join the others and to have them head overboard when he slowed the ship.

He counted four minutes and then stopped the *Goliath's* shafts. Putting on a backing bell to drag his ship towards motionlessness, he allowed his men ease of escape, and then he stopped his engines to let the ship drift at all stop.

When life rafts appeared in the view of his external cameras, he brought the starboard engine to five knots but kept the port engine silent. Driving away from his men, he lured the torpedo from them.

He then ordered a hard turn to the left, the automated ship obeying his silent tapping of icons. He continued to turn to offer the port bow as the closest point of contact to the torpedo.

He pumped water overboard from the trim tanks to make the ship light, and then he disobeyed Renard's order and kept the presses tight against the *Kim*.

"How are you doing, Terry?" Renard asked.

"Fine, given the situation."

"What's going on? I've noticed that you've slowed."

"To let the crews off. They're safely overboard. It's just me now."

"Get off the ship."

"No. I'm staying."

"I appreciate your heroism, but consider how difficult it is for me to replace you. I'm not patronizing you for your courage. You're genuinely a nearly impossible talent to replace. Think of the missions that await you. I urge you not to get yourself killed."

"I won't. I've got a good feeling about me ship, and I don't think it wants me to leave it."

"I think you're drunk with courage if you believe that the *Goliath* is talking to you."

"It's been talking to me for days. You just have to know how to listen."

Cahill looked to the tactical display. His slowing had reduced the time to impact to less than a minute.

He had enough foresight to pile bed mattresses on the bridge's deck, to lessen the effect of an explosion. Standing on them, he expected to see the detonation on the ship's far side.

"I'm not changing your mind, am I?" Renard asked.

"No, mate."

"Well then, I can only wish you luck."

"Thanks."

He finished his reply, and the seas erupted through the port bow. The *Goliath's* prow heaved, rose from the water, and crashed back down.

When Cahill recovered from his fall to the deck, he noticed waves lapping the laser cannon and jagged metal forming rifts around the weapon. The frigate-like bow had been blown away, but the watertight bulkhead to the submarine section had held.

"Are you okay?" Renard asked.

Cahill fought to stand on sprained ankles.

"I'm fine, mate. I took the hit, but it looks like I still have control of the ship. The *Kim's* untouched and the *Goliath* has survived, at least for the moment. But I'm open to any help you can spare."

CHAPTER 25

Jake had requested that the *Gwansun* and its twins join in the search for other hostile combatants in what had been considered safe waters. He wanted to give Cahill personal protection during his slow trek to the safe haven at Donghae.

Antoine Remy's ears provided the best diagnosis of the wounded transport ship.

"There's a leak through the forward watertight bulkhead. I hear the water flow."

"Can you tell how bad it is?"

"No worse than the list you can see through the periscope. It's very hard to tell, but it's worthy of concern."

Leaning into the rail that circled the elevated conning platform, Jake called for Cahill.

"You were right, Terry. The watertight bulkhead didn't hold completely. You've got a leak."

"I've pumped as much as I can from me mid-ships trim tanks overboard to stay light, but I've also pumped to forward tanks on the starboard side to minimize stresses athwartships."

Jake knew from his approach to the *Goliath* that Cahill had lowered the starboard bow under the stormy waves, bringing the water up to his bridge dome. With the *Specter* abeam of the damaged hull, the submarine's periscope offered a profile view showing the waterline at the laser cannon and the larger waves lapping the *Kim's* bow.

"That's good thinking," he said. "Just like a surface sailor."

"Liam would be proud."

"Well, maybe you can brag to him yourself."

"I'll wait until I get this ship home before I do that. You've got a point, though. This twin hull, multi-compartment damage control crap is best left for the surface skimmers. It's not natural for me. I need to think each move through three times, and then second guess meself twice."

"You don't have to wait," Jake said. "He's grabbed a few volunteers and is coming back to help you. He's going to land on your port hull and board you for damage control – with your permission, of course."

"That's encouraging. I'll need his help lining up to pump water from the bilge. Having him aboard will be a lot better than the backup option I was planning."

"What was that?"

"Crawl to the port side and line up the pumps meself."

"Bad news, though. You'll still have to unlock the hatch for them."

"Right. Give me about five minutes. It's a slow crawl."

Through the periscope, Jake watched a helicopter approach and begin to lower Walker and the small damage control team. In the tossing seas, the loading required several attempts, but the men landed. The hatch rolled open, and Cahill's head appeared prior to retreating below decks with the first of his returned crew.

When the aircraft lowered a gasoline-powered pump, Jake felt the turn of the tide in favor of the *Goliath's* survival. Strapped to the back of the transport ship, two men unfurled and fed a hose through the hatch. Minutes later, they ignited the engine, and the pump spewed spray overboard from the ship's bilge.

Cahill sounded short of breath in his report.

"I'm back on the bridge."

"I figured."

"You may not see it," Cahill said. "But now that I can use the trim pump to suck from the bilge along with that contraption running top side, I've gained about a half meter of freeboard."

"I see it," Jake said. "You won't make it home for dinner, but you'll make it home for sure now – with your ship."

A tugboat nudged the *Specter* against the pier, and Jake took one last look towards the *Goliath* in its anchorage. Two tugs illuminated the transport ship's decks. With breakwaters providing the abatement of swells, the transport ship rolled in gentler seas, and the rain that had pelted its steel hide had also vanished.

Instead of the usual limousine that Jake expected, a white school bus awaited him on the pier. It brought him and his crew to the familiar room where he had heard the original brief. Given the late time and pandemic fatigue, the reunion between Jake, his crews, and Renard was rushed.

Admiral Cho and the same translator who had explained the mission to Jake offered him and his crew the debrief. The room reached capacity with men leaning against the walls, and people considered of lesser import were dismissed.

Jake craned his neck and surmised that the *Kim's* key survivors and the leaders of the *Gwansun* were seated around him. Rapid, public introductions proved him correct, and then the admiral began by updating his audience about their shared mission.

A diving team had already assessed the damage and the risk to human life for repair teams who would brave swimming through the jagged, cut metal. The most skilled underwater welders had agreed to the endeavor, and they had made the *Goliath* watertight in its anchorage.

The admiral added that Cahill's torpedo had finished the work of his guns, sinking the *Taechong* warship. A surprising half of the North Korean crew had survived to be taken prisoner, and initial questioning suggested they had been operating independently when venturing into South Korean waters.

They had used chaff to create fake extensions of storms, hopping from one storm to the next, to maintain a hidden position near their enemy's coast prior to ambushing the *Goliath*.

The *Kim* remained watertight with all the cannon damage above its pressure hull. It would remain aboard the *Goliath* until the transport ship could submerge for the normal unloading procedure.

The admiral declared the mission a success based upon the safe return of the survivors, their prisoner, and the damaged submarine.

Then came his barrage of questions for every crew in the room. He wanted each team to relive everything from its perspective. After rendering his answers and awaiting two-way translations with each exchange, Jake faded in and out of consciousness.

"How much longer?"

"I'll request a break and order us some coffee," Renard said.

As the hours passed, the admiral's fatigue betrayed him, and he declared his inquisition complete before dismissing the audience. Seeking rest, the foreign crews scattered to their temporary waterfront quarters, while the native crews went home.

Jake found his way to his visiting commanding officer's quarters, entered its stale confines, and collapsed onto his bed. While he retained a shred of consciousness, he called his wife, but the call went straight to voice mail. To allay her concerns, he left a message that he was safe and on shore.

The ringing phone rousted him from his slumber.

"Yeah?"

"You're not planning to sleep through lunch, are you?" Renard asked.

"No. Come to think of it, I'm starved."

"Get cleaned up and join us at noon in the officer's club. You can walk there. Attire is business casual. The fleet uniform will suffice."

"Who's going to be there?"

"Just friends. This will be a low-stress affair."

Jake arrived last at a table set for seven guests. Cahill and Walker provided the new faces since he had docked the *Specter*. After warm salutations, he sat next to Henri and grabbed a tong full of salad.

"Want me to pour you a coldie, mate?" Cahill asked.

"Hell no. I mean, no. No thanks."

Chewing his salad, he scanned the seats. Along with the pair of Australian sailors and Renard, Jake had his top three veterans with him. With the *Specter's* engineering spaces showing no hiccups underway, he had seen little of Claude LaFontaine.

"Claude, right?"

"Glad you remember. You hardly see me because I keep the heart of your ship pumping. Be grateful that I do. Those MESMA units can get tricky, but I've got them figured out."

"Speak freely, gentlemen," Renard said. "This entire club has been reserved for us."

Jake looked around and realized that his party sat alone in the room.

"What's there to talk about?" he asked.

"Whatever you want," Renard said. "Reconstruction with recommendations, so to speak."

"Well, if nobody else wants to talk," Cahill said. "I've got improvements to the *Goliath* I'd like to see."

"I was afraid of that," Renard said. "My bank account is already wincing in anticipation of the pain."

"That laser cannon is no good, mate. You've got to give me a serious close-in weapon system. I need a Phalanx or a Goalkeeper. Something with metallic rounds that will count when I hit an incoming missile and give me a chance to damage other contacts that get close."

"You're not going to be shooting your cargo very often, I trust."

"That aside, you know the laser was lackluster against the missiles. It barely took down one whereas you know a bona fide close-in weapon system would have made mincemeat out of them."

"The cost of the consumables, though," Renard said. "Have you any idea how much armor-piercing tungsten penetrator rounds would cost me? Right now, I pay nothing for your laser shots."

"I think you got a deal on that laser and stuck me with it because it was cheap. Now I understand that most warriors are fighting with hardware that was awarded to the lowest bidder, but I need hard metal rounds for me air defense."

Renard sighed and reached for a glass of Merlot.

"I'll think about it."

"That means, yes," Jake said.

His mentor shot him a gruff sideways look as he sipped.

"What about explosive rounds for me cannons?"

"I'm quite willing to consider it, as I have before. But this is more than a question of money. Explosive rounds have greater length and require more storage space, which means you'd have to roughly halve your inventory. I think you're doing fine with splintering rounds."

"You could set me up with a mix. You know, a few dozen explosives in their own storage racks, in case I need them."

"Very well. You make a good point. I'll evaluate that in our down time."

"Thanks, Pierre," Cahill said. "Next, we need to consider anti-torpedo standoff weapons."

"Dear God, man. Are you trying to bankrupt me?"

"Oh come on, Pierre," Jake said. "Hear him out. I could also use an option to take out an incoming torpedo. The world has been shooting down missiles for decades. It's about time we started taking out incoming torpedoes. The initial trials are looking promising."

"Promising, indeed, if you're a nation with a twenty trillion dollar gross domestic product defending aircraft carriers worth upwards of five billion dollars."

"But it can be done, and it's worth looking into," Jake said.

"It looks like I've found an ally," Cahill said.

"The present technology would take excessive adaptation to work on either of your ships, adding to the already enormous costs."

"I don't think he loves us anymore," Jake said.

"That statement presumes much," Renard said. "And no, I will make no promises or overtures regarding anti-torpedo defenses."

"How does the cost of repairing the *Goliath* compare to the cost of acquiring an anti-torpedo system?" Jake asked.

Renard leaned into the table.

"I'll share a trick of the trade with all of you. The repair of the *Goliath* is counted as an expense for which our clients are liable. They pay for all consumables such as fuel and ordnance, and they pay for damage or loss of capital. That's rather standard in my negotiations."

The realization struck Jake as cruel.

"So wait," he said. "You mean, if you invest upfront money to keep me, Terry, and the boys alive, it comes out of your pocket. But if we get battered around and nearly die, say, for lack of having the hardware you refuse to invest in, any loss or damage comes out of your clients' pockets?"

"Precisely."

"Well, now I know you never loved us."

"Unfair," Renard said. "As long as we're analyzing this from the perspective of cold business, you must consider the cost of replacing you all. You're all my best assets and practically irreplaceable."

"Too late, mate," Cahill said. "You've told us where you stand. We're not buying anything nice you have to say about any of us ever again."

A steward wheeled out a suckling pig and two broiled chickens, along with a plate of vegetables for the party to share family style.

"No matter," Renard said. "It's not your fickle moods that interest me at the moment."

"Then whose fickle moods are on your mind?" Jake asked.

"I need to take advantage of our client's present state of euphoria to close the details of this mission's transactions. Assuming the payments clear into my account this afternoon, this evening's celebration shall be grand."

"What's going on tonight?" Jake asked.

"A victory party. Our clients will be in their dress uniforms. But don't worry. I've got jackets and ties selected for most of you."

"Most? Not all?" Jake asked.

"Would you like to explain it, Antoine?"

"No, not me."

"How about you, Henri?"

"No, Pierre. I think it's best that you share some good news to partially recover from the hole you've dug already today."

"Very well," Renard said. "Linda forbade it. She's picked out your ensemble. She's already landed in Seoul and will be arriving on the base with the other wives today."

Jake's heart raced with anticipation.

"What about the wives never knowing where we've been?"

"I didn't see a way of pretending that the *Goliath* wasn't off the coast of Korea. There are too many witnesses. I'll have to come up with a new security scheme. But for now, enjoy your day."

CHAPTER 26

Jake felt trapped in a tie, and he reached for Linda's hand and her calming effect. She sipped a vodka martini to relax while he gulped a virgin Bloody Mary for its tanginess.

"I still can't believe you're here," he said.

"Me neither, but Pierre invited me himself. He said this mission was going public, and there was no sense in asking the wives to pretend that his ship wasn't here. So here I am."

"You look tired."

"The trip was rough, even in first class."

"Pierre bought your tickets?"

"I think so. I was so excited when he told me to get ready to fly, I didn't even think to ask."

"I'm sure he did. The question is if he's taking it out of my pay."

Jake reflected that his pay over the last two missions had been five million Euro per venture, which was nothing for a man of his wealth. He had to admit that he participated for emotional reasons.

Renard approached with his wife, Marie.

"It's been forever, Jake," she said.

She kissed the air by his cheeks and did the same with Linda.

"That's a lovely dress," Marie said.

"Thank you. I like yours, too. What's it been? Almost two years since we last saw each other?"

"At least. How was your flight?"

"Not too bad with first class, but it's still tiring. How about you?"

"The same. But at least we're here. So are the other wives."

Jake scanned the room and saw Antoine Remy, Claude LaFontaine, and Henri Lanier and their spouses. The sextet had gathered around Walker and his wife along with Cahill, the solitary bachelor on senior staff, and had taken up residence near the bar.

"This tight-lipped scoundrel I married won't speak a word about what he's been up to, even with pictures of his latest toy ship carrying a Korean submarine all over the news."

"Trust me, I get the same treatment from Jake."

"Don't these fools realize that our imaginations torment us worse than the truth?"

"I think they know but don't care," Linda said.

"Will you join me in a trip to the ladies room?"

The women departed.

"I thought they'd never stop," Jake said.

"I'm thankful they did. I wanted to share an update with you."

"Okay."

"The admiral who was the target of the *Kim's* original mission is scheduled to have a private trial. You may never hear of his fate publicly, although I will attempt to cultivate a strong enough relationship with our new clients that they'll be willing to share the results."

"What's he charged with? I mean, he was just doing his job when he sank the *Cheonan*."

"One could argue, as our new clients will, that he was a contributor to a war crime."

"If they're going that route, what defense does he have?"

"Fortunately, that's up to attorneys, judges, and power brokers beyond my realm of influence."

"The mighty Pierre Renard, a spectator."

"There are some battles for which I have neither a desired outcome nor any influence."

"It strains my imagination, but I'll believe that you really don't want to stick your nose into something."

The Frenchman sipped from his wineglass.

"Forgive my blunt segue, but I fear I must stick my nose into your business. I know full well that I ordered it, but that final escort you offered to Terry turned out to be quite an impressive rampage of death and destruction. How are you dealing with it?"

"What do you mean? I was just doing my job."

"Too well, from what I heard."

"Henri's just overreacting."

"It's not just Henri. You were out for blood. You were angry and not caring who you killed."

"My anger has been a concern for you, me, my wife, and my crew forever. So what? Do you have a magic pill that fixes it? Your last magic pill cost me my desire to drink alcohol and put out the flames when I'm wound up."

"You speak as if it were a bad thing."

"Apparently, I need any crutch I can get to deal with anger."

Jake welcomed the return of the wives.

"Come on ladies," Renard said. "It's time to sit around the dinner table. You'll find this to be quite a treat. Six types of seaweed, four types of kimchi, and all the meats and fishes you could imagine served family style. You cook your own meats to your preference on the table's central stove."

"That sounds delightful," Marie said.

"I think so, too," Linda said. "But the final judgment will be the taste test. I can't wait to try it out."

"I married a food snob," Jake said.

The food snob enjoyed her dinner, and the next day, Jake bid farewell to his comrades-in-arms and took her on a limousine ride to a hotel in Seoul. He then escorted her to the tourist area of the Korean Peninsula's Demilitarized Zone.

An atmosphere of history and hope blended with harsh reality. An unused train station passing through North Korea and a neutral zone factory staffed by workers from the north and managers from the south reflected the desire for reunification. Infiltration tunnels, minefields, and army troops provided the reminder of longstanding hostility.

Unaware of the horrors he had experienced, Linda jumped at the chance to shop in a commercial zone where she could purchase North Korean goods. Jake felt twisted as she handed him candies packaged in the nation he had wounded two days earlier in a semi-private war.

His emotions toggled between hot and cold. One moment, the North were humans worthy of camaraderie. The next, they were monsters. Both perspectives had merit.

"Don't those look good, Jake?"

His throat tightened as he choked back either tears or a scream. He couldn't be sure.

Back on exclusive South Korean soil, he helped Linda pick out her final souvenirs.

"A postcard for my mother," she said.

"Postcards are old school."

"Yeah, well so is my mother."

"Okay. Get it. Come on, people are starting to board the bus."

To avoid attention, Jake had arranged travel with the most average tourist group he could find. On the bus, his wife leaned into him and held a private conversation.

"How has your anger been?"

He grunted.

"Well, what's that mean?" she asked.

"Can't you tell when I don't want to talk?"

"You never want to talk about it."

"Fine. I don't see any improvement. In fact, it may be getting worse, and I don't know a damned thing I can do about it."

"The only answer is faith."

"I've read all the books on Christian apologetics. The arguments are strong, but not provable. I can't draw a conclusion."

"Apologies? What?"

"Apologetics. In this context, it means the logical defense of the faith, which sounds like an oxymoron when I just said it. You can't logically defend a faith, which probably explains why I'm going in circles."

The last tourist boarded, and the bus reeled forward.

"You said you once knew people smarter than you who were devout Christians, even a few Catholics, right?"

"Back at the Naval Academy. There were plenty of guys who made me look stupid, and a few of them were devout. Why?"

"What did they say?"

"The same thing. You can't prove it. You need faith."

"Well, how do these geniuses get faith?"

Jake had to ponder the question.

"I remember one guy who put it in a way that I really didn't consider until now. He said you had to experience it, and that the proof would come in the daily living."

"Interesting."

"Huh. Yeah. I guess that's an illogical proof, but it could be real if you experience things that you attribute to the act of believing."

"That's what I've been trying to tell you for years."

"No you haven't. You haven't even been close to saying that."

"Of course, I have. I've always said you had to believe and that God would take care of the rest."

"That's a gross oversimplification. That's not the argument I'm making now."

"Well, what are you saying?"

He knew he had to be careful to avoid shutting her out. His words came out harshly when he forgot to see her perspective.

"I think I reached a point of understanding that you've wanted me to get to, but I had to do it my own way."

"Okay. So tomorrow is Sunday. Can we go to church together? It's been so long since you last tried it, and I saw a nice one around the hotel."

"I don't want to go."

"You remember the routine from your childhood. And you went with me a couple years ago at home when I asked."

"That's because you asked. I did it for you."

"I'm asking now."

"It won't even be in English."

"So what? I want to go. I'm going."

He inhaled and released a long sigh.

"What's that supposed to mean?" she asked.

"It means it's fine, honey."

"What's fine?"

"It means if you're going and you want me to join you, I will. I'd go anywhere on the planet, as long as I could go there with you."

THE END

About the Author

After his graduation from the Naval Academy in 1991, John R. Monteith's career in the U.S. Navy included service aboard a nuclear ballistic missile submarine, and a tour as a top-rated instructor of combat tactics at the U.S. Naval Submarine School. Since his transition to civilian life, he has continued to pursue his interest in cutting-edge technology. He currently lives in the Detroit area, where he works in engineering management when he's not busy cranking out high-tech naval action thrillers.

Novels by John R. Monteith include ROGUE AVENGER, ROGUE BETRAYER, ROGUE CRUSADER, ROGUE DEFENDER, ROGUE ENFORCER, ROGUE FORTRESS, and ROGUE GOLIATH.

The next book in the series, ROGUE HERCULES (working title), is expected in 2016.

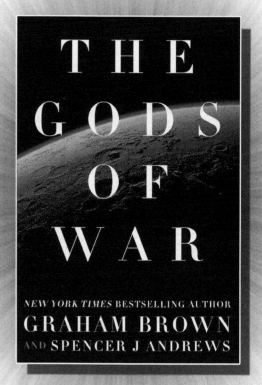

CUTTING-EDGE NAVAL THRILLERS BY

JEFF EDWARDS

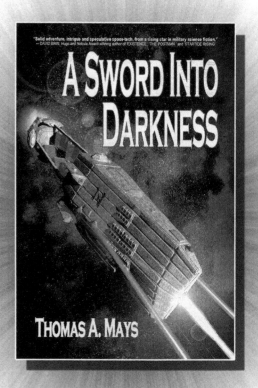

57643512R00137

Made in the USA
Lexington, KY
21 November 2016